Look for these books by award nominated author, Miriam Shumba;
"That Which Has Horns" & **"Show Me the Sun"**

Praise for *That Which Has Horns*:

… I felt obligated to say Thank you for such an AWESOME story! It felt wonderful to read a book I can totally relate to. I feel like l know all the characters personally.

—Christabel Andile Chisvo

This novel enthralled me from the very first page… Shumba has not only provided her readers with a fascinating romance but an insightful look into the beauty of Africa… this book is a must read!

—Kate Davis

I definitely recommend this book because it is well-written, full of suspense and because I had a slight smile on my face for most of it as it reminded me of home.

—Gugu Mclaren, Diasporan Darlings

***That Which has Horns** is an exhilarating and thrilling ride. I can't wait for the next book…*

—Sarai Vengesayi

… I haven't picked up a better written, easy-to-read, fascinating story in a long time. Your characters are so rich and the story line multi-layered; I was on the edge of my seat for two days.

—Kimberly

… Loved it.

—TB. Mlio

CHASING

Miriam Shumba

USA• England• South Africa

Munaii Bookworks
6565 McArthur Blvd,
Coppell, TX 75019
www.munaii.com

Publisher's Note: This is a work of fiction. Names, characters, places, and incidents are a product of the author's imagination. Locales and public names are sometimes used for atmospheric purposes. Any resemblance to actual people, living or dead, or to businesses, companies, events, institutions, or locales is completely coincidental.

Scripture quotations taken from The Holy Bible, New International Version ® (NIV) Copyright © 1973, 1978, 1984 by Biblica US, Inc. ® Used by permission.

Learn more information at:
www.miriamshumba.com

Book Layout ©2014 Munaii Bookworks

Ordering Information:
Quantity sales. Special discounts are available on quantity purchases by corporations, associations, and others. For details, contact the "Special Sales Department" at the address above.

Chasing/ Miriam Shumba – 1st ed.
ISBN 978-0-9861018-0-9

Dedication

To the Many Great Men God so generously put in my life.
I am thankful to;
My Dad, Nathan Denenga, for showing love instead
of talking about it
My husband, Gabriel Shumba, for being my love always
My son, Washe, whose very presence makes me better.
My brothers, Boni, Bernard, Michael, Aaron, Luke,
(20 cousins!!) can always count on you.
My nephews, Panashe, Darryn, Munashe, Matipa,
Natenzi, Tongai, Daniel jnr, Munashe, Tadiwa, Tanaka,
Nathan, Munya, Kundayi, Mukayi, Jack and Henry true
gentle guys who are growing to be awesome men of God.
Our God children, Jared and Thabo, good hearts and loving

In Memory of
Sekuru Boniface Mutata and Sekuru Anderson Manoah, Sekuru
Stan and Sekuru Anderson though I didn't spend enough time with
you, each interaction was priceless, beautiful and memorable.
Washe may you learn from the best that is in them, laugh at the jokes
in them, forgive their short comings and be blessed by God to be
filled with peace, joy and love.

*I have seen all the things that are done under the sun; all of them
are meaningless, a chasing after the wind.*
—Ecclesiastes 1:14

*My horizons were saturated with me, my leaving, and my going.
There was no room for what I left behind.*
Tsitsi Dangarembga

*Let your love be like misty rain; gentle in coming
but flooding the river.*
African Proverb

CHAPTER 1

Winter

I have no peace, no quietness; I have no rest, but only turmoil.

—Job 3:26

Blake glanced at the number on his phone and reluctantly answered the call. "This is Mr. Pieri," he said. He hated the irritation that crawled from somewhere deep within him, strong, gnawing, an annoying insect that he wanted to swat. He didn't want to talk to his daughter's school, but there was no avoiding it, was there? The disturbing thought that he was alone in the world crept up and he squashed it. Who else could they talk to?

"Mr. Pieri. This is Jenna Gibson from Green Lake Middle School. You need to come and pick your daughter from the school. She was involved in a physical fight in the cafeteria that resulted in a bloody nose."

Blake stopped himself before he could cuss when Jenna Gibson's words sank in. Jodi was going to ruin him. As if he was an errant boy who sent this scourge on their perfect private school, Blake had lost count of the number of times Jodi's school had called him in,. His anger continued to rise, dark red and voracious, hot enough to melt the snow clinging to his windows.

What he really wanted to know was why did he spend so much

money to pay for his daughter's education if they kept sending her home at the slightest infraction? Why couldn't they deal with her? Weren't they trained professionals in dealing with kids? He certainly wasn't.

From the moment Jodi was put in his arms thirteen years ago, he had no idea how to be a father to her. He wondered at the audacity of the hospital to just hand them the baby and send them home with no instructions, and no one coming from the hospital or state to check on them. Even now, years later, did they really think he knew what to do?

He looked at the picture of a smiling blonde girl with angelic eyes, her face too small for the wide toothy grin. That was taken eight years ago. The once beautiful blue eyes were now dark blue angry steel, the once shiny blonde hair had been dyed a dull brown. Her face and all around her was now an aura of resentment and anger. He didn't know her any more. His daughter was a stranger.

Blake rubbed his forehead to clear the tension lines that he was sure were now as deep as ditches. As he struggled to process this turn of events, another thought niggled at the back of his mind. He was supposed to do something. Something just as unpleasant as having to pick up his daughter.

"Can I come at the end of the day?"

"I'm afraid that's not possible. You have to come for her now or we are calling the police."

Blake stood. He balled his fists, fighting hard not to speak the words he really wanted to say.

"Fine, fine, I'll be right there," he said. He punched in the number to get back to Tim Dennis and cut that conversation short. He also had to get rid of the men sitting outside his office waiting for him. He called his assistant.

"Cathy, I won't be able to meet with the gentlemen waiting for me. I have to rush to Jodi's school. Please reschedule the meeting."

Before she could respond, Blake disconnected the line.

Cathy smiled at the men waiting outside Blake's office on the first floor of what she considered prime office space in Southfield Towers. She was new at the job and could easily understand why the previous assistant had not lasted. Blake Pieri was a bear to work for and not a day went by that he didn't put her in awkward situations. He was lucky because she was used to bears. She was married to one. And although her bear wasn't as handsome as Mr. Pieri, or as dark and well-muscled, bears were bears no matter their shape.

Driving to his daughter's school destroyed the enjoyment he usually had in his powerful, purring car. The wet roads added to the frustration. Jodi was angry and miserable and wanted everybody to feel the same way. He couldn't be sure whether it started when Samantha died or before. But now, her resentment permeated his whole existence.

Samantha spent all the time with their kids, so he knew as much about them as a fish knew about flying.

Blake had worked every waking moment to provide all their needs, the house by the lake, the vacations, the cars and the cleaning services. Samantha on the other hand went to the parent teacher meetings, sports games, field trips, and dealt with doctor appointments and all day-to-day issues. To him it was a fair division of labor, though Samantha seemed to hate him for providing all the luxuries that she craved, nagging him to the point of losing his mind.

Widower.

That word didn't even explain half the problems it came with. Suitcases of baggage, especially when kids were factored in. Blake could well understand men who married quickly after losing their spouse. Men who took the first available woman who could make dinner and help the kids with homework. Not that he planned to do that any time soon, but he understood why they did it.

Drowning in frustration, Blake was trying to figure out what he would do with his daughter as he neared the school. It was only 1pm and Tyler was at school and needed to be picked up at 3pm. It meant he would have to stay home with Jodi while waiting to go and pick up Tyler. Or Tyler could arrive on the bus and now, Jodi would be home for him. Surely she could be trusted to watch her brother for a short time? He really hated asking his in-laws for help. Two nannies had quite and he had no time to look for a new one.

Arranging the children's schedules was like solving a complicated puzzle. Daily. He had never, appreciated all that his late wife had been responsible for. How on earth had Samantha managed?

Green Lake Middle was a typical school building without any architectural interest or character, a two story, structure with dark gray brick facing, standing strong against the cold. Blake had never liked school when he was young and he certainly didn't like it now. He walked up the walkway, annoyed at the puddles of dirty melted snow on his path.

They probably think I am part of the staff, Blake thought as the janitor greeted him by name and when he got to the front office the office manager regarded him like a relative, albeit a complicated one. The smells in schools, too many kids, some antiseptic, markers or chalk or whatever they used these days all served to remind him how much he hated the place.

"Mr. Pieri. Good afternoon. It's wonderful to see you," Ms. Swinton said smiling at him broadly and staring at him like a movie star had walked in. He could get any woman to be agreeable except his own daughter, Blake thought. Jodi looked at him as if he was scum.

"Jodi's in the principal's office," Ms. Swinton said.

"Thank you," Blake said.

He walked towards the office and peeked in then rapped on the door lightly. Jodi sat in the side chair, arms and legs crossed. He didn't understand her attire of baggy jeans, messy T-Shirt and hooded sweaters. She looked like a rebel, a stranger, hiding from life.

"Mr. Pieri,' the principal said. "Sorry we have to meet under these circumstances, again." Her familiar face was drenched with concern. Blake wished he could get a paper towel and wipe it off her face. Beneath the apprehension, Blake detected a weariness that made him uncomfortable. He felt like he was the one who had committed the crime.

"Good afternoon, Ms. Medley," Blake responded then looked at Jodi who continued to look down as if he didn't exist. She didn't have the grace to look nervous after what she had been accused of.

"We have a written report of what happened, but I would like you to take Jodi home so she can calm down, then we can set up a meeting after the break." Victoria said calmly. She must have noticed the surprise on Drake's face. Yes, he didn't realize there was a break coming up, did he?

"That means she is only to return after winter break." Ms. Medly continued.

"Thank you. I'll call you," Blake said. "Come Jodi let's go home." Jodi glared at him then picked up her book bag and stood up.

Blake worked hard to remain calm as they walked down the path to his car, but once the car door closed shut he turned to his child.

"What on earth happened? And you better tell me the truth?"

"I didn't do anything," Jodi yelled.

"What do you mean you didn't do anything? I was told you hit somebody," Blake said, started the engine and sped out of the school grounds.

"It was a mistake!"

"A mistake? How do you make somebody bleed by mistake?"

"I wanted to leave, but I knocked him with a tray,"

"You hit a guy? What are you trying to do Jodi? Are you insane? Right now I'm supposed to be at a very important meeting, but where am I? Getting you out of another mess."

Blake stopped when he heard her sobbing beside him.

"So, now you are going to cry? Crying won't help, Jodi. This school is going to kick you out, too. Then where will you go?"

Jodi remained silent as Blake drove through the neighborhood past the lake and drove carefully up the drive that revealed his grey stone mansion. The pleasure he normally had arriving home, just seeing the beauty he had built was completely gone. Jodi knew how to take the pleasure out of everything in his life.

Now this was architectural interest, he thought humorlessly.

Slamming the door of his car without glancing at the view of the lake Blake made his way towards the house. Jodi followed listlessly behind him and he barked at her to hurry up. She walked a little faster and when he reached the landing, he turned to her.

"Your room. Now. You are grounded."

Jodi ran up the stairs and Blake walked into his office, his anger tightly coiled, though ready to spring. Before he could find something to punch his cell phone beeped. Not recognizing the number he punched the talk button.

"Blake?"

Blake recognized Kim's voice. "What?"

"Oh you've done it this time. I just spoke to Jodi and she's crying and you have the nerve to yell at her."

"What are you talking about?" Blake asked.

"Jodi's crying because you are an insensitive brute. Did you even hear her side of the story? Do you know why she hit the guy in school? You never take the time to listen to her."

"I know the school doesn't make up things like she does, Kim. Besides they are my children and you can't tell me how to run my family!"

"They are my sister's children and I won't stand by and watch you destroy their lives. Tyler needs somebody home, but you just leave them all alone. They order their own food, they clean the house. You don't even care about them do you? You never loved Sammy either."

Blake was angered by her accusations, the tone of her voice. Even if it was true, Kim had no right.

"Don't talk about my marriage like you know anything about it, Kim. Worry about your own alcoholic husband and leave my family alone."

"You can call my husband names, Blake, but I'm going to take my sister's children from you mark my words. They deserve better than a cold unfeeling man for a father."

"No court on earth will give you my kids while you live with that drunk."

"As a drunk he's ten times a better man than you."

They continued to argue, cursing at each other until Blake couldn't take any more. Talking to Kim reminded him of the last years with his wife. Dark and ugly with no end in sight.

Blake disconnected the line. He was breathing hard and heavy. Who did she think she was telling him what to do, he wondered. Jodi was his daughter and Tyler was his son and his nosy sister-in-law was not going to take his children from him.

As Blake walked to his desk, he ran through the appointments in his Blackberry, most of which he would have to reschedule because of Jodi.

It was difficult to calm down. He had to go for his run or he would do something he might regret. He ran upstairs to change, eager to be on the freezing road, the only sound his feet hitting the ground.

After changing his clothes he burst outside and took to the quiet streets, his feet hitting the ground hard. He didn't listen to music, he didn't think, he just ran, but as he made his way back something came to him, crystal clear.

He'd almost forgotten. The kids' new nanny. Wasn't she arriving today? He saw the time on the clock. He was going to be late picking her up, of that he was sure.

What was her name again? Blake tried to recall other pertinent details about her. When his mother called with the information, he had just finished meeting with the accountants and as had been the case for the past few months, the meeting had almost paralyzed him with fear. The numbers swimming in his head, his mother had told him about the girl. Where was she from again? Jamaica? No that wasn't it. Africa? But living in New York. Or was she coming straight from Africa. He guessed he would find out when he got to the airport. He also recalled that his mother had sent him a photo, but had he opened it? Did she speak English? The big question he had was, why on earth had he agreed to this anyway?

CHAPTER 2

Snow

*Delight yourself in the Lord and He will give you the
desires of your heart.*

—Psalm 37:4

Chenai drew a circle on the plane window with her index finger, her eyes gazing at the landscape below. Was that a lake or pond? How high was she from the ground?

She wasn't sure how long she still had before she landed, though she suspected it wasn't long now. With noises that disturbed her, the plane turned to indicate a change of pace and a preparation to descend. She wasn't sure. She had no watch and there were no clocks anywhere on the Delta flight. All she could see were the tops of people's heads in front of her and the ones next to her, intent on their gadgets.

Chenai refused the offer of a drink for two reasons. The last time she had a drink on a plane she had ended up soaked and very cold. Somehow, as she was reaching out for the drink, the flight attendant was thinking of putting it down and she had endured the rest of the flight wet and miserable. The second reason was that the plane was experiencing so much turbulence she had to hold her mouth so she wouldn't cry out. Nobody else was crying out.

Chenai remembered how she had felt on that flight. How she had packed her hopes and dreams along with some clothes, only to be disappointed. Brutally so.

However, she didn't know how to feel this time. She was still recovering from the traumatic events in New Jersey, still processing what had happened. Things had gone wrong very quickly. In fact, immediately. It was as if she woke up one morning and from the moment she opened her eyes to sunset disaster struck, one after the other, like continuous fireworks, except it wasn't just one day. It was a whole month of wrongness.

She sighed, still unable to believe how her life had been turned upside down, the nightmare, the shock. Chenai's heart could barely hold all that ugliness as she felt her heart race and bleakness enter in. She shifted her thinking. She tried to see the silver lining of her month in New Jersey and all she saw was Heather, the person she truly believed was an angel.

Chenai glanced out the window again, as if the ever changing landscape below would hold a clue. The light was fading and soon she wouldn't be able to track where the plane was headed. The future was now blank and totally unknown, dark. She had no idea what to expect in Michigan, who the people were, what they did, where they lived.

The landing was decent this time, she didn't have to bite her lip as hard when it touched down. With her backpack rhythmically hitting her back, Chenai followed the crowd to the baggage claim unable to shake off memories from the past few days. Still, reminders of the past weakened and she had to pause. Take a deep breath then with monumental will, not give in to the crushing feelings. Shoving memories from her mind, she walked over to wait for her bag on the carousel, glancing around at all the strangers around her. Nobody paid any attention to her or spoke to her and she felt alone, lost.

There were so many people around her, though she could have been the only person on earth, just as she felt when she stood at the gravesite the day after her mother had been put to the ground, the desire to dig her up building in her. As if in a dream, she saw an image of her mother smiling at her, teaching her to cook *sadza,* stirring the black pot filled with maize meal and water. Unlike the cooking classes she took at school, sadza cooking had no measurements, no set time or stove setting. With sadza cooking you watched and gauged with your eyes and heart. It was complicated and it took her failing many times before finally succeeding in getting the right texture. Her mother had gushed with pride like she had accomplished something grand, not mastering a meal that every young girl all over the country could cook.

She longed for her mother's guidance. Would she have advised her to fly all the way across the country to live with strangers? Was this God's will for her?

Thoughts of her mother her only companion, Chenai stood watching the bags going round and round. Memories comforted her and saddened her. Would there ever come a time when she would think of her loving mother without feeling as if her heart was being crushed by a tractor?

Bulging with the clothes Heather had given her, the bag arrived towards the end of the line. She pulled it off with an effort and stood to the side looking for someone with a sign for her. Nobody was waiting for her. Nobody came in scanning the crowd. All the other passengers from her plane seemed to know where to go as they left her standing alone. She watched loved ones hug outside as someone came to pick them up. A longing filled her heart. She felt a wind blow against her cheek and at once remembered.

Yes, heavenly Father. You are with me. No matter where I go. No matter how far I travel, you are there.

Chenai looked down at the jeans Heather had given her and the thick sweater and red coat. Chenai had refused at first. She didn't want to always feel like a charity case. Heather had reassured her, telling her that if she didn't take them, those clothes would be given away anyway. Heather's mother, Sarah had nodded.

"You look cute in that," Heather had said.

Chenai had fought very hard not to beg Heather to keep her longer. She had hoped to stay in New Jersey so that maybe her aunt could come and forgive her and take her back, but God had other plans, it seemed. Even though she feared living with her aunt, the unknown seemed worse.

After an hour of waiting, Chenai sat on her bag at the corner and waited watching as the number of people in the terminal dwindled. She took the book her father had pressed in her hands. The first time she had opened it a note stuck in the middle of the book had fallen out. It was a note her father had written to her. The simple words reminded her that although her father didn't hold her in his arms like a baby anymore, he held her in his heart, so tenderly. She knew it, felt as sure of it and secure in it as she was in each breath she took and the solid earth she stood on.

When God gave me a daughter, He filled my life with rainbows. Even though I am not there, know that the Father to all of us is with you always.

Delicately, Chenai held the book, not wanting to disturb the note and end up sobbing as she had the first time her eyes brushed on the words. It was so simple to read, but the beauty in it was astounding. She read the words her father had underlined, 'I will love the light for it shows me the way, yet I will endure the darkness because it shows me the stars'.

Being so far from home made her appreciate her parents so much, miss them more too. Why had she not realized how important they were to her? Why didn't she tell them every day? She wished she had written all the wise words her mother had whispered to her late at night or early in the morning before she set off to school. Her mother would always tell her father that all the wisdom she needed was in The Bible and that all manner of self-help books were just taking their wisdom from the Bible and not giving credit to the source. But she loved reading what her father had underlined. Even when she studied Thomas Hardy's *The Mayor of Casterbridge* and Shakespeare, she used her father's books that were full of scribbles and notes, sometimes to rival the actual words on the page. She smiled when she read the next words, 'Tomorrows is only found in the calendar of fools.' This one, her mother truly believed because she could get done in a day what others would do in a month. She was a doer and woke up running, leaving little for tomorrow.

Too nervous to read it all, Chenai closed the book. She looked in her purse for the quarters then took the little notebook with phone numbers for the Pieri family. She worried that Mr. Pieri had the wrong time or maybe she had arrived in the wrong city.

A movement caught her eye when she was about to stand up and make a call. A man who looked harried, ran through the automatic doors his dark long coat flying behind him. Chenai stared at him, hoping that he was looking for her, maybe a driver sent to pick her up.

The man stood still, and scanned the area, his eyes finally resting on her. They didn't seem friendly, though somehow she guessed he was sent for her. Chenai looked at him. From his dark pants and a white, he seemed to have so much energy, like an animal ready to spring. With a questioning, impatient look on his face he walked towards her. That's what stood out. Impatience.

"Excuse me. Are you Cheny?" he asked, his hand extended to her, pointing. It seemed to be accusatory, like she had done something wrong. Chenai looked at him and shook her head wondering. Could he be the man with the family that was falling apart? In her mind she had been expecting somebody much older, different than the young dark haired white man standing before her.

"Chenai," she said standing up and dusting her jeans as if she had been sitting on sand and not the rough carpet.

"Chenai," he said then muttered something. Chenai looked at him, stunned. "I'd forgotten all about you. Crazy day." Chenai tried to pick her bag, but he grabbed it from her so quickly she tumbled to the floor. She was too stunned to make a sound.

"Oops. You okay?" he asked and reached for her hand. Chenai

held it and stood up, her nervousness now multiplied, just like on the plane. She knew that when she was tense her clumsiness took over, dropping things and tripping while walking on flat ground. She had to breathe and calm down.

"I'm fine." Chenai rubbed her hands. They had hit the ground first as she tried to break her fall.

"I've got it." He held her bag as if it was a basket of leaves and started walking towards the sliding doors. He didn't glance back to see if she followed. Chenai sprinted to keep up with his long strides. The cold slammed into her the moment she stepped through the sliding doors.

A two door black car stood on the curb and when the man went towards the back to open the door she noticed it was a BMW. She had heard of such cars, but never been in one. Her brother had talked of BMWs like they were chariots from heaven.

When he walked to the front he said something under his breath again as he pulled a piece of paper on the front of his car.

"They gave me a ticket!" He scrunched it up in his hands, the anger towards that piece of paper seemed to come from nowhere making Chenai nervous and fascinated at the same time. "I was only gone for two seconds." He groaned and cursed again as Chenai now stood on the curb, looking around to see who had given him a ticket. She saw the brake lights of a police car in front of them and suspected that was the culprit.

"Well, get in," he said and opened his own front door. His deep voice was laced with impatience that increased Chenai's anxiety, sending her temperature soaring to boiling point. With her bag on her lap, Chenai sat on the leather seat and smelt the clean smell that new cars must have. Another scent too that must have been his cologne filled the car. The warmth of the car was supposed to relax her, but her insides were filled with dancing butterflies.

The man came and sat next to her on the driver's seat.

"I'm Blake Pieri," he said pulling his seat belt around him.

"Nice to meet you," Chenai said quietly getting her own seat belt. *Blake. Blake Pieri. This was the man with the struggling family. The one who needed God?*

Blake threw the ticket on the dashboard with another angry huff then started the powerful engine, a purring sound, and with fluid speed and ease they were moving.

Chenai had never seen a man with such a bad disposition. She didn't feel at ease, sensing his frustration, as she sat next to him. It rose from him like steam from a boiling pot, and filled the air inside the small car. With shocking realization she remembered when she had last felt that way. In Rutendo's kitchen. Rutendo, her aunt who had thrown her out in the snow, somehow starting her journey to the Pieri family. The thought of her deepened her sadness. At the same time, Chenai remembered that she didn't want to focus on that.

Her mother often told her that it didn't take too long to sense someone's spirit. They didn't have to say anything. What they were inside, if you paid attention, came to you, flowed from their body like words written on the chalk board in the classroom. Her first impression of Blake didn't comfort her.

Chenai was further troubled by the way Blake Pieri drove. He was irritated by the drivers as he drove away from the airport. Chenai looked out the window as the car sped on to the highway and swerved in and out of traffic with the speed and agility of a dragonfly. Her heart was racing at both his driving and his temperament. She had to resist holding on the sides of the car for dear life as she watched him approach a huge truck and then swerve quickly to another lane.

"Did you wait a while?" he asked after about ten minutes of silence.

"About an hour," she said her eyes glued nervously on the road. Or was it two hours? She wasn't sure anymore. Snow had begun to fall from the sky, like angry white bees with no place to go, but to dance in the air. Chenai kept her eyes on it, mesmerized.

"Your flight must've been early," Blake said, turning on the wipers. The sound of fast water hitting the windshield gripped her. She watched as the wipers cleaned the windscreen only to be covered with more drops of snow.

"No. It was on time," she replied then turned to catch him turn on the radio to listen to a basketball game. After that they drove in silence along the busy highway until they got to a quiet residential area. She felt more relaxed once they moved at a slower pace, stopped by traffic lights and other cars.

Chenai felt as if she was in some kind of dream. She couldn't quite take in the sights nor the man who was driving the car. Everything had an unreal quality about it. She wondered if she would wake up and be at the farm ready to make breakfast for her father and brothers or take maize to feed her mother's chickens. That thought tightened her heart in pain and she turned to her window to see the barren trees and the house appearing before her eyes.

Blake drove the car into one of the four, car garages getting a quick glimpse of three cars, bikes, tools and toys. He got out after turning off the engine. Chenai looked at the clock as she pulled off the seat belt. It was 8pm. She hadn't managed to look at the house but had glimpsed strong rock walls, dark wood, big windows and evergreens that hid it from the street.

Chenai stepped out of the car and stood by while Blake walked to the door. She pointed towards the car.

"Your bag." He walked back pulled it out quickly and marched with it towards the house. He opened the door then turned on the lights to a dark laundry room then strode into a kitchen that was lit by tiny lights on the ceiling. Chenai quickly took in the dark kitchen cabinets and the huge family room. Both rooms combined seemed as big as a soccer field. It was a beautiful place. It was warm and inviting, especially after the cold outside. It seemed to envelope her in its multi-colored walls of autumn. Before she could study the black and white photographs on all the walls, Blake called out.

"Tyler. I'm home." His deep voice bounced off the walls. A young boy came from around the corner dressed in pajamas, hesitant and shy. His curly brown hair was falling in his eyes and he shook it free.

"Hey Dad," he said. She had expected him to jump into his arms and horse around like they do on television, but Tyler just stood with his arms on his side looking serious and lost. Later, Chenai would always play back this scene. Her first impression of Tyler was his lost puppy look mixed with curiosity as he regarded her.

"This is Cheny," Blake said.

Chenai wanted to correct him. Instead, she leaned over and said to Tyler, "My name is Chenai."

She held out her hand to him. Tyler hesitated a while then stepped forward and shook her hand. He smiled shyly then stepped back looking down.

"Where's your sister?" Blake asked looking through the mail that was on the kitchen counter.

"Upstairs," Tyler said.

"Go and tell her to come here and meet her nanny," Blake said and Chenai just raised her eyebrows at the term. *So that's what I am here. A Nanny.*

That definitely made more sense than a superhero destined to save some family, Chenai thought.

The movement from the stairs drew Chenai and a young girl sauntered towards them. As she got closer, Chenai was struck by her lovely blue eyes which the unusually red blotches on her face didn't disguise. Her brown hair was tossed above her head messily and she wore torn jeans and a sweater with a big "M" on it.

"Jodi. Why didn't you come down when I called?" Blake asked throwing the mail down and looking at his daughter.

"I didn't hear you call my name," Jodi said sulkily. She pulled the earphones from her ears.

"I said I'm home," Blake said his chin tight with anger. Chenai looked from one to the other then decided to look away when Jodi folded her arms and looked at her father with loathing. Chenai wasn't sure she had read her expression correctly.

"Anyway this is your new nanny, Cheny," Blake said pointing to Chenai.

"I don't need a nanny," Jodi hissed flashes of light coming from her eyes.

"You don't decide," Blake said. "Now, say hello to her."

"Hi Cheny," she said, "I'm going upstairs. Remember I'm grounded." She stomped from the room and up the stairs. Chenai watched her go then after a quick glance at Blake she looked at her feet. She didn't want to embarrass him so she tried to pretend she had not just witnessed that whole scene where a daughter spoke to her father as if he was a herd boy. Chenai wouldn't have been more surprised if Jodi had spat at her father and hit him over the head with a belt.

"You'll sleep upstairs for now. We have a guest quarters," Blake said picking up her bag, also ignoring his daughter's behavior. "This way."

Chenai walked a few steps behind Blake and made her way up the stairs, her hands on the dark wooden rail. The first floor had two passages, one hallway led to the East and the other to the North East. He stopped at the two double doors and opened one side so she could step in.

The room took her breath away. Chenai had never seen any-thing like it. She looked at the bed in front of her with awe, the two heavily curtained windows on the other side of the bed and the dresser that matched the desk. The colors endowed the room with a warmth that competed with the heat.

"This is the guest room you'll be using," Blake said putting the bag down. Chenai didn't know what to say at first wondering if he had taken her to the wrong room.

"Thank you, Mr. Pieri."

"Blake. Call me Blake. Mr. Pieri is probably what they call my father where ever he is."

"Blake."

"I'll leave you to settle in. You are in charge of the kids and the house. I leave early for the office so you can entertain them for a week until their break is over."

"Thank you," Chenai said again, not sure how to express how she really felt. Gratitude yes, excitement and anxiety all cooked up to make the butterflies in her stomach painful. He was looking at her oddly, as if he was trying to figure her out. Strangers meeting for the first time, but being forced to live in such close proximity. It was a strange situation. She looked away disconcerted by his dark eyes. They felt like shards of light trying to get into her brain.

Chenai had never been in contact with white men. At the farm, there was Mr. Millard, but she never had to talk to him and really didn't know what his habits were, except that he was the boss at the farm. She tried to compare the two men, Mr. Millard, always in shorts and long socks and skin as red as ripe tomatoes and hair as light as the sun. Mr. Pieri was dark, no redness to him, dark hair, eyes, but still white, which was for sure. The Millards world was as closed off to her and to be in this close contact with another white person, who actually saw her as a person, was disconcerting. Back then, the Millards, Mr. Millard was the one who ruled over all of them, until he didn't.

"You don't have to work or anything tonight. I'm sure you want to settle down. You can start work tomorrow."

Blake turned and left her standing in the room. Chenai turned and looked around again once the door handle had clicked.   Her stomach growled from hunger as she walked slowly towards the bed, sat down her hands resting on the tall bed post, dark wood, solid as a tree.

She opened the cupboards. They were empty except for some towels and fresh linen. The closet covered one whole side of the wall. She was surprised to find a bathroom when she opened the door behind the bed. Her eyes were drawn into the serene green and cream room with a huge tub and shower.

Chenai had never ever seen such opulence. Even the white owners' farm house in Zimbabwe was nothing like this though she used to admire it and tried to imagine what it was like to live in that house. Now Mr. Pieri's house was in another league completely. Judging by what she saw in her bedroom she could only imagine what his bedroom must be like.

After the quick exploration she didn't know what to do.

Chenai didn't turn on the TV in the cabinet, but she took out her night dress and went to take a bath. She always had to bath before bed. Her aunt had complained that she smelt like Zimbabwe, the smoke and paraffin they sometimes cooked with the first week she arrived there. Her aunt wanted to throw her clothes away initially and when Chenai protested, insisted she washed them in hot water and soaked them in a strong smelling blue liquid. She was so self-conscious about smelling right that she bathed and scrubbed her skin then put the roll on and powders her aunt had insisted she use.

After she was satisfied that she smelled clean, the last traces of Zimbabwe air and sun gone, she went to the huge bed and pulled back the covers. Her mind whirled with thoughts of home, her father and brothers, though mainly her mother. She would not think about her aunt, but skipped to Heather, and then to the mysterious looking man she would be working for. Finally she thought of little Tyler and her heart warmed. He seemed so sweet and innocent.

The daughter. Jodi. She seemed so angry and unhappy. She glanced at her door. Should she go and see the kids again? Should she stay in her room? Chenai finally decided that she would face them the next day.

Chenai knelt on the thick white carpet and begun her hour of prayer for her new home and family. As she prayed she heard a car start and when she looked at the dark driveway she saw Blake's black car driving out at high speed.

CHAPTER 3

Subzero

Why are you in despair, my soul?
— *Psalm 42:5*

Chenai stepped out of Tyler's room just as Blake walked out of his bedroom. He seemed surprised to see her, as if he had forgotten that he picked her up from the airport and brought her home. It was almost seven and the light from the window in Tyler's room rested on the walls.

"Good morning," Chenai said. She wished she could speak more confidently, but at that moment she felt as if her voice could disturb the peace, ruffle feathers. Blake grunted in response. He clearly was not a morning person. She didn't hear him drive back, so he must've arrived when she was already asleep.

"Daddy. I was showing Chenai around," Tyler said the delicate pride coming through his high voice.

"Where's your sister? She should be showing Cheny around," Blake slipped on the sweater he had been holding.

"I don't know," Tyler said hanging his head. Chenai didn't know what to say so she just kept quiet and put her hand gently on Tyler's shoulder.

"Can you drive?" Blake directed the question to her.

"No. I've never been taught," she replied, knowing it was the wrong answer.

"That's not helpful. If I'd known you don't drive I wouldn't have let my mother bully me into this arrangement."

Blake sighed and Chenai looked at her feet, totally at loss for words.

"You'll have to learn. You'll be responsible for the kids, picking them up, cooking and making sure they don't get in trouble. Especially Jodi. You have to keep an eye on her."

"Yes sir," Chenai answered automatically, the way she would have answered the headmaster at boarding school. Blake raised his eyebrows at her and she bit her lip.

"Do you have any questions?"

"I'd like to know what you want me to do with the kids on a daily basis," Chenai said.

"I don't know. You're the one skilled at looking after kids. That's what my mother told me so I leave it all to you." With those words Blake walked back to his bedroom.

Blake's phone rang.

"Hello, mother."

"Blake. You were supposed to call me last night. Did Chenai arrive safely?"

"She's here with the kids."

"Oh thank God. God is good. I'm so relieved. I was going to come there, but I feel better now that she's there. Chenai's had many troubles. I know she will be wonderful for the kids."

"She looks like a kid herself," Blake grumbled. He sat on his bed and slipped on running shoes.

"Well, she's older than some of the baby sitters you've had in the past. She's nineteen I think."

"Another teenager in the house."

"She'll be 20 before you know it."

"I hope she works out. That means I can focus on my work and not worry all the time about what Jodi's up to."

"You still have to be there for your kids. They're yours."

"I'm here. It's not easy dealing with their psychological problems while trying to keep my business running. I'm a single parent, now."

"I know."

"I don't think you get it. I just need a couple of months to a year to focus on the business."

Blake heard his mother's sigh. She had not lectured him in a while. About not taking vacations with the family or even going to visit her. Blake knew all his own short comings and really didn't need to hear them from someone else's mouth.

"Blake. You have never stopped working. I know you even missed Tyler's birth. It's consuming you."

"I have responsibilities. To investors, employees and yes, the kids. They are in private school."

Blake listened to the silence. Which meant his mother wasn't buying what he was saying. Was that disapproval breathing down the phone line?

"Will you come and visit us?" Marylyn asked instead of saying what she really wanted to say to him. He knew. He had heard it before. *Slow down son. Listen to God telling you to slow down.*

"It'll be a while. I can send the kids. I'm not going to be able to take a break any time soon."

"I see. Well, I'd like to speak to Chenai if that's okay. What's she like?"

Blake heard the excitement in his mother's voice and shook his head. He hadn't looked at her. She just came. He had more things to do than study what his kids' nanny looked like. "She's African Mother. She speaks with an accent. Quiet. Timid. Very dark brown too, with huge lips, very skinny. Looks like a kid to me."

"She's dark? Why like Oprah?"

"I don't know. I don't think I know that many black people?"

"That's a shame, Blake."

"You only know Oprah."

"No. I know others."

· ❧ ·

Chenai startled when the door to her bedroom opened. She had left Tyler as he watched a movie that had machines that moved like people. Jodi was in her room with a sign on her door that read, "Keep out!"

"Cheny are you there?" She heard Blake's voice just as she looked up. He was about to say something, but he stopped, glaring at her. She watched him press a button on his phone then asked, "What are you doing?"

Chenai sat up straighter on her bed, wondering what she had

done wrong now. Wasn't she supposed to be in the room? Was she meant to be with Jodi or Tyler? She moved her feet off the bed, wondering if that's what the problem was. For some reason she felt her mouth go dry and had to swallow before she could speak.

"Reading my Bible." His expression made her feel guilty as if he had caught her stealing, or worse.

"I hope you do that privately. I don't want you to influence my kids with that. We don't believe that here."

Chenai didn't know what to say. She closed the Bible with a thud, heart racing. Blake still wore the disapproval painted on his face, grasping the cell phone in his left hand. Her shock and fear must have been evident because he sighed, though he seemed determined to follow his convictions

"Can- can I read in here?"

"Yes, yes. Just don't try and influence my kids. I don't want them growing up weak and bigoted. You might as well know how I feel about that entire nuisance from the beginning."

"Yes." Chenai said tears threatening to fall from her eyes.

"Oh. My mother wants to talk to you." Blake held out the phone to her. Chenai stood up and walked towards him. Her hand shook as she took the phone and put it to her ear. She noticed that Blake watched her for a second before he decided to leave.

"I'm going for a run. Put the phone in my room when you're done," he said.

Chenai sat back on the bed as Blake closed the door with a soft click. She cleared her throat willing her heart to stop beating with fear.

"Hello," Chenai finally spoke into the phone, just as the sound of the furnace clicked on. She felt the heat from the vent near her bed flow down to her, almost like fingers running down her body from her head to her toes.

"Chenai. It's so wonderful to hear you are there safely," Marylyn said. Her remembered voice gave some reassurance. It sounded sweet and soothing, a hug from a distance that she desperately needed. She swallowed hard. Crying on the phone would worry this lovely woman.

"Yes."

"Did you have a safe flight?"

"It was fine."

"How's my son treating you?"

Chenai wanted to bawl, but she held herself together by biting the inside of her lip. She tasted blood. Chenai recalled the first time they spoke, when Marylyn, who somehow knew Heather's grandmother from years past, told Chenai about Blake and his poor kids. She had convinced Chenai to fly to Michigan. Chenai had not really had a choice, had she?

"Fine."

"How's Tyler?"

"Tyler. He's fine. He took me around the house and this morning we made pancakes together." Chenai braced herself as Marylyn's voice grew serious and deeper.

"Chenai. I know you're going to be good for my grandkids do you hear me? Don't worry about Jodi. I'm praying for her. She needs someone to love her. She misses her mother and she misses her Dad, too. You're an answer to prayer. I've been praying for an intervention and that intervention is you. You don't know this but you have brought Christ into my son's home. He is now in that big house and Christ will work through you."

Chenai felt tears sting her eyes then roll down her cheeks, salt in her mouth. She was an answer to prayer? Why did she feel like Blake was the Devil and she was going to be eaten alive in his house? His disapproving stare a few minutes earlier still stung, just as his words cut her to the core.

Then there was Jodi. There was no life or warmth in her eyes. What could she do to bring joy back into the young girl's life? Jodi terrified her and she had no clue how to help her.

"Just think about how we connected. My friend's daughter helps you, that night. That seems like divine intervention to me, don't you think? Don't be discouraged young lady. I'm going to give you my cell phone number and email. Call me any time do you hear me? I'll be praying for you."

"Thank you," Chenai said. She was comforted by those words even though questions fought for answers in her head. Could she deal with this?

Not you, she remembered, but *God through you.*

Yes, Chenai thought. God had already proven true. Just a week before she was homeless, walking the snowy streets of New Jersey with nowhere to go. Before that, she had left the only home she knew and embarked on a journey to the unknown. Now, she was in this beautiful house, albeit with broken people. But God had a plan. As Chenai recalled her journey to that moment, she held on to the thought that God would provide everything for her. Answers. A future. He had said it. God had great plans for her. She just had to let his love remove the fear in her heart. When she was preparing to leave the father and brothers she adored, she never in her wildest dreams thought she would end up where she was now. Never.

CHAPTER 4

Foggy

The day is yours, and yours also the night; you
established the sun and moon. -

—*Psalm 74:16*

Leaving Zimbabwe she sat on the plane months before, Chenai was amazed at all the steps she had taken to get to that point. The unending application forms, SATs, essays, trips to travel agents and those last sad goodbyes.

"What do I do when I get to London? How do I know where to go?" Chenai had asked Jackie, the travel agent who gave her the tickets, while her father sat quietly next to her. He was looking at the pictures on the walls, giant blow ups of Victoria Falls, Lake Kariba, and Cape Town. All the places neither had ever visited.

"They have many signs at the airport. It's quite easy," Jackie explained stuffing the tickets and itinerary in a plastic folder.

"Where? Will someone escort her," this time her father asked. Frank had always been a quiet man, letting his wife do most of the talking throughout their marriage, though now, Chenai realized he was the single parent who had to find it in himself to protect his only daughter by speaking out. She smiled at him as he continued. "How will she know which flight will take her to New York?"

Jackie had laughed then took out all the papers again and began going through the itinerary one more time, her patience as long as the Zambezi River. After all that Chenai was still confused.

How am I going to know where to go?

Chenai closed her eyes as she sat on the plane. It continued along the brightly lit runway, the fast moving scenery engaging her and reducing her fear of the future.

This was her first time leaving the country, leaving Zimbabwe on her way to unknown parts of the world. Places she had studied about mainly in history books.

As the butterflies in her stomach increased with the phenomenal speed of the plane, Chenai knew she couldn't look outside her little window any more. Her heart raised and she felt as if it would jump into her mouth when the plane suddenly sailed up. Fear, excitement and panic all danced around in her belly. It was a potent mixture that she knew would lead to days of stomach pain.

Chenai closed her eyes and her mother's face flashed instantly behind her lids, trying to imagine she was with her. Loss had deepened her dreams, always vivid of her mother. Her daydreams were of her. It was a terrible club to be part of. The motherless. It was the loneliest place to be. If Lois had been on the plane she would have struck up conversation with the man next to her. She would be excited.

"America! We are going to America. God has so much in store for us."

Her mother's confidence would have eased her mind, instead of the fierce trepidation that held her captive her waking and sleeping moments. Her mother had a way of turning the darkest day into sun filled bliss. Her fondest memory came to her as she the plane took off into the African sky, a bit shaky, a leaf floating from a tree at first but settling down beyond the clouds.

Had five years passed already since she'd spent an afternoon of laughter with her mother? Indeed it was. She was fifteen when she felt most awkward at school, with few friends and not excelling in anything outside the classroom.

It had been during the midterm break in October. She'd been thin as the grass that grew in the savannah and awkward like a new born bird. Chenai was happy to jump out of the mini bus that had stuffed almost thirty people in the 10 seats. She began the long walk on the main road and after failing to get a lift for an hour, she began the long walk home past hectares of baby maize fields and cows grazing in the fields. On that long dusty road not a single car came by and she never passed a single person, alone with her thoughts of home.

As she got closer to their brick farmhouse surrounded by a high wall she'd felt eager to see her family. Spotting the three-bedroom farmhouse with a corrugated roof and corn growing on the front yard and backyard, her steps increased. Her feet were dusty and aching from the long walk and her heart sore from the experiences as a student at St John's High School just outside Harare. During her days at boarding school she lived for the moment she would be home again.

When she opened the gate she could hear chickens clucking in the background and further down the road young girls were singing "*Shiri yakanaka*" a song about a flying bird, their enjoyment evident in the sweet voices. After that song, they broke into another one getting louder as they got closer to her.

The metal gate squeaked when she opened it and her mother who must have seen her from the kitchen window ran out, nearly slipping on the polished verandah. She caught her daughter in her arms picking her up and twirling her and sending the chickens scuttling away from them and the dog yelping in surprise.

"Chenai. Oh Chenai," her mother cried joyfully, holding her. Chenai just held on to her, smelling her hair, her lovely perfume and the smell of soap and baking.

"Come. You must be hungry. I made your favorite scones and I even bought jam." Chenai smiled walking into the house. The rich smell of fresh baking greeted her at the door, making her mouth water instantly.

"It smells nice," Chenai said putting her bag on the ground. Her school uniform, a green shapeless skirt and white shirt and green tie hung on her lanky body. On her feet were her dusty, ugly brown shoes and green socks she had worn for almost two years.

"What's wrong?" her mother asked looking into her eyes. Chenai looked down at the tiled floor noticing a few more missing tiles.

"Nothing." Was her short answer, which her mother did not accept.

"I know something is bothering you. I could see it in your step as you walked down the dusty road." Her mother gestured toward the road but didn't take her eyes off her even as she placed a scone on a plate. Her mother gave her *the look*.

"You better tell me."

"The girls were making fun of me at school," Chenai said finally. She didn't like to admit it. Her mother always told her she was a queen just like Esther in the Bible. She told her to always remember that God didn't make garbage whenever she felt ugly or someone made fun of her.

"What did they say?"

"They called my mouth fat. They called me chicken legs because I'm so skinny." In her mother's eyes was love and determination. Her eyes were like a salve on a burning wound.

"You are a very lovely girl, Chenai my dearest," she said. Chenai just stared at her, disbelieving. "Come with me." Chenai allowed her mother to lead her to her bedroom at the end of a narrow passage. The afternoon sun shimmered through and left a carpet of warmth in the room. Chenai walked around her parents' bed and ended up by the mirror standing next to her mother.

"Look at yourself," Lois said and picked up her daughter's chin when she tried to look down.

"Chenai look."

Chenai slowly raised her eyes to her image in the mirror. She critically gazed at her wide brown eyes that sat above high sharp cheekbones. Her nose was slightly flared. Her lips seemed to cover the width of her dark mahogany brown face and they appeared darker and fuller.

"You, my dear look exactly as I did when I was your age," Lois said.

"I do?"

"Yes. You have a beauty that is deeper than just your skin. I see your heart Chenai. You have warmth, tenderness and your eyes are sincere and beautiful. I'm your mother would I lie to you?"

Chenai shook her head, a smile forming on her lips.

"At this age you feel a bit awkward because your body is changing and everything hasn't fallen into place. And the girls who make fun of you are unhappy. God didn't make anything ugly. Everything God made is beautiful and you, my baby are one of those masterpieces. He loves you and always remember that, no matter what anybody else says to you."

Chenai felt comfortable enough to tell her mother everything else that had happened at school. Lois listened attentively with her daughter's hand in hers.

"All the boys like light girls like you Amai. I'm so dark," Chenai said. Lois looked at her again.

"Dark skin, light skin has nothing to do with your heart. God just loves variety. Look at your father. He has the rich chocolate brown skin. Evans is like me and you and Petros take after your father. It's your heart that counts and my angel you have the most beautiful heart." Lois paused and looked as if she had the most brilliant idea.

"Wait here," she said and walked out of the bedroom. Chenai looked at the family picture that stood on her dressing table. She was about ten when it was taken and then she never worried about how she looked. She had a huge smile on her face and her eyes sparkled with confidence and joy.

Lois returned. "I turned off the stove. We can eat later. Now I want you to try something. Lois opened her wooden wardrobe whose doors creaked loudly and took out her favorite suit. She pulled out a blouse and high-heeled shoes.

"Try them on," she said.

"Mai, it's yours."

"I know. I want to see how it looks on you."

Chenai quickly took off her uniform and put on the outfit and the high-heeled shoes. Her mother untied her hair which stood up straight and she combed it back flat.

They stood there in front of the mirror for a while. Chenai felt transformed in her mother's creamy suit. She caught her mother's eye in the mirror. Her mother gazed at her with adoring eyes. Something shifted in her, as she saw the similarities in the slant of cheekbones, fullness of lips and crispness of hair. The only difference was in the skin tone, a shade darker here, more brown paint mixed into the black, smooth as polished wood and shiny below the eyes.

They spent that afternoon trying on clothes until her father returned from the fields. Supper was eaten very late that day, but Chenai had laughed with her mother, the memory of their voices now filling the droning plane she sat in. Voices like music from a favorite song, filled with sweetness and bitterness.

Chenai sat and willed the confidence to come, her favorite memory fading. When she closed her eyes, the dreams of the farm were strong. A place where she grew up with the cows and goats that she knew by name. She remembered the cows that belonged to the Millards, their barns, their dams, their school, everything belonged to the Millards. Then she forced herself to forget the darkest time of her life on a farm that had been mostly filled with joy. She didn't want to allow the memories of that time, or her pain would shutter the plane's engines and send her plummeting down to earth.

CHAPTER 5

Frozen

But those who wait in the Lord will renew their strength. They will soar on wings like eagles; they will run and not grow weary, they will walk and not be faint. In my weakness his strength is made perfect."

—*Romans 8: 9*

"Chenai wake up! I didn't bring you to America to just sleep. Wake up!"

Chenai opened her eyes feeling disoriented. She scrunched up her nose as the damp smell, mixed with laundry detergent wafted to her. Looking around the dark room she glanced at the pile of boxes around her sleeping pad then remembered that she was now in America. This was her fifth night in her aunt's huge house.

The basement was cold and cluttered, but Chenai had managed to sleep deeply, dreaming of the warmth of the sun in Zimbabwe and cooking sadza and pumpkin leaves with her mother.

She had never slept underground like a mouse before. It was a new experience and at first had been terrified going down there, as if the house would fall on her. So far so good, Chenai thought touching the low roof.

Before her aunt screamed again Chenai, darted upstairs, dressed in her thick cotton pajamas. She tripped once on her still wobbly legs, the dizziness attacking like buzzing bees.

Panting from the fall, she reached the landing and marched into the kitchen wiping her dreams away with her hand.

Rutendo stood in the kitchen with a sour expression on her coffee colored face. Jumbo. Yes. Her face reminded Chenai of one of their temperamental bulls on the farm. Chenai trembled at Rutendo's heavy and imposing stature. Every part of her seemed to send her messages of disapproval, anger and stress. Her face hinted at battles, vicious struggles that she wore in her eyes as one would wear shoes for a perilous journey.

Rutendo worked as a nurse in the ER and was very dedicated and proud of her job. She was also a very dedicated and proud mother. Chenai was forced to care for Rutendo's children her every waking moment.

"You were still sleeping?" Rutendo asked sipping her tea. The clock by the electric stove read 7 am, although the darkness outside the window looked as if it were still night.

"So sorry. I overslept."

Rutendo clucked her tongue like the chickens did on the farm. Chenai recalled how her mother never tolerated that sound from anyone as she said it was more insulting than a curse. It was a sound that was meant to demean and added with the slanted eyes and scowl, it worked very well. Making such a sound in front of her mother was cause for a slap and a disappointed look on her face. Lois didn't hit them much, especially as they grew older, but that sound drew her wrath. Besides, as they grew older, none of her three children ever wanted to disappoint Lois.

"My children are about to wake up. Make them some breakfast and feed the baby." Rutendo spoke in a mixture of English and Shona and jarred Chenai from her slip into the past. The Shona came out quickly with many "r" sounds that tinkled like a song or the wind ruffling through leaves. However to Chenai's ears it was the rumble of thunder.

"Yes Aunty," Chenai blinked rapidly wishing the sleep to leave her eyes faster and headed towards the sink to wash her hands.

"You should wash your hands in the bathroom. This is not Zimbabwe. People here wash their hands in the bathroom sink. I don't want your germs where I cook my food."

Chenai barely glanced at her reflection, puffy red eyes, lips full with the taste of dreams of home. She rubbed some water over the eyes, hoping to bring life into them and retied the scarf she had on her head, one her mother used to wear to funerals. After washing her hands, Chenai went to the kitchen and opened a few cupboards to find a pan.

"What are you looking for?" Rutendo's deep voice landed on her back. Chenai half turned.

"A pan." Rutendo moved hurriedly to the cupboard where Chenai was about to check and flung the door open.

"Here. You don't remember where the pots are?" Chenai didn't answer as she walked to the huge fridge and pulled out the eggs and bacon. She was so jet legged sometimes she could not remember where her clothes were. Even her aunt's orders and insults only half registered through her confused and tired mind. Was she dreaming or was this really her reality? Her jumbled emotions jousted in her heart. Disbelief, exhaustion, fear, sadness and confusion.

Rutendo left the room after clicking her tongue again and Chenai felt the air in the room thin. She let out a breath and focused on making the eggs and bacon the way her cousins liked it, fighting fatigue and something else. Something that hung around her body like a cloak, so heavy it pressed her down, lower and lower with each minute. Dread. Yes. That's what it was. It sucked her energy and like eternal fog, would not lift. She was in its belly and couldn't find a way out.

Rutendo's children were all born in the United States and didn't speak their native language or even understand it. Chenai could barely understand the two older ones as they spoke with a drawl and pronounced their words so differently and spoke so fast, faster than flies. Rutendo had explained the reason why the other two children had English names.

"The Americans struggled pronouncing their names so I went English with the middle two but with Chipo, I didn't care. I love my culture. No more English names."

Figuring out their needs was her other task. She walked in to wake up the oldest one first.

"No," The oldest boy, Tino said after Chenai whispered to him that it was time for school. Chenai left him hidden under his spider man comforter but after turning on the light she rounded back and pulled the covers off his bed onto a floor filled with toys, from guns, swords and helmets. Isaac was also difficult to wake up in the next bed, and last she went to Janet's room and got her clothes for school. They didn't wear a school uniform, though it seemed all the children dressed the same anyway in jeans, sweaters and sneakers.

About fifteen minutes later they all walked into the kitchen and she passed out the food and continued to move around as the children required different things.

"Can I have more milk?" Janet, the only girl demanded. She was four, and her hair was a tangled mess. She hated having her hair combed and even though Chenai could tell that some chemicals had been used to relax it, it still needed redoing. At four she also had to go to school.

"I don't want milk. Want juice." Tino moaned.

Isaac, the first grader just sat there and ate everything in silence. He wasn't too fussy and rarely talked.

Finally they finished eating and behind them was a storm of a mess in the tiny kitchen. Looking around the chaos reminded her of the first day she arrived. Plates, cups, glasses and spills everywhere.

Chenai went back to her basement sleeping space and dressed in her old school tracksuit while the children gathered their homework and bags then followed them outside to wait for the bus. The kids wore thick coats and boots. Chenai wore winter clothes from Zimbabwe. She quickly realized her clothes were not suitable at all for this kind of weather the moment she stepped off the plane.

Her clothes were not new-she had them in her last year of school. She felt her chest close as the cold hit her square in the face and stung her eyes. Winter could be brutal in Bindura with the mountains and the dam not too far, as well as no central heating. However, this cold was something new and deadly. Each breath felt tight in her throat, scratching it. Her fingers were already numb and it was almost impossible to hold her sweater and pull it over her fingers. The boys in their thick gloves and coat ran and pushed. She stood there shivering praying the big yellow bus would come quickly. This world was bleak, gray, dark and miserable.

Chenai worked all morning on the kitchen and also fed the baby. She carried Chipo on her back as she made the beds in all the four bedrooms, picking up toys and books and hanging up clothes. She emptied the clothes hampers. At 1pm, Rutendo emerged from her bedroom dressed in her scrubs looking professional and immaculate. Her hair was smooth on her shoulders and make up shimmered on her face, making her already smooth face perfect.

Rutendo surveyed the kitchen, the dark wood cabinets and white tile counter tops and pursed her lips in a disapproving manner. Chenai followed her eyes, trying to figure out what she had done wrong this time.

"Did you mop the floor? I don't want Chipo crawling around on the dirty floor." Chenai patted the baby on her back realizing Rutendo didn't require an answer as she took bread and margarine out of the fridge.

"I think you can do the laundry today. I'm running out of scrubs. For dinner just make something from the food in the fridge. Now that you are here the children don't have to eat Mc-Donald's anymore. And Pizza. *Maiwee*, we were tired of pizza." Rutendo laughed at her own joke, which Chenai didn't really get. "Your uncle is arriving today from Florida. He expects good food."

Scrubs. What were scrubs? After Rutendo left for work what Chenai suspected became clear. She was to be her aunt's maid and that's why Rutendo had wanted her to live with her in the States in the first place, paid for the plane ticket and the visa fees. Maybe just a slave, as no word about pay or school was ever mentioned.

Why does she seem to hate me so much? Why did she want me to come? God why am I here?

She wasn't getting a clear answer. She didn't have time to search God's face on this. She was already exhausted and when she finally threw herself on her bed, she fell asleep in seconds.

Chenai wasn't afraid of hard work. Back in Zimbabwe hard work in the house or fields was as natural as breathing. Her mother insisted it was a sign of worship. To work hard for others, to produce from the land. Laziness was not tolerated. From the time she could walk, Chenai recalled helping her mother make meals, and at about six years old she was making breakfast for the family. She worked at home and washed clothes with her bare hands and even worked in the fields but there was always joy as she did it. She was finding hard to find the joy.

Father, Please talk to me.

When baby Chipo was sleeping Chenai sat next to the baby and picked up her Bible. Her hand on the familiar pages, the thin rustling paper calmed her. She stopped in the Psalms. She loved the Psalms. Every anguish was there, every hope was available for her, waiting for her ears and heart to receive it. Her mother loved the Psalms. The Bible she held had been her mother's and notes covered most of the pages. It seemed each word in that book spoke to her and filled her up. Her eyes rested on Psalm 53. She enjoyed the easy translation, the words that she understood.

"When I am afraid I will trust in you."

God's words always had a way of calming her fears. Why would those words be in the Bible if not true? She had to remember that she had chosen to believe God in every situation, not what she saw with her eyes.

She had to push the overwhelming panic out of her or it would eat her up and leave her a shivering useless mess. With determination, she remembered her mother's words as if she whispered them to her just, as she did on her first day of high school.

"No matter what happens always find a purpose. What can you do to glorify God in every situation? Ask Him and He will show you."

"Amai I don't see what I am supposed to be doing here. I have only been here for a week and I feel like it's been a year!" Chenai stifled a sob. In that second, she knew she would do anything just to see her mother's face again.

The headache was coming back, throbbing strong, bulging through her skull fighting for release. She had started feeling sick when she landed in London. Somehow, the hours of sitting on the plane, not moving had affected her. The landing had also been scary and she had writhed with pain in her ears, wondering why everybody else seemed fine, watching the movie or reading with their night lights.

She had followed the passengers when it was time to disembark and the "ding" signaled it was safe to get up. She moved along with them like a fish following the tide. She didn't know where she was going, but she kept moving with the throng, putting one leg in front of the other with as much purpose as all the other people. Then, there were lines where she had to go through immigration and they asked her questions, just as they had done when she applied for her student visa.

"Where are you going? What do you want to study? Why couldn't you study in your own country? Where is the letter from your school?" The questions were endless and she had endured the same interrogation when she arrived in America. With a throbbing head she had answered their questions, showed them her papers, endured the search through her private bags and now here she was. In hell.

Though she was feeling like a duck in a chicken pen in America, her aunt's resentment was the most shocking thing of all. Chenai had spent little time with her in Zimbabwe but Rutendo had always been sweet as honey when she came to visit the farm. Chenai's mother and Rutendo would laugh, peels of sound and talk late into the night.

"Lois, you should bring Chenai to the States. She can do very well in the colleges there and she can also help me with the kids," Rutendo would say to Lois in her confident, well-traveled and seen-the-world voice.

Chenai would overhear this each time Rutendo visited them

on her way to Kariba to stay on a boat with her friends. After Rutendo left the last time her mother had walked with her to feed the chickens and asked her what she felt about going to the States. "I want to go America. Just for a short time. Get my degree and then come back here. I want to send money to you like Uncle Jerry used to when he went to England."

Chenai wasn't sure if mentioning her uncle to her mother was a good idea. He had gone to study in Europe, in Belgium after the war, then he had moved to England. In the beginning he had sent money home to the family, but then he got married to a woman from there, and he had not returned. He never called, he never wrote. He simply vanished into the cold frigid English air.

"Money's not everything, Chenai. We are doing fine," Lois said as she threw the corn to the chickens in the coop her eyes in the distance. Chenai watched the brown, black and gray birds scamper and eat greedily with their beaks pressed to the ground.

"I know. But then, you won't have to work at the Millards anymore. They work you too hard."

"It's just work. It doesn't kill me."

"It kills Baba."

Lois had remained quiet. They both knew that Frank detested her working in the Millards home. Chenai only knew what she overheard once in a while when her parents thought they couldn't be heard in their bedroom. One disagreement, had been when Mrs. Millard threw her dinner party for the other farmers in the area. Lois had worked until 3 am, and then had had to wake up again at 6 am to go back to the Millard home and make breakfast for them and clean the house and feed the dogs and whatever else

Mrs. Millard could demand of her. Chenai had heard her father speak strongly, though he never shouted.

"You are getting so thin. You don't sleep. I sleep alone."

"I know Frank but we need the money. Chenai needs exam fees and uniforms, so do the children. Your mother in the village needs medication and a borehole. The list is endless."

Yes, she had heard them talk. They had also discussed her coming to America. How that might help the family in the future, and how they would miss their only girl. And they had prayed.

And so almost eight years later, here she was in a place her mother only dreamed of and wished for her child to go and make something of her life. Planning the trip to America was like preparing to go a land of magic, joy, and abundance. Now, the reality was something else. Where was the magic? The education. The joy.

Now, she thought of her cousins, all four of Rutendo's children. They were just children, she thought, but was she like that as a child? Did her mother do almost everything for her while she whined and complained about everything? She remembered her youngest brother. He was spoiled and he loved to mess up the house bringing sand from outside. But she loved him and cleaning after him was not so bad because he was so cute. Her aunt's children had many sweet moments, though she noticed that they were beginning to treat her the way their mother did, with contempt. Baby Chipo was adorable. As she thought about the baby, Chipo let out a cry from her crib and Chenai dropped her Bible and ran to fetch her.

Chenai looked at Chipo's big brown eyes as they stared back at her with trust and love. She inhaled that feeling like a fragrance from her mother's flowers filling her heart with it because this love was so rare in the home she was living in. Rutendo seemed to resent her even though she needed her at the same time. Chenai had no idea that things were about to get worse.

CHAPTER 6

Icy

*You, O Lord keep my lamp burning; my God turns
my darkness into light."*

—Psalm 18:28

"There is Chenai," Rutendo said when Chenai came up from the basement. She had been ironing Rutendo's scrubs and folding laundry, the hot iron warming the usually frigid space. "Come and say hello, Chenai."

Chenai put the basket of clothes down on her hip and walked into the lounge to meet James Kameno, who reclined on the leather sofa. James wore his handsome smile easy, like a comfortable shirt. At once Chenai sensed his kindness, a man with a quiet, gentle air about him. Chenai almost felt like she was shaking her father's hand. It was a pleasant, reassuring feeling though instantly felt deeply how much she missed her father.

"Nice to meet you, Chenai. Whenever I came to Zimbabwe I never got to meet you," James Kameno said, his voice warm and sincere.

"*Makadii?*" Chenai clapped her hands together, asking after his health, the way she was taught at home, a way to greet everyone older than her. James waved it off, clearly a man who had shaken off his culture and past and now preferred the American way of greeting. What was it the kids said, "Wass up?"

The children were all gathered around him like chickens in the coop. Obviously, they missed their father. He had to tell them to sit still and listen for a minute while he talked to Chenai, but he kept his arm around Janet. Janet would not move an inch from Daddy and James wore all this love with an ease that was surprising.

"So have you been around New York City? Seen the lights and the people?" Chenai looked at her aunt. She had barely sat in that living room, with its huge TV and Zimbabwean sculptures that looked out of place. She seemed to be working every waking moment.

"She's been too busy," Rutendo said, her smile as indulging to James as it was to Tino and the rest of the kids. "Maybe next week."

"You must take her to the city. It's nothing like Africa, young girl." James went on to tell them all about New York City. Chenai listened with trepidation and excitement. She had work to do, as always, but knew she also had to hear what her uncle had to say. She felt the electrical current of indecision tingle her feet, the sound reminding her of a buzzing mosquito. But she remained, sitting with her basket of clothes on her lap.

Chenai could only imagine this city, the lights. She had seen so many buildings and lights when she landed, full of hope and anxiety. With her aunt she had gone as far as Walmart to buy groceries. Of course she wanted to see the statue of liberty and the kids talked so much about the incredible lights in Times Square. Their favorite place was China Town because their mother always bought them toys there. She was curious and wanted to see something besides the grocery store, though at the same time, she didn't mind. There was so much to learn just living in Rutendo's house. Still a little thrill found its way into her heart, filling it with anticipation.

"Can you go and make tea, Chenai. Your uncle is too excited about this whole New York thing as if you have nothing to do."

Chenai's excitement faded. She would probably never go five miles beyond the house.

When she brought in the tea with scones she had made, James asked her about her father.

"He's still headmaster at Chikomega Primary School. He said he was applying to move to the city." Chenai could have added that her father found farm life difficult since her mother passed or that the memories were too great, but she didn't say anything. It wasn't easy for her to talk about yet or ever. She remembered seeing him, surrounded by his books, but reading none of them, soon after her mother died.

"He doesn't want to live at the farm anymore?"

"When I left the people who took over the farm were not doing much with the land. It seems the man, Mr. Turefu just wanted to sell all the equipment and move into the old farm house where the Millard family used to live."

James reached for his tea and took a sip. "Yes, we heard about the land redistribution program and how only a few were getting land. CNN talked about it all the time like World War III had started. Now everybody at work is always asking about Zimbabwe and why the black people took the land from the British. Did anybody ever ask why the British took the land from the black people first?"

Chenai nodded. This subject was very difficult for her to talk about. It brought back difficult memories and distress thinking that the whole land situation was what caused her loss. It was what took away her mother. She didn't want to think about it at all. Her father was the one who looked at everything philosophically, always saying that history would continue to repeat itself because people don't live forever. Young men and women are born and they don't know of the past, and would continue to do the same things.

To him, nothing was new under the sun. He would say things like, "Right now we are all going to America. There was a time when there were other super powers. Right here in Africa. Egypt, the Greeks, The Romans. Unfortunately we never learn from history and it repeats itself."

And life is lost, Chenai would think. In the scheme of time, the whole world with billions of people, who cared what happened to a young girl living on a farm in Bindura who after losing her mother was uprooted to America? Nobody.

"I'm going to wash the plates," Chenai excused herself and made her way to the kitchen after dropping the clothes in the laundry room. When she started washing the dishes, she wanted to block her ears as her aunt began to talk.

"Many innocent people lost their lives because of that whole business. Lois had to suffer so unnecessarily all because people were greedy and didn't care what happened to innocent women. What a horrible way to die, in front of your kids, *maiwee*. Now I'm stuck with her daughter, who is so ungrateful…"

Chenai gasped, reeling from her aunt's words. From the kitchen, Chenai heard James's inquiring voice, "She's giving you problems?"

"She's just so – so rural. I have to teach her everything. How to vacuum, how to open the bath water for goodness sake."

"Oh. The taps are different here."

"Yes. The faucets. Everything is new. How to answer the phone properly. Eish this whole thing seems more trouble than I anticipated. She works hard once you have taught her, but it's too much to teach."

"But isn't she supposed to go to school. We promised her father."

"Oh please. How can she go to school when she can't even use a computer or the internet? You know James. I think I know what's best for Chenai. Right now, she needs to be grateful that she's in America. Zimbabwe is on its way down since the whites were kicked off their land. There's no food, did you hear. At least she has food to eat and a roof over her head. Zimbabwe is a mess right now and Lois would be grateful for just getting her only daughter away from the chaos over there. Lois was smart and sensible unlike her husband. He reminds me of that character from that book, remember that book, by the Nigerian…"

"Things Fall Apart," Uncle said.

"Yes. Unoka. A lazy man who played music but didn't work. I guess in her case Frank just reads books. Books don't buy anything. Just fill your head with stories. What for?"

Chenai was furious. Her father loved that book and Chenai remembered the character in question, who didn't believe in keeping money for tomorrow. Her father did. He saved and he looked after his kids and didn't drink like the many teachers from the school, who when they received their pay check, couldn't drink it fast enough until the wives came crying to the headmaster. Her father then instituted a plan that the wives had to get some money before their buffoon husbands drank it all.

Chenai felt her neck tense hearing her mother's name on Rutendo's tongue and her father talked about in such untrue, negative ways. Her heart was racing with distress as she recalled what her aunt said about Zimbabwe. Rutendo didn't know her own country's history. She had gone to school when history was taught from the white man's perspective only, all lies. Her father had told her the truth, because her father had fought in the war, to get back Zimbabwe. Her father had told her how Zimbabwe was stolen from her great grandfather, taken from them in the middle of the day by men on horses who stole not only their land, but all their livelihood and fought over their livestock. Her father had fought to liberate his own people, return to them what had been grabbed.

It annoyed Chenai when people talked and laughed at Zimbabwe's economic woes, not knowing that children were affected, families torn, people killed! Especially people who were not even in Zimbabwe. Blaming their own people for failing to farm the land as if it was ever meant to be easy, or to work in a day. A country wasn't built in a day, or a year. Rhodesia that everybody seemed to long for, was built over many years, with help from the British

Queen and the suppression of a whole nation.

She took deep breaths, controlling the urge to throw the kettle and smash the window. Her anger shocked her even as it built in giant waves, that threatened to drown her.

Was she meant to be grateful, Lord? All she wanted was to get on the next plane and go back to Zimbabwe and starve with her father and brothers.

She took deep breaths praying for the Holy Spirit to bring her peace. Slowly, like a mist of warm water, a feeling of calm washed over her, a broom sweeping away scum, cleansing and purifying.

CHAPTER 7

Chill

Better is a dry morsel with quietness, than a house full of feasting with strife."

—Proverbs 17: 1

The mess from the bridal shower lay all over the floor like debris washed up from the ocean. Strewn in the living room, dining room and kitchen were plastic cups, plates and cans. Chenai picked up the big pieces and put them in the trash bags. There were wine stains that needed to be taken care of and she sprayed the chemicals that could absorb the smell and color from the white carpet. She coughed from the pungent smell, eyes stinging.

Chenai wanted to finish quickly so she could go to church. James had told her about the closest church to the house. He had never been there, but said he saw many cars parked there.

"You should take the kids," he said to her before he left the night before. James told her that he was going to spend the night in a hotel because he did not want to be part of the crazy bridal shower that his wife was hosting for a Zambian friend of hers whom she met at the hospital. The young woman, Tabitha, was marrying a Zimbabwean doctor who worked at the same hospital.

The shower started at 7pm, but true to African time, the first guest arrived at 8pm and the guest of honor at about 9pm at which time the food was served.

Chenai spent the whole day preparing. Roasted chicken, stewed beef, vegetables, *samosas*, and lasagna. She had also baked three cakes and helped to decorate the living room with balloons and posters.

While they shopped at Wal-Mart, filling the trolley with food and paper goods, Rutendo had given Chenai the details. "This is a very good friend of mine, Chenai. I want everything to look good. She's marrying a wonderful man. I introduced them."

Chenai nodded, pushing the cart next to Rutendo.

"Have you been to a kitchen tea before?" Rutendo asked.

Chenai shook her head. "Well, you are probably too young and you will be too busy to really see it."

Rutendo was right. Chenai barely had time to talk to anybody as she ran from kitchen to living room serving food, cleaning and at midnight Rutendo told her to make another pot of sadza for her friends. The women, loud and excited about the wedding laughed raucously, but never talked to her. She could have been invisible as she heard them talk about ways to please a man in bed. She was embarrassed though she noticed that none of the women found it unusual to talk about such intimate things in front of each other.

"A man wants a wild woman in bed, but not out of it," the main speaker was saying. "Especially African men."

"I've dated American men. They are a totally different animal," Rutendo said just as Chenai walked in. When she saw her she said. "I'll tell you when the kid is out."

That wasn't all. When they were all inebriated and inhibitions gone, they began to do physical demonstrations that would make a woman ready for marriage. Chenai witnessed a woman standing on her hands and trying to remove the beaded necklace from a hook on the wall with her feet, while the others cheered and laughed. This woman was so big that she fell over and broke Rutendo's side table with her effort. When Rutendo saw Chenai's shocked face she had laughed, then told her to leave, just as another woman, this one more nimble tried the move. Chenai sat in the kitchen listening to the dancing and laughing voices, curious and lonely.

According to her aunt, the party had been a huge success and would be talked about for years to come. Chenai surveyed the living room after hours of cleaning. It was almost back to normal and the broken table placed in the basement. She looked at the time. It was already nine am and the church started at ten. She would have to hurry.

She walked into the kids' bathroom and took a bath. The youngest two were awake so she washed them quickly and then told the older ones to get ready.

When Chenai was ready to leave, Rutendo still slept, so she left her a note. The kids were bundled up warmly and she wore all her sweaters. Her aunt had still not bought her a coat and it looked like she wasn't getting any payment for being the maid. She couldn't send any money home to help her family. Chenai officially felt trapped. With that depressing thought, Chenai stepped outside with her three charges in tow.

The kids were excited as they walked beside her. It was sunny outside, but the air was freezing cold. She had to stop the boys from running into the mountains of snow by the side of the road. As she pulled Janet's hand from following her brothers she noticed the drops of moisture frozen on the evergreen branches, twinkling in the sun. Chenai now understood that the sunshine was deceiving. From inside the house, it looked warm, but when she stepped outside the cold was numbing.

Respect the cold, Respect the cold, she kept reminding herself as they walked past colonial homes, with mostly white sidings and black roofs. She was mesmerized by the chimneys that let out smoke, floating into the cold sky.

It took them five minutes to reach the church and they had to cross one major street then they were there. It was a small Assembly of God, the size of some of the houses she had seen, but it was comforting to see the words "Jesus Saves" on the front display. A young lady at the door smiled at her.

"Welcome," she said. She shook the hands of the kids then asked her.

"Do you think the children would enjoy being in the children's church?"

"Can we?" Tino asked.

"Fine, but Janet can stay with me," Chenai said taking the little girl's hand. The lady showed her where the children's ministry was and Chenai had to sign some papers before leaving the boys in the charge of a lady dressed as a clown. In the children's church, Chenai noticed many happy children playing games and having a good time. She felt comfortable leaving them there. After waving, Chenai walked towards the music.

Chenai walked into the main sanctuary just as they started

singing another song to praise God. She could see the words, "It is well, with my soul," and remembered the hymn. She felt happy as she found a seat right at the back of the sanctuary and held Janet's hand. It wasn't long before she was also raising her hands and praising God and Janet, not wanting to be left out, did the same, her tiny fingers waving. The church had about 300 people all intent on singing and getting lost in worship. Nobody looked around at the late arrivals except for the greeters. They all just sang and lifted their hands praising their Creator.

The same overwhelming peace filled her, just as it did at the church her father had founded at the school where he taught. He was not the pastor, but his mother had encouraged him to find one and begin services, several years after they moved to the farm. Chenai felt at home for the first time since she had arrived in America. She knew these people. She knew their Savior and she knew they loved Him just as she did or wanted to love Him as much as He loved them!

They sang Amazing Grace, a hymn that she used to sing at school. Then they sang some new songs that she didn't know yet the words spoke to her heart.

After a while, the congregation sat down and the pastor started speaking. Bible pages rustled and she could hear a child make gurgling noises behind her. The pastor's message was simple but heartwarming. He reminded her about God's promise to them all.

"God never said we wouldn't have troubles. That everything would be smooth and easy. But he promised that he would never leave us nor forsake us. Take those words and put them in your heart each day. A God that wants to be with you each step of the way, each thing that you do." Pastor Redman continued to speak with quiet confidence. He began telling a story that Chenai had never heard before.

"God once told a young man who lived up in the mountains to move a rock that was in front of his home. The rock was huge. The man began to push the rock, but it never budged. For years he worked hard each day to move the rock to no avail. After a while, he asked God,

"I've tried and tried, but this rock does not move." God moved it for him and the young man was confused. Why had he spent all the time trying to move the rock? God told him to look at his arms. They were strong and muscled. His legs were, too.

"Look how strong you have become my son. I just wanted you to get strong for any future trials you may face. I move the mountain. Your job is to obey."

Chenai smiled, thinking of all that she had been going through, wondering if God had prepared this message just for her. She was beginning to weaken a little, but now she felt her strength turning, like a flower that was dying, but was beginning to stand strong from outpouring of rain from heaven. In my weakness He is strong, Chenai thought.

The pastor was young and dressed casually in jeans. She was used to preachers wearing a suit on the pulpit, but realized that his jeans didn't take away from the message.

He continued, "My decision to follow Christ is not based on how things are going in my life, but in my relationship with Him. In my conviction that He died for me on that cross so I can have life and have it more abundantly!"

People cheered and clapped. God's words had the power to do that and Chenai found herself clapping and smiling, too. Yes God's word was living water that refreshed her soul and made her feel so alive.

After the service Chenai felt like she was swimming in a sea of hope. She had missed hearing God's word and being among other Christians who believed what she believed and talked of God's promises and love. As she was walking out the lady who had greeted her asked her if she was new. Chenai was about to ask how she knew when she remembered that she had not seen any black people in the service. She hadn't felt like they stared, as they probably would have done in Zimbabwe.

"Yes. Today was my first day," Chenai said.

"My name is Heather. We would like to welcome you. Can you come for coffee?"

"I have to get the kids," Chenai said.

"They'll be fine. There's somebody looking after them for about twenty more minutes. Come this way." Chenai followed Heather, her hand in Janet's, then was introduced to the pastor, David Redman who had warm eyes and a friendly smile up close. Heather also told her about the youth evening meetings.

"You should come this Wednesday. We are having a social first then we will have a speaker. You'll like it and you can meet everybody."

"I'll come," Chenai said, feeling the first real welcome since she arrived in America. She felt a little excitement build inside her. These Americans were nice! Much better than her own aunt.

After meeting a few more people, Chenai decided to leave and get the children. After picking them up from Children's church they walked home. They were all excited about Church and told her they had learned about Elijah from the Bible. They waved drawings they had made in their gloved hands.

Before she could open the door to the house her aunt swung it open with the baby on one hip.

"Where have you been?" The children stared at their mother then turned to look at Chenai. Rutendo's anger jumped out to bite.

"We went to church," Tino replied with a smile.

"I'm not talking to you. Tino, take the kids and leave. Go to your room all of you," Rutendo glared at Chenai as the children ran past her to their rooms. Chenai was rooted to the spot, her heart racing.

"Who gave you the right to take my children without asking me?" Rutendo asked. Before she could open her mouth Rutendo continued, "You think you can just leave this house with my children? Who do you think you are? To church? What church? Do you even know which church I go to?"

Chenai stood there freezing, her mouth open to speak silent protests. Rutendo gripped her upper arm and pulled her roughly in side and closed the door.

"Answer me!"

"I'm sorry. Uncle, he- he said I could go to church and I didn't want to wake you up," Chenai stammered.

"Uncle? He's not your husband! You do what I tell you not what he tells you, do you hear me?" Rutendo pushed her finger against Chenai's head so hard she banged on the wall.

"In America there are cults. You think you are walking into a church, but you could be walking into a trap. Ask me first."

Chenai's eyes filled with tears and her lips trembled. Chenai nodded waiting for a blow in the face but in the end, Rutendo walked away muttering, "Stupid girl. Stupid girl."

Chenai rushed to her basement room feeling like an idiot. All the joy she had felt being in church, feeling God's love was instead replaced with anger, confusion and deep loneliness. In that moment she felt as if her heart was broken into a million pieces and the fragments were sprinkled all over Africa, the Atlantic Ocean, and the airports. The last piece had just been dropped in Redondo's house.

"Father, I came looking for you, but all I get is grief," she said throwing herself on the hard floor and sobbing. "Why does she treat me like that? Was I wrong? Should I not have sought you Father? Was I wrong?"

Trickling in, peace began to invade her heart even as she didn't get a clear answer. Before she could enjoy it, her aunt's voice assaulted her senses from the kitchen demanding that she make food.

CHAPTER 8

Storm

Peace I leave with you, my peace I give to you; not as the world gives do I give to you.

—John 14:27

Chenai's mother, in her breathy voice, liked to tell Chenai that the only thing predictable in life was death.

"We don't know the future, Chenai. So I don't worry about it. I work hard for you my kids, but nothing is ever certain."

Those words would haunt Chenai when her life took a shocking turn in her stay in New Jersey. She would never have predicted what happened next, just as she had never imagined a life without her mother.

Weeks had gone by, Christmas lights twinkling, kids getting presents and Chenai had not gone to church. Heather called the house one day to ask her about coming to the Wednesday meetings, but Chenai would tell her that it was not possible.

She wanted to experience the feelings she had in church, singing praises to God and being with happy people. Rutendo was always angry with her. No matter what she did, it was wrong or not good enough. Chenai entertained thoughts of using her return ticket and going back home, but her father had really hoped she would attend college and experience a different life. More than anything she really wanted to provide for her father and brothers. If she could just get a job with pay, she could do it. She didn't want to give up and yet, if he knew her current situation would he let her stay, she wondered.

One Wednesday afternoon Chenai had not summoned the courage to ask her aunt about going to church again. She somehow knew the answer would be no and swallowed her sadness humming a hymn to herself.

She started making dinner early, just in case a miracle happened and her aunt would release her from her never ending chores. While she was cooking the rice and frying beef cubes for a stew, she heard the key in the door and her uncle came in.

"It smells nice in here," James Kameno greeted closing the door that led to the laundry and garage.

"Thank you. Good evening," Chenai said, wiping the stove to remove the oil that had splattered there. It was only around six in the evening so dark it could have been midnight. Chenai continued to stir the pot of stew and added a dash of paprika. The sizzling sounds filled the kitchen.

"So have you talked about College with your aunt?" James asked putting his bag on the table and sitting on one of the kitchen chairs. The chair creaked from his weight. She hardly saw her uncle. He worked in the city sometimes, though often he seemed to be traveling for the insurance business. Rutendo had tried to explain his job, that involved selling and training in different states, leaving her alone with the kids most of the time.

"No. She hasn't said anything. I was accepted for April at the community college. I still have time."

"Which courses did you choose?"

"Nursing and afterwards, medical school."

"Impressive. I saw the prospectus upstairs. I'll get it for you so you can see what classes to take." James stood and began to walk out of the room.

"You can get a head start and start preparing." He added before he bounded upstairs.

Chenai looked over her shoulder then turned off the stove. The kids were in their rooms. They spent time on Play Station which they had tried to teach her though they didn't want to leave it long enough for her to learn. The baby was sleeping so she decided to put the dishes away before she woke up.

"I found them," James's voice startled her. "Come and take a look." Chenai wiped her hands on the paper towel and left the kitchen. She glanced at the clock and stood by his chair in the living room.

"Sit down Chenai. I won't bite." Chenai sat down next to him and watched as he turned the pages of the book for the Community College Courses.

"Here it is," James said pointing at the glossy page. "You'll do introduction to biology for the first semester here."

"I already did biology," Chenai said. "I also took math and chemistry at A levels."

"Wow. You are a smart girl. Did you pass?"

"I got two As and a B. Chemistry was the hardest."

James patted her on the shoulder saying, "Good for you girl. Good for you."

Neither of them saw Rutendo standing by the door watching them until her voice shattered the peace.

"What's going on?"

Chenai stood up nervously smoothing her skirt down.

"I was just showing her subjects for school," James said holding up the prospectus.

"Who do you think you are Chenai? I'm at work and you are trying to get your hands all over my husband?"

Chenai shook her head at a loss for words. Rutendo had stunned her before, but this was so insulting no word could come out of her mouth. Rutendo was looking at her as if she had done something bad. With James!

"Come on Rutendo, you know that didn't happen," James said standing up also. Rutendo held up her hand to stop James from speaking and looked at Chenai.

"You stay out of it, James. This is between me and Chenai. Besides, I don't know why you are wasting time with all this college nonsense. Who will pay for it? She's not going to college and she's not going to be taking my husband away!"

"She didn't do anything. You shouldn't be yelling at her," James tried to block Chenai from Rutendo's venom.

"James. This is my relative not yours, so it would be good for you to leave this room and let me deal with my relative alone. Just leave us alone."

James stood stubbornly for a while then shook his head. He turned to leave, seemingly disgusted. Now Chenai worried even more. She didn't want to be left alone to face Rutendo's wrath. Rutendo's voice was hard enough to grind corn into powder.

"Don't worry Chenai. You didn't do anything wrong and nor did I for that matter."

As soon as he was out of earshot, Rutendo stepped forward and slapped Chenai hard on the cheek. The force sent Chenai's head swinging to the side. Tears sprung suddenly to her eyes as she gasped with pain and shock.

"You imbecile! I should have known! I want you to leave my house this instant. What have I brought to my house, here to destroy my family? Get out now!"

"Auntie please…I didn't do anything."

"Of all your stupidity and lack of sophistication do you know what I hate the most about you? You are so naïve and gullible you make me sick. You really do. I want you out of my house. *Buda*!"

Chenai stared, confused and distraught. Surely she didn't want her to go outside. Chenai turned towards the basement door, but Rutendo roughly propelled her towards the front door, her strong pinching hands causing sharp pain in her shoulder and arm.

"Get out! I mean out the door and don't ever come back!" She opened the door and shoved her out into the cold night.

Chenai shivered dressed in the skirt that seemed to turn to instantly turn to ice against her bare legs. Her breath caught in her throat as the cold invaded her body.

This couldn't be happening.

Fresh tears flowed out of her eyes when Rutendo slammed the door shut, the sound ringing in her ears and deep in her heart. She looked at the silent driveway and sobbed, catching her breath from the cold as she tried to rub warmth into her skin.

The nightmare had all happened so fast. One minute she was

thinking hopefully about going to school and furthering her education and the next she was seen as a harlot and tossed out in the cold. She didn't know where to go, which way to turn. She could already see the ice clinging to her clothes and skin the way it latched on to the Evergreens and roofs of the houses, burying her alive.

After a few minutes, the door opened again and Chenai looked, hope filtering in. Rutendo threw her bag out to her. It landed with a thud close to her feet and she walked towards it as the door slammed shut again, dizzying her, stealing her hope as death does loved ones.

Chenai reached for her bag, opened it and took out her sweater and slipped on two pairs of socks over stiff toes then slipped them back into her shoes. Her purse that held her passport and important papers and return ticket was there, but not some of the things that she had put up in the basement to make it like home. The photos of her family in the thin plastic album form Foto Inn, the quick photo place from Harare.

After standing for a few more minutes, leaning against the door searching for its warmth, Chenai realized Rutendo was not coming to open the door. She had kicked her out of her warm house on a cold January evening. Forever.

She picked up her bag and started walking, the rhythmic crunching noise filling her ears. Crunch, crunch, crunch. Her ears, her brain filled with the crunching as the pain from the cold threatened to take her mind. She walked out the driveway and turned right on the dark street. A car drove past her, tires throwing snow up to her, but didn't stop. Even if a car did stop for her,

where would she tell the driver to take her? She didn't know anybody in America except Rutendo. Rutendo didn't want her.

Chapter 9

Arctic

The Horse is made ready for the day of battle, but victory is mine,
says the Lord.

—Proverbs 21:31

Chenai felt disoriented when she woke up, in that moment that is the land between dreams and waking. Swimming through layers and clouds of sleep, she tried to figure out where she was as she wrestled out of her dreams. Was she at the farm? No, had to be in New Jersey in her aunt's basement? No, she was no longer there. Was she at Heather's small but cozy house? Sometimes she felt as if her mind was saturated in water. It started a month or so after her mother died. She felt as if grief had disfigured her both mentally and physically. In the early days, when the loss of her mother consumed her, she couldn't form sentences fully, or stand up straight. She imagined how a city felt after a hurricane, destroyed, shattered, never sure what to fix first.

The thoughts kept tumbling into her head. She knew she was somewhere else, she just wasn't sure where in her sleepy state. As most nights she had dreamt of life at the farm, this night her dream had been so vivid that she even felt the dry sun on her skin, and could hear the chickens in the back garden as she ran ahead to the fields with her mother. She turned around and her mother kept getting further and further away.

"Mai!" She called her, but somehow she grew further away. Chenai wanted to run back to her, but the more she ran to her, the further away she grew, getting smaller and smaller on the dusty road. She started panicking and screamed her name as rivers and mountains separated her from her mother.

She opened her eyes, the feeling of abandonment covering her in a thin film of sweat. Had she called her mother out loud? She held her dry throat and swallowed hard looking at the beautiful room. Memories flooded back. Boarding the plane for the second time, arriving at the airport and suddenly her trepidation increased. Mr. Pieri was not going to be easy to live with, of that she was certain. Still, she had to remember that being in this warm bed was in itself a miracle. She accepted this as her mind took her back to the moment her aunt had thrown her out into the snow.

That night was probably the closest she felt to dying. As she walked, the freezing wind entered her bones and turned her very center to ice. All she could hear were Rutendo's words, mocking, rendering her unable to pray.

"I didn't have anyone. I bought the plane ticket by myself after working for the city council and getting nowhere in Harare. You, I bought a ticket for. I gave you my house. You should be grateful."

Chenai took another step and as much as she wanted to shut out Rutendo's voice it kept on filling her mind. She couldn't push the force of her words away.

"I worked night and day. I put myself through school. I didn't have a father like you do. I did it myself. I didn't need anyone. Not even my husband. I helped him get where he is or he would have spent all his life working in kitchens."

"I came here and had fees for just one term of school. Money I had saved. In America, nobody will help you. You have to be tough and talk to people. How did they do it? What jobs can you get? Your father is weak. He has been on the farm for how many years? A headmaster for a small farm school and has not progressed. Now that the blacks have taken the land, why didn't your father also start farming? Your mother would have started farming."

Rutendo laughed as she continued to lecture. "Chenai, you mother is a character. Lois married down that one. She grew up in a rich family. Her father was an entrepreneur. Smart man. Lost everything in the war and what does Lois do? Marry a teacher who keeps his nose buried in a book as if he doesn't want to smell real life."

Her words kept dropping in her heart like snow bombs exploding, spreading anguish and humiliation coursing through her whole body. She didn't want them. She didn't want to die and the last conscious thought to be Rutendo's 'words of wisdom.'

However once she was inside the church, the young girl she had met at church practically ran into her and her life changed. Heather had taken her. She didn't die in the snow. Another miracle had taken place. Because of Heather, Chenai was now once again safe and sound in another state, another bed.

Still, early morning always filled her with deep, overwhelming feelings of bewilderment and loneliness. She felt as if she had slept with all the loss and pain of her life and it had grown overnight into a huge dark tree that covered the sun and hope from above. With the coming of the dawn she had to shake it off before she got out of bed, leaving it on the ground like falling leaves. Shake away her dreams, her fear, her lack of faith. Remembering what happened in New Jersey added to those feelings.

Still lying in bed with her eyes closed, Chenai prayed for grace, courage and fortitude to be able to face the new day. Once she did that she let her feet touch the floor with some confidence. It wasn't much, but enough for the next few minutes

"I'm not alone."

It was still dark out when Chenai left the luxurious linen on her bed and ran her bath. After a twenty minute soak she dressed in a cotton dress and sandals. She tied her thick bushy hair on her head thinking her head looked so small and her eyes too big and lost. What bothered her most about herself was not how she looked. How her eyes and mouth seemed too big for her face. How black her skin was, no hint of brightness anywhere.

She had learned to accept her appearance, but she loathed her weakness, her lack of faith and her lack of courage. She wished she could be stronger like Esther and other remarkable women that were written about in the Bible. They faced tougher obstacles than her. She longed to be like her mother. With her mother gone, the one who had bolstered her up, filled her with strength, Chenai sometimes feared that the wind would just knock her down and flatten her, and then she wouldn't be any use to anyone, always being rescued and flung from house to house like she had been in one week. From Rutendo's house, to Heather and now, the Pieris.

As quietly as possible, Chenai made her way down the stairs and was once again struck by the lovely hallway greeting her, the warm colors on the walls, clearly chosen very carefully to compliment the black and white photographs of European architecture, she guessed. She nearly jumped when she unexpectedly heard movement in the kitchen.

She walked in and found Tyler standing by the kitchen counter with a box of cereal.

"Good morning," Chenai said her hand to her chest.

"Morning." The little boy appeared sullen. He coughed and his eyes looked filmy.

"Are you okay?"

"My throat," Tyler croaked. Chenai looked around, wondering if Blake was around. She knew that throat issues could be dangerous. One of the children at the farm had died from a throat infection.

"When did it start hurting?" Chenai asked. She walked closer and felt his forehead. He was hot. Where was the thermometer? Where was Blake?

"What did you say? Are you speaking English?" Tyler asked, staring at her. Chenai was puzzled then remembered. Her accent. Yes, she spoke differently, didn't she?

"Yes," Chenai said slowly. "Did you understand me?"

"Yes."

"When did your throat start to hurt?"

"Yesterday."

"Where is the thermometer?"

"I'm hot?" Tyler touched his forehead. He still wore his pajamas from the night before, but looked like he had been awake for a long time. He poured the cereal, which was not much in the bowl and he looked in the box to see if there were more round chips left. Chenai felt really useless. Here was a sick little boy and she had no idea what to do. Even if Blake was home, which she doubted he was, he would probably expect her to know what to do. This was only day three.

By mid-morning, Jodi was up, but she avoided both Chenai and Tyler. Chenai gave Tyler fluids and also put a compress on his forehead. She had found a thermometer. He was having a mild fever for sure. She was getting ready to ask Jodi for Blake's number when the doorbell rang. Chenai was as surprised as Tyler. Who could be coming to see them so early on a Saturday?

Jodi came down the stairs and made her way to the door. Chenai listened as the voices drew nearer, Chenai could hear another female voice.

"She's here? Okay"

"He name is Chenai but Dad, of course calls her Cheny. He's such an idiot." That was Jodi's voice.

"Oh hi," the woman spoke when she spotted Chenai. Chenai stood up to shake her hand. "You must be Chenai. I'm Kimberly. Their mother was my sister."

"Hello," Chenai said. This woman didn't look much like the photos Tyler had shone Chenai of his mother. Kimberly had dark hair, cut around her face and brown eyes, a contrast to Samantha's blue eyes and blonde hair.

"Tyler, where's my hug?" Kimberly asked. Tyler stood up and wrapped his arms around his aunt. Kimberly closed her eyes over his little back. The love was clear in the way she held the little boy.

"What's wrong? You not well?"

"My throat hurts."

"Oh," Kimberly looked at Chenai.

Chenai nodded, "He told me a few hours ago. His temperature is a bit high."

"Oh darling," Kimberly pressed the back of a ringed hand on his forehead. Chenai noted she had a ring on every finger except for the thumb and pinky and wore about 5 bracelets, shiny and pretty.

"We were thinking of calling Mr. Pieri," Chenai added and immediately saw Kimberly roll her eyes. She stood up, almost as tall as Chenai.

"Blake. He's not going to come. He only cares about himself," Kimberly said in a matter of fact way, while rubbing Tyler's head. Chenai was stunned, that such careless words would just be uttered in front of a six year old, about his father.

"I'm here okay, Ty? Open your mouth? Ah good. Looks fine. I'll get you some medicine okay."

Tyler nodded. Kimberly stood up.

"It looks like you came at the right time. Glad you are here, I will give you my numbers and my parents too. They help with the kids, all the time."

Chenai nodded, grateful. She wasn't all alone.

"Blake, well, as you can imagine, has no time for his kids. So we all step in, though I have two of my own. Dylan is 16 and Tom 14, but we all have to step in for Sammy…," Kimberly said and then she stopped talking. Chenai saw the sob break before it actually came out. She seemed to cut it off as if it was a snake about to attack her then turned to Jodi who sat on the edge of one of the sofas in the family room.

"Well, Jodi, why don't you come with me? I can take you shopping after if you like."

"Daddy grounded me!" Jodi's anger was still evident.

"I'll talk to him. He has no right to do that. I can still get you something. I'll be going shopping, or we can order some stuff online together okay," Kimberly said.

"Okay," Jodi said, consoled.

"Well, let me run and get him some Tylenol and I'll be right back."

Chenai sat back down as Kimberly left the room, her arm around Jodi's waist. She returned a few seconds later.

"Tyler will have baseball in a few months. I think we need to register him. Chenai. You will be very busy, but somehow, just seeing you, I feel at peace."

And then she was gone.

As she looked after Tyler, she couldn't help comparing this home to her parents' house in Bindura. She was in a huge kitchen now, with stainless steel appliances and counters that looked like stone. What would her mother think of the place? Of the three living rooms and movie theater. She had lost count of the number of bathrooms but all around was just unimaginable luxury, though no one seemed to enjoy it. The dark wooden floors, the different color walls in each room.

There was the blue living room, full or light and comfortable chairs, where they all sat to watch TV.

The other room had pale green walls a long beige sofa and two arm chairs in the same color. Chenai had studied the artwork on the walls, dusted the interesting decorative vases and lamps. This very formal room stayed empty.

The other living room was below the house. It had huge leather chairs and a pool table. This room remained unvisited.

Next to that room Chenai had found another room that she guessed was a craft room or sewing room. It was one where a woman enjoyed sewing, making trinkets and Chenai's heart broke when she saw a half-finished cushion. Samantha's life was taken before she could finish.

Chenai had to learn so much very quickly. In the short time with the kids, Chenai already assessed what was needed. Tyler needed so much love and attention. In his beautiful eyes was the reflection of need… so deep it broke her heart. She wanted to hold him and shield him from the loss that hung over the house like a cloud.. She never wanted anyone to experience the pain of losing his mother, and not to one so little. Jodi really needed the same but Chenai already saw that she wasn't ready to receive any love or sympathy from anyone. It was so easy to see the walls she had carefully built around her heart and in a way Chenai understood. Who wanted to feel that pain day after day? It was better to pretend you didn't have a heart and feel nothing, wasn't it? Now she had to figure out Mr. Pieri. What did he really want her to do? What was her role? Was she going to be in the same situation as Rutendo's house?

She knew one thing for sure. Being away from home, meant her real self was no longer seen. She was a stranger, even to herself, playing a role with no script, no direction. What God said about taking each day and not worrying about the future was so true to her. Each day sure had enough troubles of its own.

Later, she tucked Tyler in bed and walked over to his space ship curtains.

"Should I close the curtains?"

"No," he said.

"What are those logs out there? By the tree?"

Tyler got out of bed and came to the window standing next to Chenai. Chenai felt his forehead glad that the medication had reduced his fever.

"Oh that's my tree house. Dad was supposed to build it when I was four with Mommy. But he never did."

Chenai held his disappointment in her hand and wished she could crush it to dust and bring a smile to his face.

CHAPTER 10

Frost

No one can serve two masters. Either you will hate the one and love the other, or you will be devoted to the one and despise the other. You cannot serve both God and money

—Matthew 6:24

Blake looked at the plans for the Medical Center turning them around then bunching them up and shoving them on the floor. Studying them had not brought any solutions and yet he did it anyway. All it did was add to the pressure building in his head. It felt as if his head was in a vice, as if it was ready to explode.

He knew his company was in trouble. The pressure may have been less taxing if it had been just his money invested in the medical center. But he had partners and they were not happy with his performance. Blake had exhausted every possible way to get out of this financial disaster barreling down towards him. Nobody understood the pressure he was under. Nobody in his family, and certainly not his children.

In the past, the problems had been smaller and easy to manage. As his projects grew and the money involved quadrupled so did his predicaments. He'd needed financing for the expansion and so he had accepted investments from unscrupulous partners. His latest project had been so well planned but the best laid plans always had a few surprises. He worried he was going to make the biggest loss of his career and ruin his reputation.

Though he saw no way out, he knew there had to be one. Blake wasn't going to sit by and watch his hard work of 15 years just fall flat like a house of cards. The stress was wearing him out, but he wasn't ready to throw in the towel yet. That would certainly satisfy his step father who always told him he would amount to nothing. When he felt like giving up, George's face with his permanent scowl, egged him to pursue and solve, and fight.

George Thornton liked to bring up his real father, a man that Blake barely remembered. A man who walked out on him and his mother when he was six years old. A man who after 30 years, never looked back. He could be dead, for all Blake knew. Blake refused to be compared to his father. He would never abandon his kids. He worked hard to provide for them so they wouldn't have to struggle. Ever.

Satisfied that Chenai was with the children during winter break, Blake settled in for a long day of work at his Pieri Construction offices, in Southfield.

Blake had never been comfortable in the office. He was not adept at handling the business aspects of the company.

When Blake began to build Pieri Construction he was totally hands on. He did all the dirty work.

Not finding any immediate solutions to the cash flow problem he faced, Blake allowed his mind to wonder to how far he had come. He remained grateful that soon after he graduated high school, his friend, Fred Richardson, told him about a job opportunity. Fred's uncle would employ them to build new construction projects just outside Detroit. Blake, who had always wanted to be as far away from his step father as possible, had fled the warm weather of North Carolina and began working for Ron Tabosky. Under Tabosky, Blake had learned the business. Roofing and siding, Blake did it all. He enjoyed the back breaking work, and having money in his pocket.

His freedom had only lasted a few months, because soon after moving to Michigan he'd met Samantha.

Thinking of his deceased wife was difficult for Blake. It turned his insides out and wrenched him with a mixture of emotions that he didn't want to face. Regret. Anger. Remorse. Anger. Sadness. Loss. Anger.

He should have seen her type from a mile away. He was used to women chasing him and Samantha had not been that different, though each time it happened, he always wondered what they saw in him. He was always surprised.

He'd taken an extra job adding a gym to the high school where she worked. From the moment he arrived he was bombarded by the flock of young women who worked there.

"Blake. It's so nice to meet you. What time do you go for lunch?" The 11th grade teacher, Diane Thomas, had asked him after she saw him sitting outside eating a sandwich.

"I'm eating it now," he had replied.

"You should be able to eat lunch with us in the staffroom," she said smiling and sitting down on the bench.

"I don't think so."

"Well, I'm Diane and you are..,"

"Ms. Thomas. There you are," a thin woman in a summer dress came out before Blake could reply.

"Ms. Shelby," Diane said surprised. Her annoyance was hard to ignore.

"I'm Samantha Shelby," Samantha said walking towards him and holding out her small hand. Samantha had a unique look about her and it was hard for him to tell what nationality she was. Kind of exotic, tanned, like she worked in the sun all the time.

"Blake Pieri," he replied then wiped his hands on his jeans and held hers.

"You want to come out with us after work. A few of us are meeting for drinks afterwards," Samantha said and turned to Diane. "You can come too and please, bring your boyfriend."

She was brash, she was funny and she impressed him with the way she could drink just as much as the guys and not be affected. She spoke like a truck driver and liked to shock him with inappropriateness. She was definitely out to impress and those days, girls like that impressed him. She cooked for him and brought him lunches packed in plastic containers arranged neatly like something from a magazine. Cold cut chicken sandwiches, salad with sweet dressings, freshly baked carrot cake and grapes, or strawberries. She would come outside and eat with him instead of eating in the cafeteria with the other staff.

"So what's next after building the gym?"

"Find another building project. I usually get called for different sub-contracting jobs around the city."

"Why don't you start your own thing? Why work for somebody else. My uncle needs a deck built. Maybe I can tell him about you and you can do your own work on the side."

She was ambitious for him. When he got the job to work on her uncle's deck she came out, not to bring him a cold drink on a hot day but to work beside him, for free, sweating in the sun beside him and carrying planks. She would take a break to dive in the pool to cool off then bring him food and drinks. And that's how Samantha got her life intertwined with his.

When they started sleeping together she was quick to reassure him that she was on the pill. He was stunned when five months later she excitedly announced that she was pregnant.

The look on his face angered her and she stormed out of his apartment. He stayed away for three days, thinking everything over, wondering how at twenty he was going to be a father and how much he wanted to run but he didn't. He was not his father. He refused to be that man who walked out on him when he was five, leaving his mother alone, unable to support the two of them.

He met with her in a bar after he had calmed down.

"We should get married," he said. "I didn't plan on this."

"If that's what you want," Samantha said. "I love you."

Blake didn't want a wedding, just wanted to go to court and get it done. Somehow Samantha had managed to plan a big party at her father's house.

From the beginning he had never been in love with her and their relationship seemed to get worse each month. Samantha immediately stopped cooking. That had just been bait, he thought bitterly. Her pregnancy made her so sick she seemed miserable and angry all the time and as a young man, it was hard to deal with.

After Jodi's birth, however, they both had a new focus. Things seemed okay. Samantha's parents set them up in a small two bedroom house, not far from them so they could baby-sit Jodi.

Blake continued to work in construction, doing everything, from roofing, sidings and renovations. He worked on single family homes, schools, small business offices. When he needed extra cash he would help friends who did electrical and plumbing work.

After a few years, Blake felt he was ready to take the risk and start his own business. Samantha had inherited money from her grandfather's estate and they used those funds to get the business going. As his business grew, his marriage failed.

When he started Pieri Construction he had a van with his name printed on it and he did odd renovations. By his third year in business he was being hired to work on single family homes. After several years, he transitioned to more lucrative work on commercial buildings, but he still wasn't satisfied. Blake decided to officially begin a new business model after attending a real estate workshop. He was now investing in developments and using his Pieri Construction too, which could be risky, but the returns were also astounding. In a way, he was making money on both ends. Greater risk but greater returns. Who could resist that?

Thinking back about how far he had come gave him mixed feelings. Right now he had enough to keep him busy. He tapped his laptop and opened the first of the 30 emails. Blake could feel the discomfort of being in the office, as if he was pretending to be someone else. At the same time Blake knew he had no choice but to focus, attend seminars, and even take classes if he didn't want to lose everything. The last thing he wanted to do to do was go back to ever needing anybody again. He wanted to be in control of his life. No need for his father, step father or even mother or Samantha's family. He was in charge and he controlled his destiny.

He glanced at his phone when it buzzed. It was Kimberly again. What did she want?

"Yes," Blake said.

"I was wondering if you knew that your son has a fever."

"I know that. I have Chenai looking after him."

"Chenai is not those kids' mother."

He listened to her complain, an annoying song he had listened to many times since he married Samantha.

"I want to take them to a movie."

"Jodi's grounded. Do what you want with Tyler."

"He's sick."

"Then take your own kids Kimberly."

He got off the phone regretting answering it as usual. He had bigger things to worry about than a child with a few sniffles. That's why Chenai was there.

Wintry

I have seen all the things that are done under the sun; all of them are
meaningless, a chasing after the wind.

—Ecclesiastes 1:14

"Mr. Pieri. It's Ms. Walvaren," Cathy told him. He had ig-nored Penny's call on his cell and now she had decided to call the office. Women.

"I'll take it," Blake said. He didn't really want to talk to her, but then again she could distract him from the disturbing reports he was reading.

"Hey there," Penny crooned on the other side of the city in Downtown Detroit. Penny worked hard as a CPA in one of the big firms in city. Blake liked the fact that her career was so import-ant to her that she had put off marriage in order to advance her resume.

"Women have to work twice as hard in these firms. I travel wherever they send me and work long hours. Soon I'll be man-ager," Penny would say to him over and over again. She was as hungry for success as he was and that's why they got along so well.

He met Penny in a bar when he was out with one of his clients a few months before. She had walked up to him, introduced herself and asked to join him. Just like that. At the time he had been seeing Julie Patterson, a high school teacher, but was happy to end that relationship. Julie was ready for marriage and that was the last thing he needed. Not after spending all his twenties married to a woman he didn't love or even like. After that first meeting with Penny, he stopped returning Julie's calls until she left him a message to tell him it was over. As if he hadn't already figured that out himself.

"Hey," he said.

"When I woke up you were gone," Penny crooned and he could imagine the pout on her brightly painted lips, blond hair pulled back severely to sharpen the attractive angles of her face.

"I had an early meeting. The medical Center is proving to be more challenging than I originally hoped. I have a few fires to put out."

"And you do that so well," Penny said her voice heavy with meaning. "How about tonight?"

"I'll call you. Listen I better get going. Talk to you later," Blake said and put his phone down just as Jim Litgee walked in with a stressed look on his face. Blake could feel his blood pressure rise.

"Blake. We have a problem," he said.

* * *

When Blake got into his car that evening all he could think about was having a drink. Jim never brought him good news and this had been the case since they won the bid on the medical center. The materials were more expensive, the contractors were slacking and he was over budget and way behind schedule. Groaning Blake punched in Penny's number on his cell phone and spoke as he joined the rush hour traffic.

"Are you at work?" he asked.

"Almost done. You coming tonight?"

"Let's meet at the Blues Club for a drink."

The Blues Club was one of the new establishments in Downtown Detroit. He usually liked to go to the Casino, Greektown being his favorite but tonight a blues club seemed like the best place to drown his sorrows. He only had to wait for Penny for a few minutes before she arrived. She pulled off her sable coat to reveal a two piece black suit and a silky red blouse underneath. Besides the red blouse, Penny looked like a CIA agent, tough and mean, but he knew her. He knew the fire beneath the austere hair style and tough demeanor.

"Two nights in a row. Should I thank your nanny?"

"Guess so. She's pretty efficient," he said taking a sip of his drink. "What are you having?"

"I'll have a martini," she said and gestured to the bartender. She turned to Blake her blue eyes sensual. They were the most intriguing thing about her. He liked her confidence, her steady gaze. She was smart, strong and carefree. She worked hard and needed the no strings relationship they were both enjoying. She was sophisticated and striking even with her hair pulled back tight. He noticed all the men at the bar turn and look at her. She didn't seem to notice.

"What's wrong?" she asked, giving him her steady gaze.

"Work. I'm worried that I might have some litigation against me." Blake said.

"Your father's a lawyer," Penny reminded him, lifting her glass in salute.

"Don't remind me about my step-father. He's the last person I'd ever ask for help from. You know that."

"I know how you feel about him, but family can always step in and help…"

"I think he's the kind of man who would be happy to see me fall. Don't even talk about him."

"I can give you some free advice. I work with very successful businesses. Also, I'm just trying to get you out of your funk."

"That's not helping."

"Okay, so let me tell you about my work," Penny smiled. "I did some serious damage to my coworker's image. He's in line for promotion with me, but since I was leading the last project I really gave him a lousy review. Think he can beat me. He was lulled by my sweetness. You'll be really proud of me."

Somehow Blake didn't feel as proud as he normally would feel. Actually, he felt a little disgusted. He put it down to his own problems at work. The threatening note he had found on his windshield of all places. Was it put there by mistake? He found it funny really. Was someone really planning to hurt his kids? That was insane. Stuff like that only happened in movies.

"So you think they'll choose you instead."

"I'm going to make sure. I have to be manager. I have my MBA and CPA and I've been lead on most of the projects. Baby, all those sleepless nights have paid off."

"Then we should go home and celebrate," Blake drawled with little excitement.

"Your place?" she asked hopefully.

"Too far. Your condo's best."

"You just read my mind," she said. Penny was always ready for anything. He liked that about her, though at times he wondered if he really knew her.

Blake paid the tab and got up from his seat. Blake followed Penn to her condo in Royal Oak. It was a new brick building right in the middle of all the action with bars and restaurants right below Penny's two bedroom home. Blake always wished he had built them himself. The contractor was making a killing charging almost half a million for the penthouse.

He parked in the street then met her by the door rubbing his hands from the chill in the air. Penny opened the door to her home then walked in her hand in his.

⁂

Blake left her an hour after he got into her house. As soon as he closed the door, Penny picked up her lamp and flung it against her bedroom wall. The loud thud satisfied her. She worked out every day and still she wished she had broken the lamp into little pieces.

She rubbed her shoulder angrily as she padded downstairs and then double locked the front door.

She slid to the floor, wanting to remove her anger and leave it on the floor, not take it to bed with her. She could cry and scream but she had done enough of that over Blake. Now she really needed to be clinical about this. She loved him. She desired him and she wanted to be Mrs. Blake Pieri so badly she almost choked with the desire. She shook with it, but she knew that in front of him she had to be in control. She had to play the part. She had been trained to play this part since college. Women were taught to party hard right from orientation. She understood that none of the boys were out for serious relationships. They wanted someone for the night, or maybe a few nights then move on to someone else. So girls had to join in the game or remain alone, lonely, untouched. Still, by the time she graduated she was done with pretending to be what she was not. She didn't like drinking until she passed out, she didn't like sleeping around. It was not only demeaning, it was exhausting. She wanted to get married. But she had to hide that desire. She knew that. She wasn't stupid.

Her need for Blake wasn't at all connected to his wealth and ambition, she made decent money and when she was partner she could be well above six figures. No, what she wanted was him. From the moment she set eyes on him, her heart knew that she would move heaven and earth to be his wife. She wanted to be able to lose herself in his devastating eyes, to able to console his broken heart, and to be able to kiss his lips each and every day of her life. To have every woman envy her, envy them as they walked together. She could be that wife he never had. She would not be demanding. She would let him follow his dreams. They would conquer the world together. She supposed she could learn to be a mother to his kids. After all, they were practically grown already.

"It's so hard," Penny whispered to herself, hating the anguish in her voice. She had to hold back her embraces, and tame her kisses. And when her love overflowed from her soul, she kept her eyes closed. She knew that if Blake saw it, even got a hint of it, he would flee.

CHAPTER 12

Cold

Surely everyone goes around like a mere phantom; in vain they rush about, heaping up wealth without knowing whose it will finally be.

—Psalms 39:6

"Can you call your Dad for dinner?" Chenai spoke to Tyler. Jodi looked on curiously as Chenai served the wild rice and sauce with grilled chicken she had found in the freezer.

"How did you make that?" Jodi asked looking at the pot.

"The sauce?"

"Yes."

"I use tomato paste. I usually use onions, but I didn't see any. Who does the grocery shopping?"

"We do once a week," Jodi said. "We like pizza and pasta."

"I can make pasta but not pizza."

Jodi didn't comment at Chenai's last statement. She looked away her bored expression deeper. Sometimes Jodi couldn't help being curious about Chenai, but she fought it and Chenai could see the battle in her eyes between wanting to know her and ignore her. Chenai still needed more ideas to reach her. Maybe they offered a course at university, a four year one.

"Daddy says he'll eat later," Tyler came down the stairs. She thought that maybe on Saturdays he would have time with his kids, but he worked all day and had arrived half an hour before she finished cooking.

She wanted to ask him about church and felt a sense of déjà vu. She felt the same foreboding she had had at Rutendo's house. Tomorrow was Sunday and she was excited to go to a church. Any church. They were in the middle of eating when Blake came in. Tyler refused the chicken and Jodi only ate the chicken, but removed the sauce. Chenai had observed Jodi's nauseated expression silently as she pushed the rice to the edge of the plate.

"So you cook as well?" he asked.

Chenai got up quickly and served his food. Blake sat down at the kitchen table, something she had not seen him do since she arrived in his house. She sensed his gaze on her as she put first the rice then the sauce and finally the chicken grilled tenderly on to a plate. The recipe she used was her mother's, but she feared that Blake would not like it. Jodi and Tyler had both barely eaten.

"I started cooking when I was six years old," Chenai said.

"You hear that Jodi? She started cooking at six. You can't even boil an egg." Chenai watched Jodi roll her eyes. Why did Blake have to say that? No wonder Jodi didn't like her father. Blake seemed to put her down at every opportunity. Blake took his first bite of food and Chenai tried not to look. She knew he didn't like the rice either.

"I prefer pasta and potatoes myself," Blake said after pushing his half eaten plate away. "But thanks."

Chenai filled a glass with filtered water, making a mental note to look up pasta and pizza recipes.

"I wanted to ask if you knew of any churches close by that I can attend this Sunday or next Sunday," Chenai said quickly and placed a glass in front of him. Blake glanced at Tyler, as if the little boy had any say in the matter.

"Can I go too?" Tyler asked excitedly. "We go to church with grandma."

"All they do is ask for your money at church. Didn't they tell you to put all your money in the offering last time you visited grandma?"

"Not all of it. It was to help starving children in Africa."

"She's from Africa. Does she look hungry? She's skin and bones maybe, but she's not hungry," Blake drawled looking at Chenai. Chenai looked down at her plate her fork in hand. "I don't like the church your grandma goes to, but you *Cheny* can go to any church you want. I know one, but it's too far to walk. So now I'll have to take you to church?"

"No. no. I thought there was one nearby that's all."

"We don't have any churches nearby. I'll ask for you if you like."

"Thank you."

"Don't thank me yet."

Chenai quickly learned much about Blake, most of which confused and saddened her. Kimberly had filled her in on all the other secrets. If she wrote a list it would have some of the words that she doodled in her notebook. Impatient, angry, self-centered, and insensitive, especially when it came to his children. What was worse to Chenai was the way he hated the church and anything to do with Christianity and forbade his children to have anything to do with it either. Had someone in church hurt him, she wondered. She had never come across anyone so blatantly against her beliefs and she wandered how she could function in the household.

Chenai had always thrived on her father praying for her and with her. Her father supported her. He always gave her words of wisdom from the Bible, and wanted her to grow strong in her faith.

I'll die slowly here father, Chenai prayed silently then admonished herself. *God is still with me. He's in this house with me. His spirit sees everything and He knows I need fellowship. He won't let me live in this dark house alone.*

She had already spent three days with the family and the ups and downs of each day were taking their toll. Sunday came and went with no church. On Monday Tyler played games with her all day while Jodi talked on the phone or chatted on the internet. Marylyn and Kimberly called daily and on Wednesday when Blake came from work he brought home fried chicken in a bucket then went to his office.

Chenai helped Tyler with a school project on his community on Thursday morning. While they worked they watched cartoons on the television. Jodi came down stairs dressed in jeans and a sweater. Her hair was wet and held back by a butterfly clip.

"Can I watch news?" Jodi asked.

"Okay," Tyler changed the channel. The newscast was about a shooting of a little girl in Detroit.

"The suspect is believed to be the father of the little girl..." the newscaster spoke with a serious expression.

"What? Why would anybody kill a little girl?" Chenai asked

holding the glue in her hand. Jodi looked at her as if she had lost her mind.

"People shoot each other here for no reason," Jodi said watching tears fill Chenai's eyes. "Are you crying?"

Tyler looked at Chenai.

"Change the channel Jodi. You are making her cry," Tyler shouted urgently.

"It's okay," Chenai said and got up. "I'll be right back."

Chenai went to her bedroom and bawled. She started praying for the mother she had seen on the TV. She had never heard of anything so horrific.

After a while she walked into her bathroom and took some tissues. When she walked out she saw Jodi standing by the door.

"Are you okay?"

"I'm fine. I was shocked. I'll come down now. You said people get shot all the time here?"

"Well, in some neighborhoods. Or if you are unlucky, you get shot or your parents are on drugs or criminals."

"People just go around killing their families?"

"Yes. You should watch Fox news or any news channel you'll hear many other strange things."

Jodi had found something exciting to tell Chenai and her blue eyes lit up for the first time. She made her watch news every day that week and the stories made Chenai sick at heart. A man got out of jail and stabbed his girlfriend and her children too! Chenai cried for a long time while Jodi laughed at her and deep down she knew that the grief she felt was more than what she saw. Any violence reminded her of her mother and tore her up, cutting open the wound that could take her whole life to heal.

Tyler walked to her and told her to close her eyes.

"Don't watch this Chenai. We can leave if you want to."

Tyler in his sweet way realized that maybe Chenai didn't know much about America and started educating her on anything he imagined Chenai did not know.

"Did you know that we have 50 states? It's like 50 countries but they are all in one country. Last week I saw a deer right there."

Chenai looked at the spot outside the kitchen window. She had to admit that the little 6 year old boy did know quite a few things that she didn't know about and that gap, both Jodi and Tyler were happy to fill. Jodi focused on the gory things and Tyler on the sweet things, including how candy was made and Motown music history.

On Friday night, Tyler told his father about Chenai crying because of the news as soon as he walked in.

"Who was watching the news?" he asked.

"Jodi was," Tyler said.

"She shouldn't be watching the news. Where is she?"

"It's okay, Mr. Pieri. I watched it on my own. I shouldn't watch it."

"What were you crying about? You've never seen news before?"

"Not here. In New Jersey I was working all the time and I…"

"You never saw what this world is like. Welcome to America then."

"Thank you," she said puzzled.

"I can't believe you are that naïve but it seems you are."

"I'm learning a lot of new things."

Chenai could tell that Blake was not there. His eyes had that faraway look, his heart, his thoughts all like an empty canvas.

"Anyway I have a late dinner meeting. Make sure Jodi watches the appropriate things on TV. Check on her make sure she's not doing what she shouldn't be doing."
"Daddy. Do you want to play video games with me?" Tyler asked and Chenai smiled hopefully.

"Can't. But Cheny play with him, too. Don't just focus on Jodi."

Blake went upstairs, took a shower and 20 minutes later walked towards the garage. Chenai walked to the window and watched the twin tail lights going up the road.

Where are you going? What are you running from?

Chenai turned away from the window and watched Tyler's sadness. Her heart broke for him as the sound from Blake's car faded.

CHAPTER 13

Cool

Sun and moon stood in their places; they went away at the light of Your arrows, At the radiance of Your gleaming spear.

—Habakkuk 3:11

"So you've never driven a car before. A tractor. Anything?" Blake asked, as he stood drinking a glass of orange juice. Tyler and Jodi sat at the breakfast nook their breakfast of cereal and bagels in front of them. They stared forlornly at it, as if the answers to life could be found in the food they didn't want to eat.

"No. I don't know how to drive," Chenai said. He had asked her the same question before. He obviously didn't remember.

"How old are you?"

"Twenty," she replied. Her birthday was the week before and it had passed, unknown, silently, like an ant.

"Do you have cars in Africa?" Chenai looked at him trying to keep her face straight. Cars in Africa? Did he know nothing about it? At least he didn't think she went to school on an elephant.

"Of course they do," Jodi responded looking at her father like he was stupid.

"Don't speak to me like that Missy," Blake said. "You should get going. If you miss your bus, you walk." Blake walked from the kitchen and into the hall and got his long dark coat off the hook. When he put it on over his suit jacket he seemed like a different person, almost like how superman must feel after putting on his cape. All business. He seemed so distant from his children even as he came back to give them a pep talk.

"Be good in school today Tyler," Blake said to his son, though he seemed distracted. His mind was already on work and what he had to deal with. "And you Jodi I don't want any calls about any crazy behavior from you."

Jodi's response was a smirk that Chenai caught, but Blake missed.

The silence was deep, a hole of emptiness, after Tyler and Jodi left for school. Chenai found the quietness unsettling and the only way to banish the loneliness was to keep busy. She cleaned the kitchen and when it was spotless, the granite gleaming and the stainless steel faucets sparkling, she sat staring outside looking out at the lake. The icy surface reminded her of Blake and Jodi and their chilling indifference to each other.

Next, Chenai went up the winding staircase and cleaned Tyler's room which wasn't that difficult. Jodi didn't want anybody in her room and she wasn't sure about Blake's. She walked into her own room and sat on the bed.

The silence was so new. She lay back on her bed and looked at the ceiling. It was a beautiful house. Everything seemed new and fresh. The bed was high and firm with soft pillows. The carpet deep and soft and tickled her toes. It was nothing like Bindura where she grew up. The rooms had been brick and hard cold cement. Everything was practical, nothing frivolous. Her mother bought blue and yellow fabric from Patel Fabric Store in town, made curtains that made the house pretty and sunny. It had never bothered her that they didn't live in luxury. She loved being home and couldn't wait to get there after months at boarding school.

When her father was on holiday from school he also worked in the field and even helped the farm owner, Mr. Millard to get extra money, money that never seemed to be enough. There were hungry years where the smell of mud was enticing to eat, when their stomachs were hollow, carved out by a sharp knife. The drought years when water ran out and they walked for miles to get a bucket of water. There were also good years. Years when even Mr. Millard had too much grain and gave families the extra.

Chenai shifted her thought from Mr. Millard. Thinking of him always brought pain that was unbearable even after all this time. Recalling Mrs. Millard though, wasn't as painful. His wife was a tall, dark-haired homemaker. Chenai had been fascinated by her, the way she spent almost every minute with her young children. She taught them to swim and ride bikes. Chenai had seen this when her mother worked for the Millards for a year.

"Lois," Mrs. Millard would drawl.

"Yes madam," her mother would stop hanging the clothes on the line. How old was she then? She'd watched the scene from a distance.

"Brent would like his food now. You can give them their food and also tell Patson to clean their bikes. They rode them in the mud and they are filthy. Filthy!"

Leaving the clothes on the line, her mother left and went to the kitchen to feed the babies. Chenai had wanted to help, but her mother told her not to touch their clothes. Madam didn't want her clothes touched by kids. The job had lasted a year and Chenai remembered that her mother worked long hours and would come home around 9pm. Chenai had been ten years old and had to do most of the work at home while her mother tended to the Millard family. They were not cruel people. They lived their life, needing their comforts, protected by their wealth. Mrs. Millard didn't really see her mother as a mother like herself. She was a tool, a woman who could work with a smile and serve with grace and never complain. Lois had left the job with pleas from Mrs. Millard to stay. She remembered her mother telling her.

"Mrs. Millard wanted to double my salary, but your father suffered for a year without me. The money was not worth it. Always remember that. Money is not worth the death of love."

Later, when things got tough, as they progressively do in Zimbabwe, Chenai watched her mother sell clothes she bought very cheaply from Mrs. Millard. Mrs. Millard made trips to England twice a year to buy her English foods and clothes. The old clothes, that were really new, she sold to Lois, who then took the bus to the nearest town, to Mazoe and sometimes all the way to Harare to sell.

For a time, this business venture helped. Lois was able to help Chenai's grandparents in the village and once took the whole family to the city to watch a movie. They watched The Karate Kid. It was a door into world of bullies and romance too. Good winning over evil.

Chenai wiped the tears that rolled silently down her cheeks. The thought of her mother, her gentleness, her voice always weakened her, deepened her loneliness. God knew that her heart was broken still and He was working on restoring it, but the pain still took her by surprise sometimes, like a punch in the gut.

Chenai had written her father a long letter about her life in Michigan. It had not been an easy letter. She didn't want to worry him. What could she tell him of her experiences with Rutendo? She didn't want to lie but would the truth ease her father's heart? In the end she had mentioned the move from New Jersey very briefly and focused on her new life. She wrote about Tyler, the sweet boy who missed his mother. She talked about Jodi and described her sadness and how they were both dealing with their losses in different ways. When it came to write about Blake she spent hours nibbling her pen. What could she say about him?

In the end she had also tried to look for the positive aspects and though it took her a few hours lying in her bed by morning she had come up with some positive things to say.

Mr. Pieri is a hard working father. He leaves at dawn and comes back at night, just like the farmers at home, though he doesn't have a farm. I think he builds houses of wood and is now building a medical center. He seems young, but he already has grown children. His mother knew that he would be working long hours so she is very happy that I am here with the children. I'm sure he misses his wife, who died in a car accident. The house is very big and Tyler told me that his father built it. Here people can build houses very quickly because they are made of wood. They are built almost like the kraals we keep our cows.

Just wood, no bricks or cement. And you can hear people talking even two doors away. I worry that our house will be blown away while we are sleeping. On TV we see that many of the houses burn down or get carried away by wind.

Chenai knew that she had talked more about other people than Blake. How could she tell her father that Blake reminded her of the character from 'The Mayor of Casterbridge,' A book by Thomas Hardy that she read in High school and her father had helped her with her holiday project. It seemed shocking to her that Michael Henchard would sell his wife and kids for a few guineas, but Blake had already sold his whole family for his success. He had lost everything in the end and at times, Chenai feared that was Blake's fate. He wasn't that different from Michael Henchard. He didn't seem to care for anyone, but his work and his daily jogs in the snow.

She also knew her father would know something was wrong, but there was no other way to reassure him.

Chenai wrote her aunt, a brief letter to tell her she was okay, not that Rutendo cared. Chenai wondered if communicating with her aunt had been the right decision. Chenai wondered if her aunt would read her letter, or discard it, pretending Chenai never existed.

Rutendo. She wasn't her mother's sister. More a distant relative, but in Zimbabwe, when people meet, they ask so many questions until eventually, they find a common thing to confirm their relationship.

Oh. Your aunt went to a school very close to my Uncle Moda. So, you are my cousin then. Sure. Sure. And from then on people were given titles and the relationship was stronger even though they were not blood relatives.

Thoughts of home started making her disheartened so Chenai left the room and decided to vacuum the house.

She just couldn't spend her day doing nothing. She had keep her mind and body active. The house was spotless and she wondered if she should also clean Blake's room. She walked down the hall and stopped outside his door. She just couldn't get in. She'd been there before when she dropped off his phone. The huge bed took most of the space and there was a section with couch and flat screen TV. It seemed like another little house. Somehow being in his bedroom had made her very uncomfortable.

She turned and began to walk down the stairs and screamed! A strange woman stood at the bottom of the stairs staring up at her.

CHAPTER 14

Gloomy

The fear of the LORD is the beginning of knowledge, but fools despise wisdom and instruction.

—Proverbs 1:7

The woman who had almost given her a heart attack was Elise Collins. Chenai had never heard of her, of course. Blake didn't communicate to her much and most things, she discovered accidentally or on her own. Like a cleaning woman who came to the house once every two weeks during school days and once a week during the summers. Elise had been hired by Kimberly. "I think I make more money cleaning houses than I did teaching," she said after the initial shock of meeting her.

Chenai had been confused. She thought her job was also to clean just as her mother had done for the Millards.

"You have the tough job. Being a mom to the orphans," Elise said.

"Oh."

"I mean they seem like it. With their mother gone I just know that they are truly without a parent. I'm a mom. I know that I make a house a home. I live for my little girl. Gave up a career in special education so I can be with her."

Chenai smiled at the beautiful baby girl who played in the play pen.

"May I pick her?"

"Of course," Elise said. "But I also want her to learn to play by herself. Most homes I go to are empty. Both parents work so it's just her and me. I have to let her play alone for long periods and take breaks to feed her."

Chenai nodded.

"I clean quickly. This place will be dusted and shiny in four hours."

"I already did my room."

"The guest room. Ah okay. That's never hard to clean anyway. Mr. Pieri's room is the biggest mess. He leaves his clothes on the floor."

Chenai laughed as Elise continued. "That bedroom alone takes me an hour. Everywhere else is easy as pie."

Cleaning homes could pay more than teaching? That was something. Chenai left Elise alone to clean and Elise told her to get on with her day.

After Elise's visit, the house was shiny, bathrooms sparkling and smelling like a garden of roses.

Chenai spoke to Marylyn about her role. If she didn't clean what else did she do?

"The kids. Be there for them. That's all."

The week Jodi and Tyler went back to school were filled with silences so monumental she could touch them. They filled her days with memories and thoughts of home.

She could've filled the time by watching television, but Chenai now avoided the TV. The news left her feeling disheartened; the few TV shows she had managed to find were filled with embarrassing images, naked men, and people in bed with each other or killings. Who actually enjoyed watching someone being murdered, even if it wasn't real? She had seen people killed in real life, her mother killed right in front of the whole family was all the horror she ever wanted to witness in her life. She needed God's ever lasting peace, not more turmoil and man-made misery that was for entertainment.

At the farm they did have a TV, though who had time to watch it? The last few years she remembered how the electricity was always being shut off from dawn until midnight.

With the kids gone she read her Bible, certain passages over and over, and wrote to her mother in the journal that she kept at the bottom of her suitcase. The second day after the winter break was over, she knew she had to step outside, no matter how cold it was. She was about to venture out into the frigid air when the phone started ringing.

"Pieris' residence hello," Chenai said breathlessly.

"Chenai. How are you my dear," It was Marylyn. Chenai smiled when she heard her voice. Marylyn was like a kind hearted angel who she loved hearing from even though she had never met her. Marylyn seemed to anticipate problems and though Chenai never wanted to complain, Marylyn knew her son, Blake and her grand-daughter's problems.

"Fine. It's so quiet here," she said.

"Kids gone?"

"At school."

"Well, so what are you doing? I was thinking about you. Did you get to go to church?"

"No. Mr. Pieri doesn't know any churches near his house."

"Hogwash!" Marylyn said. "He very well knows the church near there. There is a wonderful church called The Savior's Heart not far from his house. No churches near his house, what a load of...... Just ridiculous."

"The Savior's Heart?"

"Don't worry. I'll give it a call and set up something. You need someone to drive you. Take the kids."

"But he said I shouldn't do that," Chenai said. The last time she had taken someone's kids to church had been a disaster.

"Don't listen to him. You know, Chenai I really wish Blake had stayed close to me here in the South so I could see my grand-kids. I can't move to Michigan because my husband has a law practice with our son and my stepson. Their lives are here and I guess so is mine." Marylyn sighed and Chenai could sense some distress over her current situation. She continued in her Southern drawl that fascinated Chenai. "And of course Blake is all the way there in Detroit. Thank God you are there. Thank God for that."

"Yes," Chenai said, not sure if she was doing any good. They talked a long time. Or Marylyn talked for a long time while Chenai listened.

"Blake's still my baby no matter how grown he is. He hasn't had it easy, but we'll talk when you come and visit me here. Blake's younger brother Glen is getting married to another lawyer. Blake won't come. He's never been close to his half-brother nor step brother. In fact Blake's never been close to anyone."

After the long discussion Chenai knew she now had some of the pieces to the puzzle, but not the full picture. The fact that Blake had a brother was news. He had never mentioned him, but then again, it's not as if they had long discussions about life. She wondered what it was that Marylyn wasn't telling her and at the same time she didn't feel as if it was any of her business. One good thing she held on to was the possibility of going to church. Maybe she would be going to church next Sunday. She thanked God for Marylyn.

She found her coat, a gift from Heather and huddled inside it. She put on her boots and grabbed her gloves. She braved the cold and walked outside. The cold air was a surprise as it hit her face. The pale green grass was crisp under her feet. She avoided the few patches of snow still on the ground. As she walked towards the lake, Chenai wondered how amazing it would look in the summer. She hoped she could swim in the lake just like she used to at the farm. She brushed those memories aside. Though she had happy memories they were shadowed with the tragedies that came later. She could not think of much to do with the farm without sinking into despair.

Father, you know me. I am so weak when it comes to my memories. Everything still hurts. You know exactly how I feel. I will trust in you.

That evening Blake arrived when Chenai was helping Jodi in algebra. They were sitting at the table with their heads close together. Jodi was battling the subject like it was a demon.

"What are you two doing?" he asked, as he stood a few feet away.

"Homework," Chenai said. No greeting from parent to child, or vice-versa.

"Good, good. Can I talk to you alone Chenai?"

Chenai looked at Jodi anxiously. She left the table and followed Blake as he walked towards his office. He closed the door and Chenai felt the walls lined with books closing in.

"What did you tell my mother?" Blake asked before Chenai could even start to guess at the worried look on his face.

"We just talked about the kids and … church."

"There. You see. You're now adding to my problems. I have enough on my plate. I don't know how things are done in your homeland, Zimbabwe or wherever in the Dark Continent but here you either make money or get left out of the race. She's talking about you going to church with the kids and stuff about you being bored…? Did you tell her you were bored?"

"No!" Chenai cried feeling tears come to her eyes so fast, more from his angry tone than what he said.

"I'm not angry. Oh my goodness females and crying." Blake said more to himself, putting his hand on his head. Chenai looked down at her feet distress in every part of her trembling body.

She wondered why was she making everyone angry? Or, was it just Blake she angered. She wanted to leave the house that instant. Blake was impossible! In fact he was a tyrant. How could she make a difference when he questioned everything she did? She was scared to admit it, but he evoked the same emotions in her as Rutendo did.

"I was just asking," Blake said with forced quietness. Chenai nodded then looked at him. His eyes were a little softer, but there was still an edge to his look. He loosened his tie slightly then ran his hands through his dark hair. "I've never had a live in nanny or whatever you really are, au pair or whatever and I think we need to set some boundaries. I would rather you don't talk to my mother too often for one."

Chenai nodded. "Yes," she responded very quietly.

"I think she still wants to control me and what better way than to use you, right?"

"Yes."

Blake nodded and sat on the edge of the desk with his arms crossed, regarding her. Chenai tried, but failed to stop her internal turmoil from showing. She knew she looked sad and pathetic and terrified and probably made Blake uncomfortable. Females and crying, he had said like it was an infection he could not look at.

"I mean. Yes, you can go to your church and get brain washed or whatever they do over there. And maybe you need to do something when the kids are gone, but just give me time."

"I'm fine. I don't need anything."

Blake sighed shaking his head. He clearly didn't believe her.

"What did you really come to America for?" he finally asked.

"School." Chenai rubbed some of the moisture from her eyes. "My aunt promised me to go to school."

"School's not always the answer. You mean college?"

"Yes. I want to go to University. That was the plan. My father thought I could be a doctor."

"Really. Well I didn't go to college and look at me. Many

successful people didn't go to college. You can earn a reasonable amount of money without wasting four years in college trying to work for somebody else." Blake spoke with feeling. Chenai looked at him without response as he continued. "I suppose we can see about enrolling in the spring."

"Thank you." Chenai sighed. She could tell that Blake really didn't want to deal with her needs. He was a man trying to build an empire. He didn't have time for his kids and he definitely had no time for her!

When her smile came he looked at her. Chenai looked down immediately.

"What made you a Christian anyway? I thought that people in Africa worshipped other spirits and things and threw people alive in graves."

"We don't." Chenai realized he was probably referring to the Shaka Zulu movie where virgins were buried with Shaka's mother when she died. Her father had told her that story.

"But you worship spirits. I didn't go to college. I don't know much about your world, but I've seen some disturbing images."

"Most of us are Christians actually. At least in Zimbabwe."

"Are you sure? How can you believe in a God you can't see?" Blake asked suddenly.

Chenai was surprised. "I see what He does," she said finally after chewing on her lip, her voice soft and barely audible to her own ears. She cleared her throat and continued. "If I didn't believe in Jesus, right now I would be a mess. He gives me peace."

"So, are you telling me that you are going to heaven? Isn't that why you really believe?"

Chenai stopped amazed again. She still stood in front of him like a child in the principal's office. Oh God. Am I going to have to answer all sorts of difficult questions? Will I offend him with my answers? This thought ran around in her head. She had never been questioned about her beliefs like this, as if she was in court and had to prove the existence of God. She longed for her mother, right then. Lois would have answered Blake with confidence, with authority. Chenai felt that her own faith was not even a mustard seed, so small she sometimes forgot how powerful God was. When things got tough and she was alone. She had it, but knew that she was not confident enough to convince Blake Pieri.

"I want to go to heaven. The alternative is hell. Why would anybody choose hell?" Chenai finally spoke.

"Hell. Really. Fire. Eternal Damnation? That's all a fairytale. I can't believe you want to go to college and you believe in that. You telling me all the people in the world who believe in other religions are doomed."

Chenai was quiet, and Blake was so quiet they could hear the T.V from the other living room, a commercial, probably about hair or some pill to make your life better. Chenai didn't know what to say, but Blake was waiting for her to say something.

"If I believe the Bible I would have to say yes."

"The Bible. Come on. I want you to show me in that book of yours where it says that your god is the only true god."

"I'll look." Chenai said. "I'll show you. It's all there. Jesus says "I'm the way, the truth...."

Blake's phone began to beep and Chenai stopped mid-sentence. He picked it up without a word and while he listened his brow furrowed with anger.

"Those drafts are exactly what you asked for. Why are you calling me?" She heard him curse then decided to leave him alone. Chenai walked out challenged and confused. Underneath it all there was another feeling, like little bubbles bursting in the sky in a delicious "pop" sound. Yes she felt it, small, fragile. A little feeling of excitement.

Melt

Consequently you are no longer foreigners and strangers.

—Ephesians 2:19

Sometimes in life something happens and you get renewed hope and strength and believe that a change will surely come, but then something else takes place and things remain the same or get worse or nothing ever changes. Her mother had told her a story that showed this and Chenai had never forgotten it. When Chenai heard the story of her mother and father rescuing Mrs. Millard and her children, she would decide that human nature sometimes does not recognize important things, or doesn't even know what to do with miracles. It was surprising to Chenai how vivid the memory was. Chenai sank back in the memory, enjoying its willowy softness and taking comfort in it.

The day her mother surprised her with a visit in the middle of the term was the day her story came out. After the initial excitement hugging her mother, feeling her love in her smooth arms they had settled down to talk.

"Mai, I heard that you nearly drowned trying to help the Millard children," Chenai said. She enjoyed hearing stories from Lois and especially after such an unexpected visit. This didn't happen often. Money was tight and her mother only did the surprises when she had errands somewhere close to Chenai's school. She still had to walk for over 2 hours from the buses to see her, but Lois was strong and fit and when she wanted to do something, she did it.

This time Lois brought her sweet potatoes wrapped in newspaper and round nuts, cucumbers with thorny spikes and cooked pumpkin, and all her favorite foods that she didn't get at boarding school. The smell filled her dorm room and they left all the items hidden under her bed and walk around the grounds. At those times they could talk without the interruption of brothers, or fathers, or chickens. It was just their time and they did talk.

Lois laughed when Chenai asked her question, "Where did you hear that?

"Well, people talk. Is it true?"

"Partly. I better tell you the truth before someone else tells you more lies."

Chenai laughed as her mother began to speak, in her story telling voice. Her mother, when she really wanted to tell a story would leave nothing out, paint a picture for you like you were actually there.

"We had gone to a funeral when Sekuru's wife had been killed by lightning. It was a difficult journey; you know he had moved from Masvingo to Mutoko."

"Baba's Father, right?"

"Right. He wanted to go back to his people. Either way there is no address to get there and we finally found his new home after asking about 20 families walking on dusty roads that have no signs. The funeral was about 3 days and we worried about all of you alone at home so we decided to leave early right after the burial. We finally got a bus, but then the second bus that was to take us home broke down just before Bindura. We waited to see if it would get fixed. It seemed like we would spend the night and your father asked me what I wanted to do.

"I'm not going to sleep here and wake up being eaten by wild animals. Let's just walk home."

"Are you sure?' your father asked in his usual doubting way.

"Don't I look sure? Watch me take the first step and you will know how sure I am."

We began the walk and after an hour we were about 30 minutes from the house, walking in the dark, guided by the half moon over the pale sky. The ground was thick with the wet soil, sometimes my shoe got stuck and I had to rescue it. It had been raining strong for weeks and rivers were full to flooding. We were too tired to talk by then, your father holding our small bag of clothes and I held the bag of nuts a relative had given us, which I was ready to throw in the bush they were getting so heavy.

After hours of walking in the dark, we saw a car come towards us, strong lights from what seemed like a huge vehicle. We naturally stepped off the road and my foot stepped in a puddle of water as we stood close to the tall grass that tickled my elbows. The car slowed down briefly for me to see that it was Mrs. Millard in the car with her children, who slept in the back, heads looking up to the sky white necks exposed. Her eyes caught mine and for a second. I thought she would stop and give us a ride home it being late and how I had worked for her in the past, but she picked up speed and I lifted my hand to wave then slowly put it down.

Your father and I looked at each other, saying nothing as we stepped back into the road and watched the tail lights of Mrs. Millard's car disappear. We were nearing the dam and maybe we could take a drink of water when we heard a loud sound, like metal hitting a rock. We knew something must have happened to the Millards. We ran fast and got there as the car dipped and turned into the water. It was hard to tell what had happened and we could not figure it out so we just took off running after the car as we saw a panicked Mrs. Millard trying to get out of the car through the window.

Your father ran and pulled her out then the mad scramble began when we fought to reach the children as the water rose in the car that now lay on its side. I could not swim, but I ran in too, the water reaching my neck, and the kids screamed trying to get out. Your father pulled one. Then the other. At that point I lost a footing and found myself going under before I could even utter a word.

Your father came for me and caught my hand before it disappeared under the water. It seemed the drink of water I wanted earlier had come rather dramatically because by the time we all sat by the side of the road, watching the car groan and then turn upside down, I had drunk about three gallons."

Chenai had finally interrupted, "You could have died!"

"No my child. You don't die unless it's your time and it sure wasn't mine. We all sat there on the side, Mrs. Millard crying and holding her children that dripped with water, their hair pasted against their faces like tiny mosquito legs.

'I'm so sorry. Oh my children. I must have hit something and the car flipped over. I tried to right it, but it just kept going as if the dam was calling it," Mrs. Millard cried, her words coming out fast and terrified. I soothed her as our heart rates slowed down, watching the top of the silver car as it drank the water in the dam like a thirsty monster. Glug glug glug.

There was no one to witness what had happened except for that half-moon and a million stars. We walked to our house first as it was closer than the farm house so we could give them some clothes or towels. This was the first and only time the Millards entered our house. You had been sleeping and didn't quite understand why the Millards were in the house. I told you to remain in your rooms. I wiped the children and dressed them in your clothes, I gave Mrs. Millard my favorite dress and she sat drinking tea for a few minutes, looking around our house like we lived under water and she had never seen how those blacks live."

Chenai interrupted again.

"So afterwards did things change? Were they nice to you? Did they do anything?"

"No, Chenai. Nothing changed. They still drove by us and never gave us a lift. It seemed as if they were embarrassed that we had helped them, but that's not my problem. That night, God put us together for a reason. I may never know it, but I think Frank and I did what we were supposed to do. The Millards, well, I don't know what they were supposed to do."

What happened two weeks after she moved into Blake's house brought the story back to her? You may think things are going to change, but sometimes they don't. It's you who has to change, Lois had told her over and over when she seemed perplexed by the events that happened the night there was a half moon. Chenai had her own ideas about that night and only now she was beginning to really form them and understand what was going on at the farm. Her conclusion was that the Millards did not see her parents as human beings, not really. They were tools and you don't show gratitude to your tools. You just use them.

So when Blake walked in a few days later, Chenai was more relaxed. After all, the last she had talked to him he seemed open to helping her go to school and find church.

"Where's Jodi?" Blake asked. She was surprised to see him come in that early. The darkness had just settled in. There was a soft snow falling outside, falling gracefully to the ground and then disappearing. When Blake walked in and asked his question she looked up from the book she read to Tyler. Did the picture of the two of them their heads closely bother Blake. Chenai noticed the look in his eyes. Was he softening towards her?

Samantha's sister, Kimberly called often, telling Chenai that as long as Blake didn't have to worry about the kids now that she was there, he would spend even more time trying to save his lousy business. She continued to add that Chenai was more of a parent to Tyler than he could be. Those words didn't sit comfortably with Chenai.

"Towards the end of my sister's marriage they had both been preoccupied with other things other than the kids. Their marriage soured way before Tyler was born and by the time Samantha was killed it had derailed into a war zone," Kimberly said, adding that information during the last time she called.

Whenever Blake spoke, everybody's words about him came back to her. Samantha's opinions, Marylyn's soft revelations.

"She's here somewhere," Tyler said. Chenai got up looking around. She found it hard to manage Jodi, who felt she was more grown up than even Chenai herself. Jodi said she didn't need anybody watching her or helping her, except with homework.

"She came in a while ago," Chenai said walking up to Blake and automatically taking his coat. Blake passed it to her distractedly.

"I saw a bike on the side of the house. Does she have a friend?"

Blake started making his way upstairs. Chenai decided to follow, clambering up the stairs behind Blake. Her apprehension grew with each step. A bike outside. Who would ride a bike in this weather?

"Jodi," Blake tried the door but it was locked. He knocked, but there was no answer. Jodi never wanted anybody in her room where she sat with her computer and her phone.

Chenai watched Blake, without a struggle force the door open and gasped when she saw a boy in Jodi's room. He stood by the window looking out while Jodi stood by the closet.

"Daddy," she said with shock, her hair in disarray.

"What's going on here? Who the hell's that boy?" Blake yelled marching towards the skinny dark haired teenager and picking him up effortlessly by his skinny arms.

"Daddy! No! He's my friend. Leave Dave alone!"

"The hell I will."

Chenai stood by the door shocked by the scene as Jodi screamed at her Dad.

"I hate you! I wish you had died instead of Mom." Her words had made a sound like a loud gong, echoing around the house ominously.

After Jodi's angry words, the only sound was the angry breathing and shuffling as Blake dragged the boy out of Jodi's room. Chenai leaned against the wall so the boy wouldn't bump into her as he stumbled down the stairs and pulled up his bottoms that had fallen down.

The boy ran out of the house as Blake stood by the broken door of Jodi's room.

"You are grounded do you hear me. No phone! No computer! No friends!" He slammed her door which wouldn't quite close, then glared at Chenai. Wasn't Jodi already grounded from the last time?

"How did that boy get in my house?" he asked her. Chenai shook her head, her mouth a perfect circle. Even though he wasn't raising his voice at her it still sounded hard, angry and disconcerting. She felt guilty as she wondered when all this transpired? How had Jodi managed to sneak a boy into her bedroom?

"Chenai. Your job is supposed to be watching the kids. How

did a boy get in to my daughter's bedroom? Maybe you spend too much time with Tyler because he's easy to deal with and not Jodi."

"She won't let me in her room. I've tried but.."

"No buts Chenai. I'm disappointed. You need to do better."

There it was. Life with the Pieri refused to improve. Things were remaining just the same, tense, difficult, no clear ideas of how to fix things in sight.

It took a while for Chenai to find something to be happy about. A few days later, the ringing of the telephone would do just that.

CHAPTER 16

Bleak

Weeping may endure for a night; joy comes in the Morning

—Psalm 30:5

"Chenai. It's yours," Tyler called from downstairs.

Chenai would remember those words, *"Chenai it's yours"* as the beginning of her contentment. It was the moment that Blake's disappointed and heartbreaking voice would fade allowing joy to trickle in and then immediately take over.

She opened the door to her room with her towel around her and called through the crack, "I'll come, in a minute."

Without applying body cream she pulled a dress from the closet then ran down the stairs to pick up the phone sitting on the counter. Jodi could've brought the cordless up to her, but that wasn't her style. Jodi was the definition of self-absorbed.

Understandably, she had lost her mother, but how could she move on, if all she thought about was what Jodi wanted? These thoughts danced around in her mind as Chenai picked up the phone.

"Chenai?" the deep male voice asked. Chenai had no idea who it was. The voice sounded kind and warm, a deep baritone that reminded her of a radio DJ.

"Yes. Who's speaking?" Chenai took the phone to the office where she wouldn't have Jodi and Tyler looking at her.

"My name is Anderson Reeber. Many people call me Andy though."

"Anderson. Andy."

"I go to The Savior's Heart. We know you'd like to visit our church and I can come and pick you up on Sunday."

"This Sunday?"

"Yes." Anderson laughed a deep throaty laugh that tickled her and she found herself laughing too. The laugh that made her feel like she was funny, worth listening to.

"Who told you? How did you know?"

"Does it matter? Will you be ready at nine? It starts at ten but we like to get there early."

"Thank you Anderson," Chenai said happily.

"Call me Andy."

It didn't take long for Chenai to discover who had called The Savior's Heart. Marylyn. Blake's mother was like a fairy god-mother, making things happen. And yet, Chenai knew that God had a hand in all that was happening in her life. As long as she trusted in Him then there was nothing for her to fear. If only she could always remember that, because sometimes, she let her guard down and let fear and darkness fill her heart, blocking out the light like a thick blanket of uncertainty. During those times, questions fluttered like terrified birds through her mind. *What is my purpose? Will I go to school? Can I help this family? Will Blake ever change?*

When Sunday finally came Chenai knew one thing. She was drawn to Andy. What made him even more endearing was the way he seemed uncomfortable with his tall lanky frame and seemed to fight a losing battle with his curly hair. It was curious that the minute she saw him his kindness seemed to flow from his light brown eyes and warm her like the sweet heat of the sun she loved at the back of their house. *Mushanaa*. That gentle sunshine that melted the heat from the night before, warmed her bones and melted the frost and left her blissful.

She wanted to close her eyes and let this new feeling soothe her. But it was more than his looks that made her feel lighthearted and excited like a leaf dancing in the wind. It was more than his friendly smile and warm unthreatening presence. Besides Heather, he was the first safe presence she had really come across since arriving in this strange, cold country.

Andy was passionate about Jesus, as if he had walked with him 2000 years ago. The way she imagined the disciples. That's all he talked about as he drove her to church in his blue truck, a song about Jesus blaring. When Andy talked about his faith, he was so matter of fact about it that his devotion to God came naturally to him like breathing. Unlike her, he would probably tell Blake about Jesus at first meeting. That was what faith was, right?

Andy's closeness to Jesus was so real she felt it in the air around him, in every word he spoke, even in the way he drove. She immediately felt at peace, and knew that those filled with God's love, peace naturally comes out to touch the world. God knew she needed and hungered for him. God had sent her Andy, to show her faith in action. She couldn't wait to get to church.

The Savior's Heart was another surprise. She had expected a small church like the one she attended with Heather in New Jersey, picture the small brick building with tall pillars in the front, but this one was like a high school or sports arena and she stared flabbergasted. As she glanced around with some trepidation she heard Andy tell her that he would be taking her to the youth service as soon as they walked through the glass doors.

"Good morning. Welcome to Savior's Heart." The greetings were many, raining sweetly on Chenai. Inside, Chenai took in the lush carpet, the couches, the big screen TVs and the people moving around, intent on going somewhere. Little children ran around their squeals of laughter tickling her ears. She wished immediately that she had brought Tyler.

"We meet separately from the main church," Andy explained. "Is it okay if I show you that later?"

Chenai nodded. They walked and several people stopped to greet Andy, hug him, and tell him their problems or testimonies. Andy was kind enough to introduce her to each person. What might have been a quick walk took about twenty minutes. Did Andy know everyone in church?

Finally, they reached the youth center. Chenai's eyes were first drawn to the stage, filled with young people of different races all standing around waiting for the service to start. The stage was set up with many types of musical instruments, different colored lights lighting it.

Andy introduced her just the way Heather had that first day at church in New Jersey and stayed by her side as she met young adults from eighteen to thirty-five. Most of the people she shook hands with seemed friendly and excited to meet her. One or two didn't say much and seemed preoccupied or found her presence unremarkable.

"You are from Zimbabwe? I know someone from Africa too. You look a little like her, this model Oluchi or something. Do you know her?"

Chenai didn't really know who Oluchi was and the name didn't sound like a name from Zimbabwe. Even if she was from Zimbabwe the chances of her knowing this person were so slim. Did some people not know that Africa had over thirty countries and that even in one country it was impossible to know everybody? So Blake wasn't the only person who had no idea what Africa was like?

"I don't know her. Sorry."

One question that she really wanted to share with her brother Evans was when she was asked if she had lions in her back yard. She had never seen a lion except in books.

Chenai's mind swam with all the people she met that day and when the service was about to start, she was shocked to see Andy walk up to the stage after the opening prayer. He held the microphone and welcome everyone then picked up the guitar and started to lead the praise and worship, a huge band accompanying him. Drums, violins, pianos. Who was this guy? She couldn't focus on that, because the music, though new to her, relaxed her. She could worship God with all these young people. Tears filled her eyes, the stress seemed to melt away and all she was aware of, was God's overwhelming love.

It was baptism day and two people were being baptized. Chenai remembered how they were all baptized in the river, dunked under the water under the blue sky. The first girl to be baptized was handed the microphone. Chenai was amazed that the girl would speak in front of everyone.

"My name is Amanda. Just turned twenty," the girl took a deep breath and Chenai could feel her tension all the way to her toes. After a sigh she continued, "I made many bad choices. I know I always heard about the God shaped hole and I know I had one. I tried to fill it with everything that really hurt me. It looked exciting, but it was pain wrapped up in colorful gold paper. The parties, the drinking, all seemed very great, promises of a good time. I was just lured in, but the reality is different."

Amanda paused and started sobbing. Chenai's eyes filled with tears. It was a palpable feeling. She suddenly felt God's power deep in her heart and noticed others reach for the tissues too.

Amanda continued, "I was so lost, so dirty, people. I kept moving the line I had drawn, instead of escaping from my hell on earth, disgusting relationships, habits- and everyone will tell you, everyone is doing it but everyone is unhappy. Everyone loses something each time they cross that line, they do what "everyone" is doing. I was so empty, the more I drank- going back to my vomit—but God—He took me and lifted me out of that mess. So gently, just as dirty as I was, He still loved me."

She closed her eyes and the tears flowed—Chenai imagined them washing away whatever the young woman had done, a river removing all the scum and leaving her spotless. As Chenai cried along with her, she felt the water, the living water filling her. Nothing else mattered but the peace that God brought, even as she cried.

After church as Andy walked with Chenai towards his car, Amanda tagged along. In that short meeting, Chenai could see that Andy was a human magnet that drew people to him. There were many who clung to Andy, though none as persistently as Amanda, the girl who had just been baptized. Was she in love with him?

They were walking out the church when someone called Andy's name from behind them. They stopped. It was a young man flanked by two older looking gentlemen. Chenai had not seen them in the youth service, but they were probably there. It was such a huge church. So many people.

Andy made the introductions though Chenai could sense the men's eagerness to talk about other business.

"Have you given any more thought to that proposal? My Dad's lawyer looked at it. It's a solid contract."

"Imagine that, Andy. They really want you to record a single. Your song, *Amazing*. They want to sign you. Everybody is going to know you soon," Amanda said. Chenai noted the excitement in her voice.

Chenai turned to Andy wondering what the news was really about. Andy didn't seem pleased.

"Listen guys. Like I said before I don't really want to get into the music business. It's just not for me."

"I know what you said man, but you are the one they want. They really want to make us all into huge Christian super stars with you as the lead singer. The band won't work without you."

Andy looked down then back at the three men. She noticed sadness in his eyes and Chenai wished she could leave and give him privacy. She didn't know how to walk away gracefully and take Amanda with her.

"I already told you guys, come on…"

"Andy, that's pretty selfish of you.   You already sing in the church, what's wrong with just recording those songs to be enjoyed by everybody in the world, just like Michael W. Smith and Steven Curtis Chapman. Recording albums does not make them less Christian."

"I never said that… Guys can we talk about this another time?"

"Alright," the other young man relented. "Why don't we talk later? We have to decide very soon."

Scott grabbed his friend's arm and basically forced him to walk away from Andy. Amanda stared at Andy with a look of amazement. Chenai didn't know what to say.

"Let's take you home, Chenai," Andy said at last.

At the Pieris', Chenai asked Andy if he wanted to come into the house so that he could meet Blake. As soon as she walked into the living room with him, Jodi looked up from her music gadget, the tiny white headphones permanently stuck in her ears like extensions of her body. Jodi was always plugged in to it as if she couldn't walk, eat, read or even talk on the phone without it. Jodi visibly blushed when she looked at Andy and for the first time pulled off her earphones.

"Hello," Andy said.

"Hi," she smiled and Chenai could see that just like all the girls at church, Jodi was taken with Andy. "You go to church?"

"Of course. You should come too." The way Andy said it was matter of fact as if he was answering a question about whether or not he had been to the movies before. Chenai looked at Jodi who took in his answer by nodding her head.

"Okay." Jodi said and Chenai almost had a heart attack right then and there. Then she remembered the boy Jodi had in her room and she felt worried all at once.

CHAPTER 17

Frigid

*But Shem and Japheth took a garment and laid it across
their shoulders.*

—Genesis 9:23

"Turn the wheels. Chenai, Can you see the tree in front of
you?"

Chenai hated every minute of driving lessons with Blake. Two
days of pure torture. His anger erupted at every mistake. She could
feel the sweat building up as he scolded her, his words bringing
out distress instead of confidence. Her heart raced and her leg
trembled causing the car to jerk forward. She held on to the dashboard afraid that they were going to fly through the wind shield.

"Stop. Stop. Don't- don't drive another second. Park the car."
Blake said, and then he stepped out of the car. He stood outside
and ran both his hands through his hair with frustration, his cold
breath forming clouds in front of his face.

Chenai remained in the car with her eyes on the steering wheel
trying to control her breathing, her fear. Two weeks after meeting
Andy and going to church with him Andy had offered to teach
Chenai to drive. Blake tersely told Andy that his help wasn't needed. For some reason Blake disliked Andy. They had only met twice,

briefly when Andy came to pick her up for church and on her day off, but Blake had acted as if Andy wasn't there. He wouldn't look at him. The whole encounter left Chenai baffled and distressed. It was pure wishful thinking the two men could be friends. They were oil and water. They repelled each other. Another even more dangerous thought occurred to Chenai. Maybe Blake was incapable of relating to any human beings.

At this moment, Chenai imagined how different it would have been if Andy was teaching her to drive. His patience and kindness. She would be a pro by now. But Blake. She was nervous just stepping into the car with him.

After a few seconds, Chenai got out of the car. Her legs were still shaking. She felt humiliated. She couldn't drive, though she now knew that girls much younger than her could. Drake wanted her to go on to the highway, but she was terrified driving around the empty parking lot. The wind blew towards her and she pulled her coat closer and shoved her hands in her pockets.

"Blake," she croaked and he turned to look at her. His eyes softened a little.

"Fine," Blake said. "It's your first time."

"Shouldn't I get the written test first? I don't even know the signs."

"Everybody knows a stop sign, Chenai," he drawled. At least now he called her Chenai not Cheny. She turned away from his eyes that were filled with disappointment and looked beyond the empty parking lot at the busy street beyond, seeing the cars moving steadily on Orchard Lake road. She turned to Blake unable to hide her pleading.

"I can't do it," she finally said. She wanted to say that she couldn't learn how to drive with him, but she knew if she did he would probably bark at her like a dog. When she woke up that Saturday morning she had been planning to complete her applications for college and then go out with the people she had met at church. Andy, Michelle, a gifted musician whose family was originally from Korea, Maria who was in Medical School with Andy and Darnel another guy who led the youth choir. Blake told her that getting her license was a priority. He was tired of driving her to Wal Mart and even to the pharmacy to get her feminine things.

Blake strode towards her and grabbed her shoulders. She felt his fingers digging into her skin. Her arms went limp by her sides as his eyes bored into hers.

"Yes you can. You just want to go and spend time with those people from Church instead of learning to drive."

Chenai held her breath when he stood that close. His eyes seemed to drill into her, asking for answers. Her anxiety tripled. She shook her head.

"I-I." she muttered.

"You can do it. Even Tyler can drive. Let's try again," he said. "Do you know how I learned to drive?" Chenai shook her head, trying to calm her beating heart.

"By myself. Nobody taught me. Come on get in and drive."

She did and it was terrible.

"What happened?" Andy asked Chenai several weeks later.

"I drove into the bushes. I thought I stepped on the brake, but I stepped on the gas instead."

Andy laughed throwing his head back while holding his cup of strong coffee. Everybody in the church choir room turned to look, pausing to pack the boxes for a women's shelter in Madison Heights.

"It wasn't funny," Chenai said, but she found herself smiling as Andy laughed with Amanda next to him.

"He was so angry. He got out the car kicking the air and throwing his fist at the damage on his car"

"Why do you put up with him?" Amanda asked. Chenai looked at her face, shining with makeup. Her dark hair fell on her shoulders, gleaming.

"I live in his house," Chenai said, as Amanda stared at her, blue eyes filled with worry. The three of them were now often together, working together at church for different ministries. As they talked, they all put together items for their visit to the women's shelter. Chenai had packed several boxes and then watched in quiet shock as Amanda removed everything and repacked, the way she saw fit. That was one aspect of Amanda's personality she was not getting used to. She had to be in control of everything

"So what? He should leave you alone. He sounds really mean."

Chenai looked at Amanda trying to choose her words carefully. Somehow, no matter how unreasonable Blake was she didn't want anybody else talking negatively about him. Why was that? Was it loyalty? Or that they were on the same team, somehow, though with opposing views? She really wasn't sure.

"He's just busy. He has a lot on his plate being a single father,"

Chenai said, her voice faded off when she didn't get a response. Amanda still had the expression that she had swallowed lemons.

"And I think he has some problems at work," Chenai added.

"You know, your naiveté surprises me. I have to get used to it. He sounds like a bully," Amanda said, with her eyes moving from Chenai to Andy. Chenai didn't know what to say as Amanda continued. "You're in America. You have rights. I would never put up with that kind of behavior from anyone. I mean in college, I pretty much did what I wanted and even at home, my parents let me make my own decisions. Did I tell you that right here at church, I got the pastor to change the way we work with the kids. I came up with this new idea of doing a mini service and he agreed."

Chenai listened as Amanda went on to give her examples of how she got her way and how she didn't 'exactly' manipulate people but that she was firm and persuasive. When Amanda was on a roll, nobody else could a word in edgewise and when she finally close her mouth for a second, Andy spoke.

"You are okay, right Chenai? I've met him. He just seems lost.

Besides Amanda, Andy also introduced Chenai to a young woman from Zimbabwe. Ruva Makono's life was very different from Chenai's. Though they came from the same country they really could have been from different planets. Maybe it was her imagination, but when the three of them met for coffee, Ruva dismissed her and spoke to Andy. Chenai accepted that it was probably because Andy and Ruva were both in medical school, whereas, she was a nanny. Ruva certainly looked down on her, that was quite obvious. Ruva had asked her what her father did and then went on to talk about her wealthy father, who was benefiting even more in the new Zimbabwe.

"My father is rich beyond words, but has too many kids and women. Whenever there is calamity there are some who will prosper. Men who can see opportunities and my father is one of those. But asking him for money to come here humiliated me. Be thankful, Chenai. You don't know how it feels. I am not important to my father, because he has other children that he loves and takes care of. I am not one of the legitimate ones. I had to beg."

Chenai had remained quiet and Andy took a sip of his drink. Ruva had opinions about many things and they listened to her intently. Chenai wished she could be able to talk confidently about world issues the way Ruva did. She had traveled to Europe and Asia so could compare cultures effectively. What Chenai resonated with was how much people changed after a few years in America.

"When you come to America you have to get rid of your identity, wipe off your culture like cleaning your feet at their welcome mat. You shake off your dirt, your accent.. The Nigerians arrive in their long silk robes and huge hair pieces. The Indians arrive in their saris, but in no time they have thrown them away and all wear the American uniform, the jeans."

Chenai laughed as she looked at her jeans. It was true. She remembered her aunt telling her to wash off the smell of Zimbabwe, the smell of the earth, the sun, the water and cover it up with lotions and portions from the stores that she bought by the gallons.

When they left Ruva, Andy made a comment.

"She's a nice girl. Very different from you."

"Yes." Chenai said.

"She has many great qualities. But I prefer you."

Chenai couldn't hide her smile as she looked out the window of Andy's car.

Chapter 18

Spring

Accept him whose faith is weak, without passing judgment on disputable matters.

—Romans 14:1 NIV

Blake walked through the construction site of the medical center. The building was almost complete but work had stopped. In fact, the project had been at a standstill for a few days. Blake felt his heart race as he counted the money that was lost on an hourly basis. "We've done this before. It always works." He stopped walking and turned to look at Jim. Jim rubbed his dark black moustache as if it held the answers to Blake's questions.

"Just not comfortable with doing what we've done in the past. Besides cutting corners doesn't save us that much money. I started attending a men's group at my church….,"

"Not you too." Blake glared at Jim. He couldn't control the laugh that followed.

"What do you mean 'not you too?" Jim asked.

"Have you become one of those Bible thumping…"

"Don't mock what you don't know," Jim warned. "The Bible makes a lot sense."

"Yeah, but damn it Jim, we need to make a profit on this thing or we'll lose everything. That's what you want?"

"No."

They walked around the building looking at the almost complete structure. Blake had wanted the contractor to come, but they were demanding more money for any over time. And now Jim had suddenly grown a conscience and wouldn't do what needed to be done to keep them afloat. Simple things that nobody would notice. Taking money and returning it later. Simple things.

Attending Men's Bible class. What on earth was that? Another ploy to make men weak and spend their time listening to some preacher who never ran a business in his life.

What needed to be done was not going to hurt anyone. The investors who had come aboard with him at the start of the project were also turning out to be dishonest. He was dishonest too, but Blake knew that he wasn't brutal. Money turns even the most agreeable man into a murderer and the men he had eaten lunch with, had meetings over dinner about the project with, were no longer so friendly. In fact they were downright sinister, their former smiles replaced by snarls and vicious threats. Was this the mafia? He had to laugh at the thought. Yes, money could turn anyone into the mafia.

"I'm sorry Blake. I'm turning my life around and I have accountability brothers at church. I can't lie to them. I'm trying to clean up my life and save my marriage."

Blake glared at Jim then looked at the silent building at a loss for words. Jim was like a stranger to him now.

What on earth were accountability brothers?

The brick face of the medical center and blank windows stared back at him, black holes that sucked in all his money. There was some negotiating to be done with contractors. He had two meetings before he could even go home. The fact that Chenai was home with Tyler and Jodi eased his mind and freed him to do what needed to be done. He had nothing left, no time or energy for Jodi's sulks and Tyler's puppy dog eyes.

A few hours later, Blake drove home all the problems heavy on his heart, pressing on him from all angles. He wanted to ask Chenai about this whole men's group that had changed his business partner and friend. She seemed to spend more time in church with that clown Andy and her equally clownish group of friends. What on earth did Church give them? He was trying to be a man, work hard and feed his kids whether they deserved to be fed or not. Sitting in a pew and listening to some man preach just seemed like a waste of time.

Blake arrived home and parked his car in the garage. He no longer enjoyed the pleasure the sleek BMW once gave him. He now wished he could get rid of it. Waste of money. He should just use his truck.

It was almost eight. The kitchen was dark and empty and he looked over to the family room. That was empty, too. Often when he came home Tyler would be reading to Chenai or doing his homework right next to her. The night before, she'd been tossing a soft ball to Tyler to hit with a wooden baseball bat. Tonight he found Tyler in the formal living room playing with his action figures.

"Dad," he said and smiled. His boy never looked at him with accusation. Only the women folk in his life did that very well.

"What's up? Where's everybody?"

"Chenai's studying in the office and remember Jodi went to visit grandma." Oh yes. He had forgotten. Jodi went to her mother's parents who lived in Clinton Township as often as she could. That was fine with him. He really had nothing to say to his daughter and he needed a break from seeing the hatred in her eyes. Like mother like daughter.

"Why didn't you go too?"

"I wanted to stay with Chenai," Tyler said. Blake nodded. He liked the closeness he had seen between Tyler and Chenai. At least his little boy had someone to care for him while he was gone. He remembered, just last week when Tyler was congested, coughing through the night, he had found Chenai asleep on the floor by his bed. He didn't know how he felt, but it was quite shocking to him. That she seemed to take her role of looking after them very seriously. Including him. He gave it more thought than he thought was necessary. She was just doing her job. He paid her well to do it.

He walked into his office and saw Chenai sitting at the desk intent on her books.

Now he remembered. She had started school. His mother had forced him to help her, like he didn't have a company to run to the ground. It hadn't been easy getting her student visa transferred but after a month she finally got it. So now two things were her main focus, school and church.

"Hi," Blake said. Chenai practically jumped when she heard his voice. Her large brown eyes turned on him. Nervous fingers rushed to her neck as she tightened her sweater over her collar bone.

"Good evening," she stood up then sat back down to her essay. She often dressed in jogging suits in the evening like a school uniform. Her thick hair was tied up on the top of her head. Blake often wondered what the texture of her hair was like. He studied the dark curls, his curiosity deepening. Of course she would think he was crazy if he suddenly grabbed a handful. Lately he was as intrigued with her as he was uneasy with her. Her eyes somehow seemed to see through him, see all his darkness and corruption, like all the women in his life who resented him. Was that judgment he could read in her gaze the rare moments their eyes met. It annoyed him and challenged him.

Sometimes he wanted to find ways tarnish her lily white spirit, her indestructible morals. He wanted to see her try not to be perfect. Always doing the right thing, being perfect for his kids, perfect for him in the quiet way she served meals and then ran off to be with her "pure" holy friends like Andy. His need to know more seemed to deepen with each passing day and with her reluctance to spend time with him.

She was so different. He never had much to talk about with black people and couldn't remember speaking to anyone from Africa. They were just not in his circles. He was not racist. He just didn't have friends or business acquaintances who were black. Blake also realized in that moment that he actually didn't have any friends. Not really.

Chenai leaned onto the desk, her body slender as a giraffe bending into water, hair dark cotton, a ball on her head. For some reason he felt like he was noticing her for the first time, like something of her was now revealed to him.

"What are you doing?" he asked walking towards her. He looked at the cover of her book. 'Introduction to Biology.'

"Yes. I've an assignment. I'm going to type it at Andy's place."

"What's wrong with that computer," Blake pointed at the computer on his desk.

"It's doesn't have Microsoft word," she replied looking at it.

"Well, here's my laptop. Let's try that." Blake picked up his laptop bag and brought out the latest business tool that he had discovered he had to have along with his blackberry.

"No. I- It's okay," Chenai shook her head.

"Why? You'd rather go and use your boyfriend's computer?"

"He's not."

Blake looked at her self-conscious face. She acted as if talking to him was painful, like suddenly she was sitting on thorns. Was he such a monster? She turned away from his gaze and looked at the notes on her desk in her neat small handwriting.

"You like him?"

Chenai shook her head her eyes almost watering with shyness then glanced at Blake as he powered up the computer. Blake finished powering up his laptop then selected a blank page for her to type. He wasn't surprised when she didn't reply.

"There you go. You can start typing now. Try it out," Blake said stepping back. Chenai turned her chair around and faced the machine looking at the key as if they were going to bite her.

"Now?" she asked skeptically.

"Come on. Put your fingers on the key. You can type right?"

Chenai typed her heading. She tried to move the cursor with the mouse pad, but it kept jumping around, a flickering insect she couldn't pin down.

"Don't you know how to use this?" Blake asked. His impatience was evident and Blake could sense her nervousness. It rose off the top of her head like steam.

"I've never used it," Chenai lifted her hands in surrender, but before she could stand up Blake leaned closer and moved the mouse with his long deft fingers. "It's easy. Here put your fingers here," Blake took her hand and placed it on the mouse. "Just like this and then click. Try again," he commanded.

"I-I can't," Chenai complained. She pushed the chair back hitting Blake hard in his stomach.

"Dammit girl," Blake swore in reaction to the blow.

Flustered, Chenai apologized as she stood up.

"I can't do it," she muttered and left the room. Blake stood there holding his stomach where the chair had hit him. He looked at the laptop and then the door puzzled at her reaction. Was she afraid of him? Did she hate laptops that much?

He didn't know what to do. He had work to do and should just leave her alone. Still, he wanted to figure out what he had done to upset her. He walked into the living room and Tyler was alone.

"Where's Chenai?"

"Upstairs, Dad," Tyler said, "Can you play with me?" Tyler began flying one action figure into another and said "boom" when the figures collided. He realized he had no idea what his son en-joyed doing? But he would change that soon. When this medical center was sorted out, he would have more time to spend with his children.

"Later, Ty," he said. Right now he had to find Chenai and… apologize? For what though? What did he have to apologize for? All he had done was to try and show her how to use the lap-top. Questioning himself, he went upstairs and stood outside her room. He knocked.

"Chenai it's me. Blake. Can I talk to you?"

Silence.

"Chenai."

Blake heard some movement then the door opened slowly. She held the side of it leaning on it and hiding behind it slightly. Her eyes grazed his then looked down. For a second he just looked at the top of her head then remembered he had to ask her if she was okay.

"Are you alright. You ran out of the office."

"I'm fine."

Okay. Blake wondered what else to say to her. She continued to look down as if she wanted him gone or feared that looking at him might burn her eyes. Did they not believe in eye contact back in Zimbabwe?

"Don't you need to do your essay? When is it due?"

"A week. I wanted to be done with it."

"Do you still want me to help you with the lap top? You don't have to go all the way to wherever your friend stays if I have a computer right here. I can show you. It's not that hard. Even Tyler can show you."

At that she looked up.

"Not that you are an idiot.."

Her eyes shifted.

"Damn—I mean darn it. You can learn it in two minutes if you let me show you. I won't get mad like with the driving," Blake said. He remembered that a smile might help and he smiled at her and he saw the corners of her mouth lift, though she didn't look at him. He couldn't read her, and he wondered why it mattered to him how she felt. She stepped out of the room and closed the door.

Within two minutes she had figured out how to use the mouse pad and while she typed her essay, Blake went to see his son. He would sit on the floor the way Chenai did and hold those action figures. Maybe that would help him forget his business problems.

CHAPTER 19

Warm

The sleep of laborers is sweet, whether they eat little or much.

—Ecclesiastes 5:12

School was easy for Chenai. Really a repeat of what she had studied in high school, so that didn't stress her. Initially, she had worried that she couldn't afford to pay for the semester. However, on the day she went to the billing office, the lady who ran the office, Rhonda Stevens had given her some great, but strange news.

"Your whole semester has been paid in full," she said, after typing on the keyboard and staring at the screen.

"Are you sure?" Chenai's heart was racing.

"A very good looking young man came in and paid your bill, but he wants to remain anonymous."

Chenai nearly fell over with shock.

Andy. He had paid her fees. She had talked to him about her fears, and he had somehow found a way to pay them. And he didn't want her to know. So, just that simply, her worries for school had been alleviated and because she couldn't find a way to thank Andy, she thanked God, over and over again for him.

Chenai also knew she was making a difference in Tyler's life, homework, illnesses, sadness, were all hers to deal with. One day she hoped she would be able to reach Jodi, but whenever she tried to reach her, Jodi regarded her like scum.

Also, letters from home didn't give her peace of mind. She received two in the weeks she had started school. One from Evans distressed her.

Dear Chenai,

You are so lucky you are now in America. Things are really bad at home. Baba is fine, but I just couldn't stay at home anymore and keep going to school with no promise of a future. I'm now in Harare and have decided to go to the mines and make some money in diamonds or gold. I hear you can pick up gold like stones in the streets. I think I can make more money that way instead of wasting my time with school. Please send money to baba. There is really no food in the shops. He may have to travel to Mozambique to buy things like oil and sugar.

Chenai sobbed after reading that letter. If anyone was like her mother it was Evans. He was fearless. He would travel anywhere, just as Mai had done, going to South Africa one year to buy food to sell. Her mother liked to tell them that they were not trees. She told them that they could move and hunt and search for a better future. The Colonialists had traveled all around the world in search of a better life, better land, better opportunities; the children of Zimbabwe could to. Why stay and watch your family starve? So Evans was proving that. But why was she so afraid for him?

Chenai couldn't eat for days, each morsel in her mouth turning to cardboard when the contents of the letter filled her waking thought. Chenai sent her whole pay to Zimbabwe, hoping it would help, but the guilt was still huge. She was living in absolute luxury and now driving a shiny new car. She had her future looking brighter than before, but what of her brother? What kind of life would he have at the mines? He was so young. She felt terrified and tried to bury it in the business of life in America. School, the children, Blake, Andy, Church, Amanda, Kimberly, and sometimes, Ruva. They all kept her busy.

Chenai would bury her distress in the moments she played ball with Tyler, on cool afternoons. She hid her fear with Jodi, helping her in algebra as well as trying to find ways to reach her, though Andy was the only interest that they had in common. Chenai wondered if Jodi had a crush on Andy.

Chenai had never understood love, the way her mother seemed to and her father lived it. Her father seemed to spend so much time in silent pursuits, reading, fishing, no real grand gestures, but she would glimpse her parents lost in each other. She would hear their laughter as they talked in their bedroom, her mother's laughter free and musical, and her father, more subdued yet crackling like fire.

At school there had been some girls who got pregnant and had to leave school. That had been some kind of after effect of love. Chenai tried to talk to Jodi about boyfriends, after the boy in her bedroom incident, but Jodi had smirked at her.

"You don't know anything, Chenai. Girls here are much more advanced than the girls in Africa. If you don't sleep with a boy then he won't be interested in you. Me and my friends all know about sex, and we use protection."

Chenai had been properly schooled and didn't know what to say. She felt inadequate, even as she knew the consequences of those choices. She had volunteered at the pregnancy center and seen teenagers who were pregnant and alone. At least those girls wanted to find a home for their babies. But it was more than that, one girl had spoken of her broken heart, how she had felt used, and how the boy didn't want anything to do with her. When she brought it up with Kimberly, Chenai was stunned at her reaction.

"As long as they use protection. We can't stop it. It's a moving train."

She could talk to Andy about anything. Andy didn't judge. He tried to understand her concerns about home, family.

"This is America. Unfortunately, the media and just about everybody else now lives by very "progressive" codes though I believe nothing is new under the sun. Promiscuity is nothing new. It's just now it's seen as the norm and being chaste is seen as being backward. Girls especially are being turned into sex objects very early on. It's not really Jodi's fault. But don't give up."

Everything she heard at church was contrary to how the Pieris lived. She started worrying that if she didn't diligently pray, then she would slowly be changed, slowly lose her sense of what was right and wrong. Yes, just like the story of the frog in water that became progressively hotter and it died. Would she change little by little until she couldn't recognize herself anymore?

When she studied with Andy, they would discuss the issues which she had with Jodi and Blake and get his guidance too. They didn't study alone often, but one day, she went to study at his place, against the youth group policy, about appropriate behavior between women and men. But Amanda and Andy's classmate cancelled last minute.

Chenai liked Andy's apartment. It was small, just one bedroom but the living room was spacious, one green couch a desk in one corner and small table and two chairs. Chenai took the desk while Andy studied on the floor or couch. There wasn't much to distract in the living space. No ornaments, just a simple place with bare necessities. The kitchen was even more dismal to Chenai's eyes. He didn't cook much and even if he wanted to, there was nothing to cook with. Just last week she forced him to buy a pot so they could have real home cooked food at his place.

Andy was focused especially when he had tests. But after about an hour of studying he was happy to talk, about her job with the kids, or just about life in Zimbabwe.

"What songs do you sing in your language?"

"Well, we sing a lot in English."

"Really."

"I know one Shona song."

"Can you sing it?"

Chenai looked at Andy. Sitting on the floor guitar in hand. He usually played to relax, or when he just felt like worshiping God. She felt shy, but after a while she took a deep breath, closed her eyes and began the song her mother loved. It could be sung fast or slow depending on the occasion, but Chenai sang it slowly, sadness in every note, but something else too. A belief that, yes there was no one like Jesus. He brought the flow of peace and joy, along with the bitterness of her loss, bittersweet.

"Hapana akaita sa Jesu. Hakuna akaita saye. Hakuna."

"What's it saying?"

"There is no one like Jesus. *Jesu* is Jesus."

"That's beautiful Chenai. Teach me and I will play. By the end of the evening she had taught him 3 songs in Shona and he had told her more about his life. How his parents adopted him, how he didn't know his real parents. He didn't really know his nationality but had adopted his parents' which was part Native American and English.

Weeks later Andy surprised her at church when he taught the church a few lines from one of the songs and then added the English translation. She felt tears brim her eyes. Oh Andy was so easy to love! Because she realized he made her feel loveable, as if she had something to offer. She felt as if he urgently needed to know more about her, as if the knowledge of her also filled him. She could tell him stories about home, without feeling guilty that she came from such a dysfunctional country.

Sometimes he would ask her to tell him jokes that her mother used to tell them. She would refuse because her mother had a way of making them funny.

"There was the biggest man in the village. One day he went around with a paint brush painting the villagers houses for fun. So he painted this man, Komoka's house. When Komoka came back he was really angry. "Who painted my house?" he asked the other villagers. They told him that a man who lived on top of the hill had painted the homes. Komoka, being a man of pride told everyone he was marching up there to confront this man. He walked confidently while all the villagers looked on. When he reached the hut at the top of the hill he knocked on the door.

"Come out now," Komoka yelled.

The door opened and out came this man. Komoka's eyes stopped by the man's stomach. He slowly turned his eyes up to the giant's face.

"What do you want?"

"Ah. Are you the one who painted my house?"

"Yes," the man said.

"I wanted to tell you that the paint has dried."

Andy smiled. He was amused.

"It sounds better in Shona," Chenai said.

"It's good in English. I will tell my patients this joke. They will heal faster with laughter."

❧ ⚘ ☙

She had asked Andy about his music.

"What happened with those guys? That first day at church. They wanted you to do an album?"

Andy nodded. "They don't talk to me anymore. They are mad that I refused."

"Why didn't you do it?"

"Just didn't feel right at the time."

"Now?"

"Still doesn't feel right. Some things to me, are not for sale. I am not going to sell the voice God gave me to worship him."

Another day, Andy asked Chenai about Zimbabwe. He seemed to have a genuine interest in her country.

Chenai tried to remember what her father had told her about the history of Zimbabwe. At school she'd studied Russian history and European history. She'd never studied Zimbabwe.

"This country is complicated. As you know there was a time when it was probably simpler. The issues were black and white. There were no grey areas, but now it is no longer true. Zimbabwe is a young country going through growing pains. Sometimes you have to be patient with adolescents."

Her father's words were not really helpful. She had tried to research on her own, using the internet, checking out books from the library. The truth was hard to find because it was tainted by whomever wrote the book. It had seemed impossible to find all the answers to a nation that didn't exist until the British people came and said here are its borders, now this is your country.

"It's a little difficult for me. I often wonder why God made it easy for one race to just over power another one."

"But you know it's not new in any civilization right. Look at the Egyptians. It's just human nature," Andy said.

"I know. It still feels weird that the whites in Zimbabwe and maybe even here could just hate me just because of how I look. And I can't hide it. It's all over me. My blackness."

"So Zimbabwe had racism too."

"I know right. And it's the white people, very few of them, who managed to subdue a whole nation."

"Here we only heard about apartheid in South Africa."

"They kept their racism more organized for longer in South

Africa. A war had to be fought and even though the whites lost, they still ruled the economy in Zimbabwe. The whites lived in their own world next to us another universe too."

"And now?"

"Now it's not whites who oppress. It's the powerful who oppress the weak. We exchanged one oppressor for another one."

Andy nodded then comforted her by saying, "Every country has blood on their hands. Every country has prospered on the oppression of the lesser. America tries to avoid that. But it happens. Just a few decades ago American citizens used apartheid too, and it was just as brutal. It makes me sick to think my ancestors were oppressors, too."

"You turned out okay," Chenai teased him.

"I guess so, but it's a bit embarrassing that anything to do with our history is about oppressing other cultures. It's shameful."

When Chenai arrived home, it was late. She had stayed longer than she intended, talking to Andy always so refreshing and fun. She opened the door to the living room and was surprised when Blake came to meet her by the kitchen.

"You were out late," he said glancing at the clock by the microwave. All the warm thoughts of the time she spent with Andy disappeared and the ice she saw on the lake seemed to have covered her from head to toe even though it was now spring.

"I had to study," Chenai removed her back pack. It was Saturday. It was her day off even though she rarely took her days off, preferring to spend time with Tyler, going to volunteer with church members and sometimes even taking Jodi.

"I don't think you should be out late. You are a young woman. Were you alone with that Andy?"

Chenai looked down totally embarrassed. Was she going to get a lecture? Like the one Blake gave Jodi when she was caught with a boy. Even though Andy and her were just friends, albeit close friends, she felt guilty.

"I've been reading that Bible of yours. I think it says none of that nonsense with men until you are married."

"I know."

"So you are breaking your laws?"

What Chenai really wanted to do was ask him why he wasn't out like he usually was. Running around, chasing for whatever he was looking for and running away from whatever he was running away from.

Where were the kids? She wasn't sure if they were home or they had gone to their aunt or grandparents that day. She was relieved when she heard Tyler come down the stairs.

"Chenai! You are back. I have something to show you. Come to my room."

Chenai looked at Tyler's face gratefully. Blake lifted his chin higher, his disapproval deep. Chenai began to walk towards Tyler and to avoid Blake she ran into the counter and winced in pain.

"You alright?"

"I'm fine," she said and moved quickly past him, her side stinging with pain.

CHAPTER 20

Sun

There is no fear in love.

—1 John 4:18

Dear Baba,

I hope you are fine. How is the school year going? Did you get a new grade 7 teacher? How is Evans? He sent me a letter about his move. Did he get the letter I sent him? I know he is not good at writing letters, is he?

I have started school now and I am getting all As. It's much easier than what I did in High school. I get paid quite well so I will also be sending money for Petros to pay for his exams. All my fees for this year were paid. I think I got a scholarship. I'm not really sure.

I wanted to tell you about life here. It's very nice. The winter is gone so it's much warmer and nicer. The trees are starting to grow leaves, they are pretty, not like the Jacarandas, but they bloom pink and white and yellow. Anderson is always taking me to see different places with Amanda too. Jodi likes spending time with me when Anderson is there. Mr. Pieri is very busy with work so I am usually home with Tyler. Tyler likes the lake which is right by the house. It reminds me of the dam near the farm though with no boats. I am a mother to Tyler, sometimes it's surprising to me. I go to his parent teacher con-

ferences and bake things for his bake sales and I even meet with Jodi's teachers when Aunt Kimberly is not there. The teachers are always surprised, but I am now legally their guardian so Mr. Pieri has given me the power of a mother. Can you imagine me as a mother to a thirteen year old and 6 year old white child?

We now have a family camp coming up at church. Jodi and Tyler want to come. I'll write to you when we come back. I better go and get lunch ready for Tyler and Jodi. They like cold sandwiches for lunch.
I love you Baba and I will phone you again soon.
Your daughter
Chenai

In her letter Chenai didn't say anything about how uncomfortable Blake made her feel, or how Kimberly filled her head with negative stories about Blake dishing her storied that made her wary. She didn't want to judge Blake and she wished they would stop. She hated that their words were affecting her view of him.

"He's not a nice man, Chenai. He only cares about himself. He's selfish and mean," Kimberly would say. She didn't tell her father much detail about Andy who seemed to love God the way David in the Bible did and want to do His will no matter what everybody else was doing. Blake's voice caught her by surprise as she folded her letter at the kitchen table. She never heard his car. Why was he home so early?

"What is this camp Tyler's talking about?"

"It's a family camp. The church does one every year."

"That sounds really lame."

Lame. He thought everything she did at church was lame, or stupid, or senseless. Chenai knew not to comment on Blake's statement.

In her short time at school. she now understood that Christians and most of what they stood for or did was considered a waste of time, backward, dumb, intolerant, and small-minded by many of the students and lecturers as well. Andy told her some scary stories about College and how he was laughed at because he didn't sleep around and didn't drink. She was shocked when he told her of a girl who had tried to spike his drink so he would get drunk and she could sleep with him.

"You'll see when you go to college. They'll try and change you to fit their lifestyle. And God warned us in the Bible that we wouldn't be popular. Don't try and fit in at school okay. We are not called to fit in but to stand out. Even Jesus wasn't popular when He walked on earth and He is God. Jesus makes people living in the dark very uncomfortable that's why they call us names," Andy had told her a few weeks after she met him.

"But it hurts. I get mad at Mr. Pieri sometimes. He is the worst..."

"Don't worry about him Chenai. Just pray for him. He's lost. He's in the dark and he's afraid of the light from you because you are somehow helping him see himself. You are like a mirror and he doesn't like what he sees and he will hide it by being mean to you. Sometimes people don't want to come face to face with who they are."

After Blake's comment she stood up calmly though inside she was about to explode.

"What do you do there anyway? Why's Tyler all excited?"

Chenai sighed. She wasn't in the mood to spar with him. It was exhausting. But Blake was waiting for an answer so he could argue with her. She could sense it just as a chameleon changed color in times of danger.

"It's time for families to get together and …." She didn't want to say the rest as Blake looked at her with a smirk on his face that demanded answers. "Pray and praise God."

"What?" his perplexed statement raised her temperature. "What are you trying to do to my son? Make him believe in some god who allows things like September 11th to happen. A god who makes rules that no sane man can follow…"

"At least the people at church care more about Tyler than you've ever shown," Chenai blurted out then covered her mouth shocked when she saw anger distort Blake's face.

"What do you know about being a father? How dare you tell me how to raise my boy…"

Chenai looked around hoping Jodi or Tyler would come in again, but they were both out by the lake with some friends from school. She was alone with Blake's anger.

"You think you can do a better job than me with your Christian friends like Andy and all the other narrow-minded people from your church?"

"I'm sorry. I didn't mean you were not a good Dad. I just think you need to spend more time with him."

"That's what I pay you for, right? I have to make money so my son won't have to struggle and depend on anybody else for money. A man has to provide for his family or he's nothing. And you come here and judge me."

"I didn't mean to," Chenai said, her hands in tight fists. "I- I must go."

Chenai walked towards the door, but Blake walked towards her and pulled her arms. His hands were above her elbows grasping her so tight she felt like a rag doll. She remembered the doll that she had that her mother had made for her with fabric and stuffed with wool. She remembered how when she held it at the waist the arms would fall back useless.

"Don't run away from what you started," Blake said his face close to hers. "Maybe I can finish it for you."

"Daddy. What you doing?"

Blake let Chenai go as if she was hot coals. Chenai stumbled away from Blake and looked at Tyler who held a bucket which he had been collecting different creatures in. It seemed Tyler could sense whenever there was trouble or whenever she was sad. When she would be crying thinking of her mother, Tyler would suddenly show up and just put his arm around her. He didn't say anything, but his big brown eyes would be filled with understanding. Chenai would think that he is so young and yet he seemed to understand more than a kid should and comfort her.

Now, Chenai looked at him and could see his confusion. Tyler had just saved her from a situation that could have damaged her relationship with Blake forever.

"Go and play, Tyler," Blake ground out then glanced at Chenai who stood leaning against the counter and holding her arm.

Blake walked out the door, grabbing his keys though he had just come home. As he drove aimlessly he felt angry. Angrier than he had ever been with anyone. He didn't understand what Chenai's presence was doing to his senses. It was her constant praying, not eating or fasting or whatever they call it around his house that was driving him crazy even as he longed to get home and spar with her about her beliefs. How dare she call him a bad father? He had to get away from her. He was a father who remained. He didn't run away from his kids and he provided for them. Worked night and day for them.

CHAPTER 21

Blossom

*In his heart a man plans his course, but the LORD
determines his steps.*

—Proverbs 16:9

Spring. She had always associated spring with flowers bloom-
ing, butterflies fluttering and birds singing. Spring in Michi-
gan, however, was still too chilly for her liking, especially today.
Chenai wondered if Blake's bad temper was due to the weather.
Tonight, however, Chenai decided to put Blake out of her mind.
Tonight she focused on serving dinner in the church gymnasium.

The huge room had windows placed so high, not much light
came in. The many over-head lights in the room did little to improve the darkness. Chenai and other young people had placed
balloons and streamers around the gym in an attempt to brighten
the room for the fundraiser.

There were many ways this church served the community and
Chenai had decided to give her time to help with the pregnancy
center as well as two other programs. The dinner would raise funds
for the center where young girls who found themselves pregnant
could get resources and support to keep their babies or give them
up for adoption.

As she served, Andy and Amanda were greeting the arriving dinner guests. Soon, all the people who had come to support the event were served. The sounds of chatting voices and tinkling flatware filled the place. Chenai smiled when she saw Andy walking towards her with two other people.

"Hey Chenai," Andy greeted. "Great turn out."

"It is," she replied.

"Chenai this is Mark and Lisa Stafford. They have been coming to the church for years."

"Nice to meet you, Chenai. Andy's told us so much about you."

Chenai nodded smiling wondering why Andy wanted them to meet her. "Chenai they have two boys. One in first grade and one who is four. I told them you may be interested in working for them."

Chenai tried to hide her surprise as she kept her smile on her face. Work for them? Leave Tyler and Blake and Jodi. She had never said that she wanted to leave them.

"They are sweet boys," Lisa said.

"You won't really have to do much. Lisa works half a day two days a week and I am usually home by 5pm. Just get them from school, take them to activities…" Mark said.

"They have soccer and piano. Nothing too hectic."

"Lisa is a physician but has her own practice now so her time is more flexible."

"So, what do you think? I just wanted them to meet you. You can talk to them later."

"Andy. I still work for the Pieris," Chenai managed to say. She was struck by Andy's eagerness.

"I know how difficult that situation is..,"

"Are you still serving?" someone asked behind Andy and the Staffords.

"I'm sorry. I can serve you. Yes," Chenai said and smiled apologetically to the Staffords.

"We can talk later," Lisa said. She walked away talking to Mark. Chenai liked the Staffords, she truly did. From appearances they seemed ten times better than Blake. They seemed to have joy and seemed to love their kids. They were as different from Blake as a jackal from a dove.

Who should she choose to work for, the dove or the jackal?

As Chenai finished serving and cleaning up, she warily watched Andy walk towards her. Their work was done and another team was responsible for putting the tables and chairs away.

"Are you ready to go?"

"Sure," she picked up her bag and walked out of the gym towards Andy's car.

"Are you okay? What did you think of Lisa and Mark?"

"They are nice."

Andy chuckled. Chenai hoped he couldn't tell how conflicted she was. The moment Andy told her his plans for her and the Staffords', Chenai's first thought was, no! She didn't want to leave Tyler. She almost shouted it out. She didn't want to leave that family. It would be like abandoning them. As they cleaned up after the dinner she thought some more. Maybe it would be better to leave Blake's home. He stressed her out, didn't he? Jodi also. Why would she want to stay in a home where she was not comfortable? Why not go and live with a wonderful Christian family and be surrounded by love, prayers, smiles..?

"Well. They are willing to pay you more, too. You would be so much happier there."

Chenai nodded and Andy was encouraged to say more.

"More time to study. You know you will actually be off in the evenings. These parents like to be with their kids."

"I wish you had told me. I mean…"

"I know. I was just too excited. Sorry for the ambush. You will talk to them further won't you?" Andy stopped by his car looking at her. She zipped up her jacket and kicked a stick on the ground.

Chenai stifled a yawn. She had stayed up late doing an assignment because, Tyler needed to practice his soft ball and she needed to listen to him read after bath time. She had watched him do it alone, but after a while, Chenai had left her work to go and play with Tyler. It was hard, managing school, Blake's children, Blake himself and her work for church, but she knew that whatever she did for God, was the most important. That family needed her, desperately. The dream she had, or was it a vision came back to her clearly. She wasn't even sure if she had been awake or asleep. In that dream she was home and Tyler was missing. One minute he was watching Sponge Bob and the next he was gone. He wasn't in his room. She ran downstairs just as Blake walked in and saw the terrified look on her face.

"I can't find Tyler." Saying those words derailed her mind and she felt herself coming apart, running this way and that until Blake rushed to her and gripped her shoulders.

"What are you talking about?" His voice was panicked, the disbelief in his eyes terrifying her. They started running outside calling Tyler's name, to the edge of the water, and by then they were screaming their voices causing the birds to fly away in terror, violent terrified screams. Blake dialed 911 with shaky fingers and while he explained to the operator he ran to the road to take another look. Chenai ran around the front of the house checking behind every bush, under the chairs, under the logs, up the trees, up the roof of the house, under hats, everything she could pick up was upturned. Before the police arrived they both ran to the basement and then found Tyler curled up under the cabinet in the laundry room. His action figures were still gripped in his hands, superman and Spiderman. He was asleep. He opened his eyes and they both embraced him with relief, bodies sagging laughing and crying. And then she watched the whole scene, as if from a distance and felt God speaking to her.

Tyler is Blake to me. I will not leave any stone unturned to find him.

"I can't." Chenai said to Andy, now, almost in tears at the memory of the dream.

"What do you mean? You want to stay with Mr. Pieri?"

"I feel I should stay Andy. I can't abandon them."

Andy's eyes didn't leave hers when she said the words. He seemed to be searching for something. Andy seemed to sigh in resignation.

When Andy dropped her at home, she could tell he was bothered by her decision. His unspoken disapproval hung in the air thick as the porridge her mother used to make for breakfast. She knew that no matter how hard it was, she could not abandon the Pieri family. She just couldn't do it and live with herself. Andy left soon after and Chenai didn't know what to say to make him feel better about the situation.

She pushed thoughts of Andy out of her mind and after checking on Tyler who slept soundly and heard Jodi moving in her room she waited until 1 am so she could call her father as early as possible. Blake wasn't home.

She took the phone from the kitchen and using a phone card dialed Zimbabwe, to a house where her father could receive calls. The school phone had not been working for a while, just as the electricity and most things had begun to fall apart. Little by little.

She was relieved when the phone was picked up after a few rings.

"May I speak to Mr. Muvhimi? It's his daughter. Calling from America."

"Ah. I will send someone to call him."

Chenai listened to the crackling static while she waited, praying the line wouldn't suddenly cut off as it sometimes did.

Her father came on the line in five minutes, her precious phone card losing money by the second.

"How are you, Baba? Did you get my letters?" she asked trying to control the rush of questions and emotions. She leaned back on the pillows, imagining the school office, the brick walls and cement floors, all very basic, but still very special to her father. She knew he spent hours in there, repairing torn books, furniture, but mostly the books that he cherished. But he wasn't in the office, was he. He was in someone's house. Maybe standing in the hallway, holding the phone awkwardly. When he talked she remembered how little her father liked to talk. He had always been a man of a few words and sometimes she felt as if talking pained him, like he preferred being in his thoughts or lost in his books.

"We are fine. Don't worry about us."

"I can't help it. I keep hearing that there's no food, that …"

"No. We have food. The news always exaggerates. Politics."

"And, how is Evans? I got his letter. He left home?"

She heard his sigh. Her father's sighs spoke a million words.

"He's trying something else. He has friends who influence him more than me."

There was silence. Chenai didn't know what to say when her father continued.

"Thank you for the money you sent. It's a fortune. Do you have any money left? What about your school? Are you able to go now? Your mother really wanted you to go to school. More than anything she knew you were smart."

Chenai nodded then remembered to speak.

"Yes."

Her father continued, and she could imagine how much effort this speech was taking. It had been months since they last talked.

"I dreamt of her and she seemed to be telling me that you may be in trouble. Are you alright? I still don't understand what happened with *Sisi* Rutendo. Why did you have to leave?"

At those words Chenai felt her heart race and tears fill her eyes. All at once she was overwhelmed, as if waters were rising and she had no way out of the darkness. She missed her mother so sharply;

the pain was so raw she thought she might faint. If she lied to her father then she would be lying to her mother's spirit. Her mother, above all, wanted honesty. They had had a very transparent relationship, mostly because Lois could see through her.

"It's all worked out well, Baba. Don't worry."

"And this Mr. Pieri, He's a widower, too?"

"Yes. So I'm helping with his children. The boy is very young."

Chenai could sense that her father was not satisfied with her answer, and she sensed that he didn't want to stress her.

Chenai looked at the bracelet on her wrist. She fingered it remembering how it had looked on her mother's delicate wrist. Her father had bought it from Nyanga when he went there for a job interview. The jade and woven gold looked like an intricate design of grass blowing in the wind. Her mother loved to wear it with her yellow dress with green flowers and only on special occasions like weddings, parties, or prize giving day at the Takoma School.

After her mother's funeral the dress had been given to Lois's younger sister, Vivian. Chenai had been given some items during *kugova,* the ceremony of distributing the deceased's clothes and the bracelet was the most precious thing she owned. She wore it that day because it was her mother's birthday, May 2nd.

"Well, I can't talk very long. The owner will not be happy. And you found a nice church. That's very important to your mother."

Oh baba. He seemed so lost, a man without a compass. She could see him in her mind's eye, reading a book, or the paper, but his anchor gone.

How could she have left him? Who was making his favorite sadza and okra? Or frying his matemba fish and spicing it with strong spice mhiripiri that Lois grew just for him.

She knew Evans and his playfulness. Her younger brother just needed looking after too. Who was taking care of her brothers and making sure their clothes were clean and that they bathed and studied. Her father was book smart but her mother had brought life and beauty into their lives, and ran the house in her strict but humorous way. She felt worse when she remembered that Evans had left too. Only Petros remained. Would he run away too? He was so young.

Now she was in this foreign land, and her family was being blown about by the wind, possibly starving. The last time she had managed to speak to her youngest brother, Petros, he had sounded so sad, too.

"I'll send you some money. You can buy whatever you like," Chenai had told him.

"I don't want money. Only you, Chenai."

After hanging up the phone Chenai sobbed, trying to stifle her anguish by burying her face in a pillow. Somehow Jodi heard her, because when she looked up Jodi stood by the door, her expression questioning and concerned. Such tenderness from Jodi increased her tears.

"Chenai?"

"Sorry," Chenai said sitting up and wiping her tears. "Did I wake you?"

Jodi walked past her into the adjoining bathroom and brought a wad of toilet paper and handed it to her. She seemed uncomfortable now.

"Were you on the phone?" she asked

"Yes, I was speaking with my father. I- I miss him?"

Jodi wrinkled her nose. She clearly didn't share the same sentiments on fathers. Chenai looked up thinking of what to say to Jodi. She was still a child and needed guidance. Chenai still didn't have a clue how to help the girl. She wondered if Jodi would ever open up to her about her feelings.

Jodi's question seemed like the opening she needed. "You miss your mom?"

"We all miss her," Jodi said.

The girl folded her arms. The softness Chenai had seen earlier was disappearing.

"I know how hard it is," Chenai said. Jodi shrugged but there was some emotion on her face, a glimmer of sadness trying to push past her sullen, angry gaze. It was as if the sun was trying to fight the dark clouds and make an appearance. Chenai didn't say anything and after a while Jodi spoke again.

"I do. They should have just divorced then maybe, maybe my mom would still be here."

Chenai didn't know how to respond to Jodi's last statement, but decided to ask her something else instead. In a book Andy had given her, she had read some advice about dealing with teens. How to listen without judgment, and how to follow their lead. Teens in America were the bosses it seemed. If you didn't march to the sound of their drum you could lose them. Especially the troubled ones. They could run away, or resort to drugs, if they were not already doing that. "Were you and your mom close?"

"We were. She liked to take me shopping. Almost every week we went shopping. We could spend hours in Somerset mall shopping. Have you been there?"

"No. Is it nice?"

Jodi seemed to light up as she talked, "Yes. They have loads of designer clothes. We can go sometime. Mom and I could drop a thousand in one spree if we wished. That's if she wasn't buying a shoe that cost a thousand."

Jodi laughed when she saw Chenai's eyes. *A thousand dollars on shoes?*

"Dad didn't like it. They always fought about it, but what does he know about fashion? He wants me to buy my clothes at Target. And have everybody laugh at me at school."

Chenai listened as Jodi talked animatedly about fashion realizing that she was passionate about it. It helped her forget her sadness and even though it was way too late to be talking, they probably both needed this moment.

"I can be a stylist I think. I can help you with your clothes. You look like a model, but you dress like a house maid."

"I am a nanny." Chenai wasn't even offended. She laughed.

"No you are not. You are an au pair. We've had au pairs from Paris who spoke French and dressed like models. It's about mixing and finding the right clothes. You tend to wear dresses all the time even when it's 20 degrees. You need a rocking pair of jeans. You look like a size zero."

"Okay. I have jeans."

"Do you have a photo of your mum?"

Chenai blinked at the change of topic. She took the single photo by the side of her bed. Jodi stared at the black and white studio portrait of her mother and father. Very stiff expressions.

There was no hint in the photo of her mother's vibrant personality. Maybe a little in her eyes that seemed to sparkle.

"She looks like you," Jodi said. "I'll show you my mom. I have loads of albums."

Jodi left and came back her arm full of four big albums.

"She loved to scrapbook. So here are the family ones she did."

"She was very pretty," Chenai said.

"I know. She knew how to enhance what she had. She could do her make up in 20 minutes and look like Paris Hilton."

"Is that you?" Chenai asked pointing to a photo of a little girl standing next to Samantha.

"Yep. As you can see, my Dad wasn't in many photos. He is always working."

Chenai looked at Jodi, not sure what to say. Her silent prayer always in her heart, *God give me wisdom with this child.* She had spent so much time thinking of ways to reach her and now there seemed to be cracks in the wall and Chenai said a silent 'thank you' to God as she spent precious moments with Jodi.

CHAPTER 22

Breeze

And though she spoke to him day after day, he refused to go to bed with her or even be with her.

—Genesis 39:10

The threatening notes were getting more ominous by the week. Blake read the note a few days after his argument with Chenai.

He had gone to Penny's after he had quarreled with Chenai, but something had changed with Penny. For the first time since he met Penny, their time together had left him feeling cold and unsatisfied. He could tell that she sensed the change as well.

Penny had begged him to stay for dinner. She had promised a better performance in bed, but he had left her wondering why he wasn't enticed by her promises. He could tell she had been angry, but he didn't care. He had just wanted to get out of her Condo.

Blake turned over the note in his hand again and collapsed in his chair. He studied the words.

You think you can get away with what you did? Think again. We'll make you pay. We know where you live. We know where your kids are. You'll pay.

Blake had fired a lot of people especially when business was slow and he had burned a lot of bridges in his career. Two brothers had threatened him before because they thought he owed them money, even though the courts had decided otherwise. Blake hated the way he had created enemies of one of the most dangerous families, if indeed they were the ones sending the notes. He called Jim Litgee.

"I got another one," he said immediately.

"A threatening note?"

"Yeah," Blake said and rubbed his forehead. His gaze fell on another balance due letter from the bank that lay on his desk.

"I don't like this one. It mentions the kids."

"Where are they?"

"They are leaving for camp today with the nanny. Some church thing."

"You should go," Jim said quietly.

"Nah," Blake said.

"And I think we should tell the police about these letters. Maybe they can do some forensics and figure out who's sending them?"

"Unless a crime is committed I don't think the police care."

Blake arrived home expecting to be greeted by delicious cooking as he often was since Chenai moved in, but instead the house was empty.

Camp. Blake remembered opening the fridge. His cell phone buzzed and he looked at the number. It was Penny. He could finally invite her over, but the thought of her didn't interest him as it once did. He didn't have the time to figure out why.

On the counter he saw the newsletter from the church giving directions to the camp. He knew the Lake by Tenby Bay. It would take less than an hour to get there. If he stayed home, the weekend stretched ahead of him in the huge house. He had some work to do, but he told himself that he would rather be with the kids and make sure they were safe.

Without questioning his motives or his sanity he rushed up to his room and grabbed a bag. He threw in a pair of shorts and changed into loose fitting jeans and a T-shirt. In the garage he decided to grab a tent and folding chair. He hadn't done any camping in years. Once in his car he dialed Chenai's number, but there was no answer.

Chenai drove behind Andy. It was her first time driving such a long distance. It was one of those days poets would enjoy describing, Chenai thought, clear blue skies with the dusting of pure white clouds, the air tinged with the sweetness of birds, light and breezes. Days this beautiful, Chenai was sure she could feel her mother's presence more.

After they checked in at the camp site entrance Chenai drove through the gate and entered a nature wonderland. Shadows of tall trees danced on the windshield. Chenai breathed in the pine tinged fragrance delivered by the wind that came in through the windows.

After driving for about a mile Andy parked by a camping site. The blue of the water didn't disappoint, inviting, refreshing and clear. Though Chenai lived by a lake and enjoyed seeing the water daily, the natural surroundings were breathtaking. There were no homes built around the lake and all they could see was the clear water, trees and endless sky.

Chenai parked at the site and then took a moment to look around. Tyler smiled at her through her rearview mirror. Jodi still had her earphones and was asleep.

Chenai got out of the car and stretched. Her back and neck hurt from concentrating on the highway. She hated driving and was always terrified. She couldn't wait to be a confident driver, the way Blake could talk on the phone and at the same time navigate curves on the highway at high speed.

Andy stretched too and smiled at her over the roof of his truck. She smiled shyly back and wondered if Andy was still unhappy about her decision not to leave the Pieris.

Still, Andy was the balance. She had to find time in her often busy days now to reflect on God's goodness. How He had brought Andy to her life to balance it out. She had Blake to make her strong in her faith and Andy was the opposite. He was the sunshine to Blake's darkness. Andy, whenever they were both free he would plan many fun activities. He reminded her that she was only twenty, still new in this state that had so much to offer. Take her to free concerts in the park or canoeing on Kent Lake. He loved to take her out to nature with Amanda too. To sit still under tall trees and listen to the birds and follow the trail of ants. Or during the last snow storm of winter, deep into the forest to gaze in wonderment at its peaceful piling up, to be in a white enchanted land, that took her breath away. Before she had viewed snow with such fear, after her aunt threw her out in the storm, certain she would die in it, but with Andy she lay in it and drew what he called 'Snow Angels' and sled down hills on it, screaming and laughing at the same time. She knew that Andy always took time to gaze at creation and be still. She looked forward to those moments at camp as she took a deep breath of the fresh air. She glanced at Andy now. Yes, she was truly blessed.

They were early. The rest of the families would arrive soon, but Andy had told her he wanted them to go on the beach before too many people arrived.

"This looks lovely," Chenai sighed gazing at the water. It sparkled like jewels. The wind was much stronger this close to the water and it was welcome. The wind seemed to blow away any bad feelings they may have brought with them, casting them into the water and burying their troubles beneath the sand.

"Can I swim?" Tyler asked. Chenai held his hand laughing then looked back in the car. Jodi was now up. She remained seated in the car with her head phones in her ears.

"We will," Andy said and laughed. He then picked a screaming Tyler up and ran towards the water. Chenai ran after them laughing as Andy threatened to throw the boy in the water.

Smiling Chenai watched Andy as she walked on the beach picking up tiny rocks. Tyler reminded her of her younger brother, Evans was soft hearted, adventurous and had a loving nature. Evans was just like their mother.

A wave of sadness passed through her body like an electric

current as she remembered the letter from Evans. Where was he? Where had he gone?

She jumped when she felt Andy's arm on her shoulder. She tried to focus on the wind and the way the waves moved at its command, rippling against their feet.

"Are you okay?" he asked. She turned and looked in his beautiful, understanding eyes. His short hair danced in the wind that played with his clothes and her dress, a slapping sound, like sails on a ship, she imagined. She smiled, happy for the distraction he brought. She still didn't know what he wanted, he was her friend, though sometimes, like now he would put his arm around her and he felt like so much more. He kept it there and she felt its weight on her shoulders, a strange but comforting feeling.

"It's great to be here with you," he said.

Chenai looked down embarrassed.

"Were you thinking about…"

He now knew not to say it. Her mother. She nodded then crouched down to pick up a smooth stone. She stood up again and Andy reached for her. When it came to that subject he didn't force her to talk. He was just a comforting presence. She could talk about Zimbabwe, talk about life before the tragedy, but not what happened to her mother. It was not easy to utter. It was not easy to think about.

"Come here," Andy said and then held her in his arms.

She let him hold her, and she began to feel relaxed. In Andy's arms, memories of her mother still flooded forcefully into her mind. She could hear her mother's voice as clearly as if she was there with them at that moment.

She wanted to share the story with Andy as they sat there quietly. She wanted to tell him of her mother and father's love story. She felt as if she was falling for Andy.

Was she falling in love with Andy? Was that what love was. Comfort. Tenderness.

She knew what love was like. She saw it, though her mother and father never really called it love. Lois could get her father to look up from his book. She would do extraordinary things for her family. The story of Lois and Frank always brought a smile to her face and she smiled now as she recalled her mother telling her.

"Chenai. I have a story to tell you," Lois had told her as they dug for sweet potatoes on the small plot of land, they were given. Lois had decided to grow sweet potatoes on one side and corn on the other. "I think you are ready to know about me."

Chenai remembered sitting up straight on the mound of soil where green leaves sprouted out, no hint of the bounty hidden underneath. Her mother looked small, kneeling next to her basket filled with red sweet potatoes caked with mud. She preferred to leave them that way so they would stay fresh longer.

"There were two young women. I will call them Nyara and Tanetsa". Chenai nodded. She knew that someone called Nyara was probably shy and sweet like her mother and Tanetsa could only mean trouble. Her mother continued.

"Nyara was a kind, beautiful girl, the kind of woman a man wants to take to be his wife. Do you know what I mean?"

Chenai nodded. Women who were too loud, too excited, too happy were regarded suspiciously. Her mother always told her to listen more and speak less. To think before acting. To dress modestly. To respect herself.

"So is this about you? Where is baba in the story?"

"Be patient. Yes, it is about me, but I want to tell it to you like a story. You know *ngano* that *ambuya* tells you when you go to the village. Don't you like those?"

"I do."

"Maybe you can pass this story on to your daughter," Lois said and laughed when Chenai giggled. "You don't see yourself as a mother do you? You are right. It's a long way away. You are too smart like your father. You will probably go to University and be a teacher like your father."

"Or a doctor," Chenai said and Lois nodded.

"Yes you can be that. Now, back to my story. No more interruptions?"

"No." Chenai covered her mouth with her hand.

"So, one fantastic summer just before the rains, both women found themselves at the school where Frank taught. Nyara was from Frank's village near Gutu. Her family knew him and had already talked about the two of them getting married. Nyara was doing everything right according to the customs. When Frank left to teach the grade seven children she would enter his house, pick his clothes from the floor, wash them, and then at lunch time she would make him sadza and *mbowora*, his favorite."

Chenai smiled, but didn't say anything. She knew her father still enjoyed eating the pumpkin leaves that she herself only tolerated.

Lois continued with her story, "Nyara would call one of the students and they would take the food to Frank who liked to sit away from the other teachers under a tree and read his favorite books.

One day Tanetsa also arrived, and if Nyara told the story, she would call Tanetsa, *mhene*, lightning, coming from the area near the shops. Years before, Tanetsa had attended the school and was visiting when she spotted Frank. Tanetsa wore beautiful clothes from the city that no one had ever seen. Her hair looked like it flowed down her back and she would go and talk to the other teachers, because she was famous. Her uncle owned the grocery store and all the teachers bought their cold drinks from him.

Now, Tanetsa would never have noticed Frank if it wasn't for the fact that he didn't notice her. She wanted Frank to see her and she would wear bright colors, red blouses and green skirts, but Frank kept his head in his book. She would talk and laugh loudly with the other teachers, regaling them with stories of the city, the opportunities, especially in Highfields where she lived."

At this point of the story Chenai had already decided she didn't like Tanetsa. She knew her mother was Nyara because her mother was a lady. Tanetsa was clearly one of those women, the attention seekers that always got into trouble. Chenai didn't interrupt the story or tell her mother her thoughts.

Lois continued, "Nyara could see what Tanetsa was doing and she would smile inwardly because Nyara never liked to show her emotion. Nyara's laughter would bubble inside when she caught Tanetsa trying to get Frank's attention, but all Frank ever did was swat the flies away and continue to turn the page of some thick volume of plays by Shakespeare, seeming to want to fit inside the book and not have anything to do with the world.

One day Nyara saw Tanetsa coming from the stores holding a cold drink and she loudly spoke to the other teachers so that Frank could hear her. Frank barely glanced up and Nyara watched Tanetsa almost stomp her feet in anger."

Chenai giggled at the image of this woman who lacked wisdom and tact.

"So the next day, Tanetsa came to the school again and this time she had wrapped a cloth around her waist to accentuate her hips. She held a drum and she called all the girls who had been sitting under a tree at the end of the school day. They all ran to her and she whispered something to them. Nyara had just come from the river to fetch water and she stopped in her tracks, the can of water on her head. She wondered what Tanetsa was going to do this time and stood to watch her. One of the young girls began to beat the drum and Tanetsa began singing a song that the other young girls echoed. They danced in a circle and like magic, Frank looked up. Tanetsa must have caught his attention from the corner of her eye because she began to dance with more energy; swaying her hips from side to side and her head around and around like a peacock. Nyara watched in shock as Frank put his book down and stared at the dancing in earnest. When Tanetsa was done she said good bye to the kids and took off her wrap to reveal a stunning skirt underneath. She shook it as if to shake it off all inhibition and decency then rewrapped herself. Nyara watched in horror as Frank smiled, then after a few minutes, got up from the where he sat and slowly walked towards Tanetsa. Nyara watched them walk away as the water she had been carrying on her head tilted to one side and drenched her."

Chenai looked at her mother with shock. So then how did she get to marry her father, if this Tanetsa person walked away with him?

"What do you think?" Lois had asked.

"I don't like this dancing woman. So how did Nyara get Frank? Baba?"

"She never did. I am Tanetsa." Lois said.

"Daddy!"

Tyler's voice broke into Chenai's reverie. Chenai spun and in her scramble to get out of Andy's arms, her legs tousled with Andy's. They both tumbled to the ground. Chenai fought to get out of the entanglement and stood up at attention like a soldier looking at Blake while Andy remained on the ground staring. Sure enough Blake stood outside his car watching them his displeasure the only dark cloud on an otherwise clear day.

CHAPTER 23

Wind

When the Queen of Sheba heard about the fame of Solomon and his relationship with the Lord, she came to test Solomon with hard question.

—1 Kings 10:1

Blake's arrival and his dark mood would have ruined Chenai's day, but the arrival of other families and some of her friends kept her spirits up.

As the afternoon progressed, the forceful breeze became stronger. The leaves on the trees rustled back and forth. Chenai wondered if Blake had the power to change the weather with his arrival.

The camp site, which had been fairly empty, was now coming alive with the families setting up.

Jodi and Tyler helped to get items out of the car. On their campsite they now had three cars, Blake's SUV, Andy's truck and Chenai's small sedan that Blake had purchased when she got her license. He had given up giving her lessons after three days and sent her to driving school. With a professional instructor Chenai was more relaxed. She'd managed to pass her test the first time round.

"I think I'll go and help Amanda and her family," Andy said. Did he also feel the chill of Blake's presence? Chenai glanced at Blake as he pulled out a bag that held a tent.

"Alright," she agreed, giving Andy a stiff wave.

"Andy you should stay and help me. I don't know how to set our tent up," Jodi called out. Jodi hadn't talked much to anybody. She moved around listening to her music or whatever it was she listened to. Chenai had no idea.

"I got it," Blake said quickly.

Chenai wanted to say something, but since Blake arrived she was ill at ease.

"I'll see you later," Andy said. He seemed poised to reach out and touch Chenai's arm, but then stopped. When he walked away Chenai turned to Jodi completely ignoring Blake.

"So, now I see why you wanted to come to camp. Time with your boyfriend, right," Blake said and nodded his head towards Andy's retreating back.

Chenai bit her lip. What she wanted to ask him was why he had come to ruin her time away from him. What was he doing at a Christian Family camp that he thought was pathetic? Chenai quickly corrected her thoughts.

God can work in his heart. He's here isn't he? Blake is actually at a Christian event. Wow!

"He's not my boyfriend," Chenai said instead taking the folding chairs from the trunk of the car.

"Are you telling me your beliefs don't allow boyfriends too?" Blake spoke while taking out the tent and opening it up fighting the strong breeze, which suddenly grew more powerful. When he turned around, the tent had been blown away and he let out an expletive as he tried to run after it, tripping over the dark green bag on the grass. Chenai watched, surprised as the wind picked up the tent and it began to roll towards the Lake at incredible speed.

"Daddy the tent!" Tyler cried running after it behind Blake. Chenai watched as a giggle escaped her throat. She had never seen Blake running around and never seen him chasing anything. So to see him sprinting after the tent had her laughing so hard. She screamed in horror when she saw the tent land on the water, and began to sink.

Andy and the other men left their own tents and started running towards the Lake. Chenai squealed when Blake jumped in the lake, the water reaching his waist and started fighting to pull the tent out. By then three other people were helping him. Blake walked out of the water with his clothes clinging to him. He was soaked from head to toe. He dragged the wet tent in his hands, frustration on his face.

"Are you okay, man?" Andy asked.

"Fine, fine," Blake grumbled and walked to where Chenai stood by their cars.

"This whole camp thing is ridiculous," Blake complained reminding Chenai of Tyler. He looked like a little boy, not his usual intimidating self. He flung the wet heavy tent down on the grass and the vision she had of Tyler lost filled her thoughts again.

Why did you come? Chenai wanted to ask, but bit her lip. She opened the door and pulled out the only bath towel she had brought. She hoped he would refuse it, but Blake grabbed it from her and began wiping his hair and arms. His clothes clung to him. Chenai turned away and looked at the crowd of people that would occasionally glance in their direction.

"If you think it's so stupid why are you here?" Jodi asked and Chenai turned to face her, praying that she wouldn't start another confrontation. Their arguments were now part of everyday life in the Pieri household and Chenai couldn't stomach them. She longed for peace and often the only people who provided her with peace were Andy and Tyler. There was only peace if Blake and Jodi were not in the house.

"None of your business."

"That's why your stupid tent got wet. So where are you going to sleep now?

"In your tent," Blake said absently taking off his shirt. Chenai looked at her feet and caught the smile from Blake. He obviously knew how uncomfortable she was.

"I'm not staying here," Jodi said and started to walk away. "I'll stay with my friends."

Blake stared at her, his anger still evident. And then he sneezed. He continued to wipe his arms and Chenai turned away and busied herself with her bags.

That night after a dinner of sandwiches and fruit, , the first meeting took place in a huge tent set up further from the lake than the other tents. When Chenai left, Blake remained behind alone. She had hoped he would at least attend the church service, but he wasn't interested.

When she arrived, Andy called her over. Jodi was sitting next to him and Amanda wasn't too far either. The tent was filled with happy voices, chatting and excited to be out in a beautiful setting to worship God and get closer to His Power. The strong breeze seemed even stronger now, flapping the tent roof over their heads but not strong enough to pull the tent down. At least Chenai hoped so. Chenai sat down and when the opening prayer began she kept thinking of Blake alone setting up the family tent. The beginning strums of a song she loved reached her ears and pushed Blake out her mind.

"He's turned my mourning, into dancing again. He's lifted my sorrow…"

They all stood up and started singing and Chenai saw that Jodi was clapping her hands and had removed the earphones that were usually a part of her hair style. God was working miracles, she suddenly realized. The whole Pieri family was there, at this Christian camp. God was indeed God.

After the service, Tyler talked to some of the kids around the tent. The kids and adults were all served hot chocolate and doughnuts. Chenai, Amanda, Jodi and Andy all sat together by the lake enjoying the reflection of the moonlight on the water, the wind getting stronger by the minute. Amanda snuggled close to Andy and Jodi was doing her best to engage him in conversation. Chenai watched the two women, their hair tossed to and fro by the wind, vying for Andy's attention,.

"Did Mr. Pieri tell you why he came?" Andy asked Chenai. Amanda looked at her.

"No."

"He's gorgeous. When you told me about him I was pictured some old scrooge not a Tom Cruise look-alike."

Chenai laughed at Amanda's comment. Jodi rolled her eyes to reflect her annoyance.

"I don't get him. He comes to a Christian camp, but doesn't attend the meeting," Andy looked at Chenai, concern in his eyes. "Are you going to sleep in the same tent as him?"

"I don't think so," Chenai shifted on the grass then looked at Andy's beautiful face. He was perfect. A perfect godly man who cared about her and made her feel safe. "Will his tent be dry?"

"What about Jodi?"

"I can stay with you right?" Jodi turned to Amanda who nodded then she turned to Andy. "I was going to come with you, but yours is a one man tent."

"No sharing tents with opposite sex, unless they are family," Andy said. Chenai wouldn't meet his eyes. She kept trying to understand Jodi's comment. Share with Andy? Was she insane?

"That's true," Amanda said, turning to Chenai.

"Tyler?" Andy asked.

"He'll stay with me," Chenai responded. "I'm sure Mr. Pieri will sleep in the car."

Chenai was uncomfortable with the whole discussion on sleeping arrangements. She didn't want to discuss them with Andy because she didn't really know the answers. She turned to him just as he scratched his curly head with confusion in his eyes.

"It's almost bed time I better get Tyler. I'll see you tomorrow?" Chenai stood up and dusted herself off. Andy stood up next to her. She could sense he wanted to do something or say something, but he didn't so she said good night to the group and walked to get Tyler. Tyler ran ahead of her to the tent and Chenai stopped by her car to see if she had forgotten anything else. Chenai was surprised to find Blake and Tyler working together putting items in the tent.

"We made your bed," Tyler said excitedly looking at his father proudly. Blake seemed more relaxed. He was dry, wearing a pair of shorts and a t-shirt. His hair was still wet in some spots.

The other girls thought he was cute, Amanda's voice came to remind her. *Cute? They must like scowling, angry lips, dark, unkind eyes that never have much humor.*

"Thank you," Chenai replied arms folded.

"We all get to sleep together," Tyler continued, enthusiastically. "I wanted to sleep by the window so I can see outside. You are in the middle so you can be safe and Daddy is on the end."

Chenai nodded unable to speak. She noticed Blake watching her from the light of the moon and the flash light Tyler now held up.

"Don't you need the restroom Ty?" she pulled her toiletry bag out. "I need a shower."

"Now?" Blake asked surprised.

"Quick one," she said then turned to Tyler and ruffled his hair, "Thanks for making my bed. I'll be right back."

When Chenai got back from the communal bathroom a few yards away she glanced at the car, wondering if she should just sleep there. But it would not be as comfortable. She had her own sleeping bag and she would scoot closer to Tyler.

Later, Chenai flashed her light into the tent. Tyler was already fast asleep, but Blake turned to her as if surprised. She had really hoped he would sleep in the car. But now what could she do? She was so tired. Just wanted to collapse and sleep.

"Sorry." She turned off the flash light, but the tent went dark. It was meant for 5 people and she noted with relief that there was plenty of space separating her from Blake. She had never seen him lying down. Blake was constantly in motion at home, or he was away from home in motion somewhere else so to see him looking relaxed and not in a rush to go   anywhere unsettled her. She had become used to the old Blake, the one who was always running to something and away from home.

"You can turn it on. Don't want you to end up in the wrong sleeping bag," Blake drawled. She felt his voice as if he was whispering in her ear. Chenai squirmed as she turned on her flash light. She didn't want to end up in the wrong place either. In her T-shirt and sweatpants she unzipped her sleeping bag and climbed in. She reached out to close the zipper and Blake leaned forward.

"Here," he said and she lay very still while he pulled it up.

"Thanks," Chenai mumbled then looked at Tyler. She wished Tyler was awake. He was good at diffusing tension with his sweet voice and innocent comments, but after how active he had been all day chasing other little boys and girls and dancing like lightning at the service, she knew he wouldn't budge. He was exhausted.

"How was your service?" Blake asked after a while. Chenai glanced in Blake's direction. She could see his outline now that she had adjusted to the dark.

"It was good,"

"It was loud enough for me to hear, too. I'm sure they put up the volume so I could hear about the power of your God," Blake said. Chenai wasn't sure she was ready for another sparring session. The evening had been so great, and she had felt God's presence and sometimes Blake's cynicism drained her. He liked to challenge her and she remembered how she would read up on topics before he came home, just in case he had another impossible question.

Last week, for example, he had almost stumped her.

"So you believe that only those who believe in Jesus will go to heaven. So how about people who've never heard of God. How about some tribe in the middle of nowhere, Africa or Asia or some island. Do they just go to hell, as if it's their fault?"

Chenai had been astounded by that question. That was a difficult question that many theologians debated and argued about. But Blake was looking at her, hoping she would have nothing to say. His eagerness to hear her response encouraged her.

"That's a hard question and I don't have all the answers," Chenai began and Blake smirked. She was quiet for a while, trying to get her thoughts in order, biting her lower lip. Finally, she thought she could continue, still fearful of Blake's reaction to anything she had to say on the subject.

She took a deep breath and plunged ahead. "I know that God wants us, those who know Him and his power to go and tell as many people as possible. Some people go the dangerous places, like China, the Middle East just to spread God's love, his promises and I'm afraid to share it with you, right in this house." Chenai spoke hesitantly, but with conviction. Blake didn't really look like he had been listening. He looked as if he was thinking of something else to say.

"Because I'm not like those people living in the middle of no-where. I've heard all I can stand about your religion right here in America. You didn't really answer my question, Chenai."

Chenai remained quiet. She had to bite her tongue. It was not really up to her to convince him. Blake had to see God's work through her or God would talk to him. He was not ready to re-ceive God anyway.

After that she had gone and read all she could about the sub-ject. She knew that God was just and fair and He would not let a whole world of people perish if they had not heard about Him, but what she discovered challenged her. She was responsible to let others know about Jesus and spread the good news. But she really struggled in sharing it with Blake, one man. How about a whole world of lost people?

His argument to her was that people like her from African obviously needed God.

"I can understand the need to believe in a savior over there in Africa. I mean you have poverty, war, dictators. I mean you die from malaria. It's easy to see why all the people there need to lean on something bigger, a crutch to keep them going. Yep, it's only weak minded people who need a crutch. People in America are inventors, scientists, we go into space and we can grow a chicken in a week and grow lettuce without soil. We are now in the process of cloning people."

She had listened to him in dismay, unable to say anything to his train of thought. He had told her a hundred reasons why they didn't need God and had not given her a chance to answer.

When she talked with Amanda and Andy they had been sympathetic. Chenai wished Andy was there to talk to Blake. She was reminded also how her father had talked about the subject. How he had initially struggled with Christianity because it was brought to them by people who wanted nothing, but to take over their land and enslave them. People who discriminated against them and called everything they did evil. These missionaries commanded them all to change their names. As if their own given Shona and Ndebele names were not holy enough, could not be stomached by God.

But no matter who bought Jesus there, Jesus remains pure and his message remains pure, no matter how evil people are in the name of Christ, Chenai thought.

So much to think about, yet the message was so simple. Andy had also talked about Blake's arguments.

"You can't argue with someone. You can't make him believe. Only God can. In his heart there is a place only God can fill and Blake will try and fill it, but one day every knee will bow, including Mr. Pieri."

Chenai now thought of Blake's question about the service. It wasn't that difficult a question but she knew he was probably just warming up.

"The service was about God's presence. How it fills us with his goodness and peace and makes everything alright."

Blake snorted, "How can you talk about a presence when you can't see Him? How do you know you get peace and such?"

Chenai thought for a while, not sure she should bring up what happened earlier but unable to resist. "Well, it's like your tent. Something was moving it towards the water even though you couldn't see it right?"

Blake's burst of laughter took Chenai by surprise and she found herself laughing too, but trying to block it with her hands lest she woke up Tyler. Blake, however, didn't seem to care if he woke up the whole camp.

"Are you making fun of me?" Blake asked.

"No, no. Just showing you that God is like that wind. You can't see him, but you can see the results of his presence."

"Well, maybe God moved that tent in the water so I could speak to you tonight. It's the closest I've felt to you."

The joy that had filled Chenai fled as Jodi did from her Dad. Now she was tense again, holding her breath. Did Blake sense her tension?

"Are you missing your boyfriend? Do you wish he was here instead of me?"

"Andy's not my boyfriend. He's a good person,"

Blake didn't respond and Chenai wanted to hide deeper in the sleeping bag so she could sort through all her feelings.

"We're just friends," she added.

"I see the way he looks at you. It's okay to have a boyfriend Chenai. Don't tell me your religion doesn't allow that, too."

"It does. But not in the way other people do it."

"Can you kiss?"

"No."

"Hold hands?"

"That's okay."

Blake shook his head in the dark, "By the time I was your age I had done more than kissing and holding hands. Man, I had Jodi already."

"That was very young," Chenai said. She looked at Blake who now stared at the ceiling. She could see the outline of his face, but not the details. She couldn't imagine having a child and Blake was already married by the time he was her age. He turned to look in her direction.

"So you've never been kissed?" Blake asked.

"No. I don't like it," Chenai responded starting to feel the stress increase.

"How can you know you don't like it if you've never done it?"

Blake was surprised when Chenai pulled her sleeping bag zipper down and stood up. She grabbed a sweater and after finding the flap to the tent, crawled out.

"Oh God give me strength to deal with this man. He's driving me crazy," She muttered then stood staring at the water in the distance. It was getting close to midnight and the camping grounds were quiet. The sounds of crickets and the wind filled the air, a striking concert that matched the wind and waves on the water. This was supposed to have been a wonderful, peaceful camp, where she felt closer to God, but all she felt was confusion and stress because of Blake. Her eyes found the full moon that rested on thin clouds, as if it was half dressed. It mesmerized her and she felt calmer, just staring at the sky breathing in the crisp air.

She gasped when she felt strong hands on her shoulders.

"It's me," he spoke close to her ear and Chenai nearly buckled with shock. "You seem stressed."

"I'm okay," Chenai shook her head and moved Blake's hands away. Blake walked in front of her and faced her bending low so his face was on the same level as her face was.

"Why did you leave the tent?" he asked. "Did all that talk about kissing make you uncomfortable?"

Chenai shook her head then froze when he touched her face. His eyes seemed to hold her frozen, unable to think or breathe as he licked his lips.

"Relax," he coaxed. Chenai swallowed hard. She wanted to look away, but found she was unable to move from his gaze. "It's just a kiss."

He leaned close to her. She felt his hands resting on her temples and ears.

His lips touched her tightly closed ones. With that one touch he seemed to take her breath with him and she felt her heart thud with fear.

"No," Chenai muttered even though she leaned in to him, allowing him to mold her to him. When he left her lips to trail kisses down her throat, she tried to speak again. "Can't do this."

"It's just a kiss, Chenai. You see, no big deal."

His voice was strange to her ears and then she felt his lips again, deeper. In the back of her mind she remembered feeling this way. When she was about 14 and she sat on the raft with two of her brothers and without warning, a flood of water had come terrifying all of them. Their raft had been thrown up and their screams and howls of terror covered the river and surrounding trees. But besides her alarm she had never felt so alive, her heart lurching up almost into her mouth and when they didn't drown, they had laughed and held on to floating logs and the raft, her knees weak with bewilderment and her heart beating wildly. The water took them high and low, completely out of their control.

Afterwards they talked about the incident, describing the feelings like they were the most incredible, unbelievable emotions they had ever felt. She felt just the same now. Bewildered, out of control, scared, confused.

"Daddy. Chenai," Tyler called from the tent.

"Blake stop," Chenai said then realized that Blake wasn't holding her, but she was the one leaning into him, like he held the magnet that was pulling her. Embarrassed she stepped back from him trying to come back to earth and shake off the fog that had taken over her brain.

"Tyler needs me," she stumbled away from Blake, and then moved towards the tent, heart beating wildly. She reassured Tyler who smiled and fell asleep and lay in her sleeping bag, ears tuned to the outside, her heart continuing to race. She tried to pray, but couldn't settle herself. She was still in the river on the raft, unsure if she would make it out alive? Her mother's warnings came clear to her.

"Don't take a bath if there's lightning." She may as well have added, "Don't sleep in the same tent as Blake Pieri. Or, leave his house now!"

Blake didn't come in and she couldn't sleep for a long time. She never knew when and if she fell asleep, but when she woke up in the morning Blake, his car and wet tent had disappeared from the camping grounds.

CHAPTER 24

Humid

For where your treasure is, there your heart will be also.

—Matthew 6:21

The warmer spring days that followed didn't ease the pressure on Blake. The only positive was that it was two weeks since the camp and he had not received any more threats. The main pressure was coming from one of his investors. The man who was turning out to be more of a criminal than a business man.

Blake acknowledged that he had made mistakes by using money that should have stayed in escrow, but he had shifted the funds in an effort to reduce costs. The contractor had messed up the foundation. Blake had had to pay another company to redo the work. The project continued to hemorrhage money.

Before he could go into panic mode again, Blake knew he had to come up with another plan. The taste of a life of inconsequence and poverty threatened him each morning. Blake vowed, however, that he would not go down without a fight.

To that end, Blake had arranged a meeting with Penny. The CPA was as beautiful as she was smart and well connected. Blake needed an increase in his line of credit and contacts in the city to expedite the permit for the next phase of his project. He knew that Penny could help with both.

One thing was certain. He would do anything in his power to ensure that his fortune never ran out. Blake was furious that someone was trying to scare him off, and when he really thought about it he could narrow it down to two people. His former builder, Troy Smith. Troy demanded payment when he had messed up on the supporting structures. Blake had to redo most of his work with another company. Then there was Charlie Henson. They had been friends before, working together on many renovations. Charlie was a skilled electrician, but for some reason when it came to Blake's medical center, Charlie had been totally unprofessional, doubling his estimates and not turning up for work with his crew. Eventually, Blake had to replace him and then the animosity began. It's as if they had never been friends with Charlie calling him names and stating that he thought he was too good for them all. It could have been any number of contractors he had fired. Yes, during this project Blake had made many enemies.

To make matters worse Chenai was now making his life even more uncomfortable, adding a complication that he just didn't have time for. He was irritated that the kiss that he meant as a joke had gotten out of hand. He had planned to play with her a little, tease her, rock her confidence. Now it was him who was dominated by the kiss. He hated the way he had lost control as if he was in middle school. Now the joke was on him.

He found himself thinking about ways to challenge her when he got home. He even bought a Bible and was amazed about the people he read about. The Old Testament was filled with stories of war, adultery, and people crying out to God and God saving them from horrific mistakes like murder. His mother had been surprised the last time they talked.

"I thought you would come to the wedding. It's your brother's wedding."

"I'm busy Mother. I have a lot of work to do. I'm sending the kids aren't I?"

"I know. I just thought your brother meant something to you."

"Your Bible says God is more important than family."

"Blake what Bible are you reading? Since when …..That's wonderful!" Marylyn spoke excitedly. "I knew God would answer my prayers. I just knew it…"

Blake remembered that his mother had gone on and on and he had lied that he had a meeting and hung up. He didn't have to spend hours talking about the Bible with his mother, too. He had enough of that with Chenai.

Penny lifted her eyes from her menu and glanced at Blake. She could see the tension on his face and hoped that with her help, he would be more relaxed again. Fishbones was crowded at lunch time, but all her focus was on the man opposite her. He had called her that morning. She hadn't seen him since he went on that camping trip two weeks earlier. At his request, she had done some research to see how she could help him with his project. He just needed an extension of his loan and she had contacts. She would even cosign for him. She knew someone from his bank who could help with extending his loan so he could finish the medical center.

"I can help you Blake. I know you don't want your company to fail," she said. Blake nodded but didn't reply.

"Your step-father's predictions would come true."

Penny could see that mentioning Blake's step dad was all she needed to do to get him angry, and then spur him on to do even better … and to rely on her.

"That's enough Penny. You can talk to your guy…"

Penny smiled at him, but noticed Blake wasn't even looking at her. He stared out the window. Penny wondered who he was looking at. She saw a skinny black girl walk past with a young white girl chatting up a storm next to her.

"Who are you looking at? Those young girls?" Penny asked. Blake turned to her lost in thought.

"Did you see a ghost? You know them?"

"That was – the kids' nanny," Blake said. "What is she doing down town? She's a long, long way from home."

"That's Chenai? I didn't expect her to look like that," Penny said studying Blake. She saw something in his eyes that surprised her. Was he acting like a 14 year old with a crush on a girl?

Penny glanced at the door and saw Chenai and the girls enter the restaurant, speak to the hostess and then walk to a table. Penny could see that the African nanny had seen Blake. The girl's eyes widened with shock, and then she averted them just as quickly.

Penny had to meet this woman who made Blake act like he was sitting on porcupines. She lifted her hand and waved her over. Blake stared at her with disapproval, but she ignored him. Chenai and the other young women walked to their table. Penny studied her as she got closer. She wore a long skirt and a peasant blouse on her skinny frame. Penny took in her thick hair that sat on her head like a stiff hat. No makeup. No jewelry except for the bright jade bangle on her wrist. She was young and a shade of dark brown that reminded her of her coffee in the morning. If Blake was into this exotic creature whose eyes looked like a lost puppy then she didn't know him at all. She had to revise her view of men.

"Hi," Penny smiled broadly. "You are the kids' nanny?"

"Hello," Chenai said.

"I'm Amanda." Amanda introduced herself to Penny and then blushed as she looked shyly at Blake. That annoyed Penny. Amanda's crush on the much older man was obvious. Her body language gave her away. Oh to be young, Penny thought.

"Hello Mr. Pieri." Chenai greeted.

"I'm Penny." Penny held out her hand. "It's so good to meet you."

The introductions done Penny asked the next question.

"What are you doing so far from home? Where are the kids Chenai?"

"They had camp today." Chenai took a deep breath then continued. "We were working at the homeless shelter and decided to come here for lunch."

"Oh. How sweet," Penny crooned. Blake didn't say anything, but Penny had already seen all she had needed to. She was as attuned to Blake as shark was to blood. Something was going on between Blake and that cute little nanny of his. She couldn't look in Blake's eyes and he looked uncomfortable and tense when she approached. Was he taking advantage of that poor girl? She wouldn't know how to handle a man with Blake's experience and sophistication. Blake could charm anybody. She knew. Even the young Amanda was taken with him. She had some work to do to make sure he would always be hers. Not much because these girls would bore Blake very quickly. Chenai was really too unsophisticated, too immature to even know what hit her. Penny would have to figure out a plan. Blake was hers and her plan to be Mrs. Pieri was about to get more interesting.

"We better go. Nice to meet you,' Chenai said turning away.

"Bye Mr. Pieri and Penny," Amanda said, and then they went to their own table which unfortunately was right in view of Blake.

"She's a sweetie. Very quiet," Penny crooned glancing in Chenai's direction then stealing a peek back at Blake. Blake took a gulp of his water then focused his eyes on Penny.

"Too quiet," Blake agreed then sat back and looked in Chenai's direction as if he couldn't help himself. Chenai had been looking at her menu, but stole a glance his way and when she saw him staring she quickly looked back at her menu. Penny swallowed her knowing smile. She couldn't help grinning when she saw Blake's expression change when a tall handsome young man came in and squeezed next to Chenai and took her hand. My, my, my, this was even more interesting than she originally thought. She glanced at Blake and wondered if he was about to have a heart attack. Penny stifled a laugh at the thought.

That evening when Blake got home it was quiet and silent.

The kids were away at sleep overs with friends. He had hoped to find Chenai at home. He remembered her in the restaurant and scowled. He wondered if she remembered the kiss. He hadn't forgotten it. Right now he wanted to kiss her again. That thought flew from his head when he recalled how Andy walked in to join the women that afternoon. For a man who was supposed to be in medical school he seemed to be spending an awful lot of time with Chenai. It was almost as if he was her shadow. Blake was convinced that every time he turned around, there was Andy with his "holier-than-thou" attitude, and "I want to go and help people in Africa" crap. Blake nearly groaned when he saw Andy reach over and grab Chenai's hand. Why was he doing that? He remembered the feeling of jealousy that swept through him enough to knock him over, but he kept his expression as calm as he could.

What was wrong with him? The two of them deserved each other. They could go back to Africa and act holy together. He certainly had no time for their childish aspirations. He had a big investment to protect.

He heard her car drive in just after he had opened a can of his favorite drink. He took a long swig then heard her come in through the kitchen. She froze by the door when their eyes met. Blake hadn't realized how huge her eyes were. At that moment, when she spotted him, they reminded him of a startled deer ready for flight.

"Hi," he said.

"Hello," she mumbled holding the purse straps by her shoulders. Her cotton shirt and long skirt did little to hide her long slim body. She was covered from head to toe, and yet she seemed more alluring than a bikini clad Penny. Had his tastes changed?

The silence was thick.

Chenai seemed terrified of him and he didn't like that. She looked as if she might run any second and get into her car and drive away.

"I have to go and study," she said.

"How's school going?" Blake asked putting his beer down. His question seemed to take some of the tension from her body. Just a little bit.

"Fine." She tried to smile.

"It's not too hard?"

"No."

"You should have a cell phone," he said and Chenai raised her eyebrows, seemingly in surprise. Her face was always easy to read, full of expression. Whatever she was feeling was painted on her face, clear for the world to see. "It's important that I can reach you anytime. Everybody has a cell phone."

"I don't need one." Even as she spoke Blake took a cell phone out of his pocket.

"Here."

She shook her head as he walked towards her and pulled her hand. He closed her fingers around the phone. She snatched her hand away as if she had been burned. Blake smiled.

"I don't use that line much. Just keep it. Listen, it's not safe for a girl to be out alone without a phone."

Chenai looked at the razor thin phone, shiny and alien in her hand.

"Thanks," she mumbled.

"Guess it's just you and me. I'm going to bed." Blake said and turned away from her. Chenai stood in the middle of the kitchen and Blake turned to look at her still rooted to the spot, staring at the phone.

Chenai looked at the door to the garage and physically shook herself out of her reverie when she heard Blake's shower running. Never before had she felt more like Alice in Wonderland than the last few weeks. She wanted to run out of the house. How could she be alone with him in this house with his all-knowing eyes? He had made absolutely no mention of the kiss during the past two weeks.

Maybe she had dreamt it. Why had he done it? Why had she allowed it?

During the rest of the time at camp she'd been distracted. Chenai feared that his kiss had somehow ruined her spiritual life. She had prayed all night to get him and all that had transpired between them out her mind. She had prayed for forgiveness for allowing it and for even sleeping in the same tent with him in the first place. She should have slept in the car or joined Amanda's family, or the bathroom would have been better. She shouldn't have melted in his arms like she had no will power or self-control. The thought always filled her with disgust in herself for acting so foolishly. She wanted to talk to someone, but wasn't sure how Andy would take it or Amanda, who had moved from having a crush on Andy to Blake. Yes, it was true. She couldn't trust the heart. The heart was deceitful above all things, beyond cure. Who could truly understand it, Chenai wondered.

Was Blake the enemy trying to confuse her and ruin her future? She knew the verse in the Bible clearly. *the enemy comes to steal, kill and destroy.* Blake was there to steal her innocence, her focus on God. Her mother had warned her about such men, who were older and worldly. Who wanted what they could get from you. She had shown her a dirty rag that they used to clean the kitchen floor. It was torn after years of use.

"This is what they can do. They can use you up until you are like this rag and then throw you away so no one wants you."

Chenai had stared at the stained rag with holes and held together by torn strings. Her mother had not been really clear how you can get used up until you looked like a dirty rag, but she said that it was possible. Chenai had studied biology and knew some of what happened between a man and woman when married but…. Was that what Blake wanted, she wondered.

"You must wait for that one man. Only one, who will love you and cherish you the way your Father in heaven does, your Dad does and the way I do. He will treat you are like you are a treasure from heaven.

Blake was not that man, Chenai knew.

Maybe it wasn't too late to move in with the Staffords. Maybe she could still escape.

After a while, Chenai walked slowly upstairs to her room. Her room was still the same, huge bed, thick white carpet. She felt the loneliness rushing over her, covering her like a thick blanket. She wanted to talk to somebody about what was happening to her. She wanted her mother.

And yet, somehow deep down she knew. She tried to hide it, and escape from it, but she knew that she was drawn to Blake. She wanted their arguments, and she wanted to convince him that God loved him. She wanted him to realize that he didn't need to be running around like a fortune hunter who couldn't see the treasures he already had—Tyler and Jodi.

After all, he was home now wasn't he? He was home and not out with that blonde woman chasing something that he just never seemed to find.

CHAPTER 25

Thunder

Live as free people, but do not use your freedom as a cover-up for evil

—*1 Peter 2:16*

"Has Blake changed his mind about the wedding?" Marylyn asked when she called her the next evening. Chenai was still confused about Blake, scared of him and also terrified to leave him. Did she really know him? She had seen his stunning and very nice girlfriend Penny. And somehow that made sense. Him and her. They were both smart, hardworking Americans. Both were white, both were very attractive and they both deserved one another. Anything about Blake and her was totally wrong in every sense. Every single sense.

Chenai recalled Penny's eyes on her. Kind of condescending. Kind of sympathetic and kind of knowing all at the same time. What did Penny know, she wondered.

"He's very busy," Chenai said, trying to explain.

"No Chenai," Marylyn said her name in a way that it sounded like Chaynay. "I know Blake, darling. He-he's been through a lot and I know he's not able to forgive or move past things."

Chenai nodded though she knew that Marylyn couldn't see her. She didn't want to probe into Blake's life, though sometimes

Marylyn just volunteered information. They spoke so often now, Chenai felt as if she knew this mother, knew her heart and her concern for Blake. She also knew that Blake and Marylyn rarely talked. It was as if, Chenai was the only link between the mother and son.

"Well, you'll meet my other son too. My little boy, Glen's getting married. You'll come with the kids."

As the children's nanny, Chenai knew she had no choice but to go. In early June, Michigan was really hot and she had been warned that Charlotte could be even hotter. Jodi was already getting antsy and the trip would do her good. She had been getting into trouble a lot lately, little things. It was as if the warmer weather increased her mischief.

The day they were set to leave, Jodi was excited about getting away from home for a few weeks.

"I can't wait to get away from here. Daddy's getting annoying. He won't even let me go visit my friends."

Chenai nodded, but didn't say anything. Not about when she had been caught smoking, or about another day she slipped out her window to meet up with a boy in the pool house and Blake had nearly pulled his hair out. And of course the calls from her mother's family, cursing Blake out and taking Jodi's side. On that at least, Chenai knew that Blake was in the right and Jodi was playing her mother's family against her father. Her manipulative ways were sneaky and dangerous and there was nothing she could do to stop her except pray.

Jodi was going to church, though she wasn't changing. That just proved that going to church didn't mean a thing and Chenai knew that a church was just an intensive care and many people in church needed The Healer. They were far from perfect or they were completely messed up. Yes, she had to remember that and not judge Jodi too harshly. God would change her. He loved her more than she could and it wasn't Jodi's fault that she had grown up without really knowing Jesus.

"Do you need help packing?" Chenai asked. Jodi turned her blue eyes on her. Chenai had to gauge Jodi's moods that changed daily and had to pray for patience hourly.

"No. I don't need help."

Chenai left Jodi's room and walked into her own room. Tyler's bag was already packed and she had finished with her own packing. She didn't have much to take. She would only stay for a few days and then leave the kids for an extra two weeks with their grandma, who had booked a vacation in South Carolina with her grand kids. Andy had invited her to go up north with him and his whole family that included five aunts and uncles and ten cousins. She looked forward to that break because after that she would be in her intense summer classes.

"Are you ready?" Chenai jumped at Blake's voice. He stood by her door looking into her room. He seemed reluctant to step past the door.

"We are."

"We should leave soon."

She nodded then reached for her bag on the floor. Blake walked quickly into the room.

"I'll get that," he said and she had a momentary flash back to the first day she'd arrived in Michigan. The angry harried man who had met her at the airport seemed to be disappearing. She had glimpsed sides to Blake that were soft and caring. Though they were few and far between they were there and they took her breath away. Those were the moments he actually put himself aside for his kids or her.

"Thanks," she tried to smile and he stared at her. What he said increased her discomfort that seemed constant since camp, though she wasn't too surprised. He always had a way of saying things that shook her.

"When you get to Charlotte don't listen to everything my mother has to say."

"About you, you mean?"

"About anything."

As they drove to the airport, Jodi's earphones in and Tyler playing a game in the backseat, she wanted to ask him why he wasn't going to his own brother's wedding. She remembered how much her own brothers did everything together, taking on the boys who were bothering Chenai and building the chicken coop for her mother, working all hours and forgetting to eat. They would fight sometimes, but mostly they were there for each other, sometimes even against her.

She would also do anything for her family. She was spending half her income to her father so he could pay some of the school fees and she knew her brothers would mail items to her even though they could barely afford food. And Blake didn't even mention his brother's name.

The cell phone Blake had forced on her rang as they took the exit onto I94.

"Andy, hi," Chenai said and felt Blake's anger appear like smoke rising from a campfire. She leaned back into the seat. It seemed to rise like a monster from the lake.

She listened smiling as Andy told her that his family was excited that she would join them up north.

"Andy, I'll call you when I arrive. Take care."

After she hung up she stole a glance at Blake.

"Seems you're making good use of the phone, then," he commented dryly.

Chenai stole a glance at the kids who didn't seem to be paying them any attention.

"Yes," she responded, then turned away.

"Guys are only interested in one thing Chenai. You gotta be careful."

"I am," she responded when she really wanted to tell him that Andy was different from most guys. He treated her with respect and didn't make her feel tense and uncomfortable all the time. He was a good man. The man she had to be careful about was sitting next to her.

The airport reminded her of travels since she left Zimbabwe, and then leaving New York. She never spoke to her aunt again, but just last week a package had arrived with the remaining items she had left in New Jersey. No note.

Blake dropped them off and drove away without waiting for them to board. His indifference was the total opposite of Marylyn when she met them at the airport. She had flowers for her and balloons for the kids. Chenai loved her on sight.

She looked much smaller than her pictures. She was shorter than Chenai with short red hair styled around her round face. Her eyes were a blue/gray and more expressive than the images she had seen.

"Tyler, puppy. Jodi," Marylyn cried pulling the kids in a hug. Jodi seemed slightly warmer towards her grandmother.

"Chaynay," Marylyn said at last and pulled her close, too. She smelled clean and flowery, like she had been dipped in rose petals and washed in perfume.

Tyler laughed and Chenai and Marylyn both looked at him.

"Grammy, her name's not Chay chay!"

"Oh dear. What is it?"

"It's Chenai," Tyler said.

"So sorry child," Marylyn put her arm around Chenai.

"I'm not good with names. Never have been. I'll keep trying Chenai. It's so wonderful to meet you. So wonderful."

Marylyn bent down and picked up another bag then led them to the airport parking lot where her blue Ford was parked. Chenai couldn't help looking at Marylyn trying to find some similarities to Blake, but they seemed to be opposites, just as the North and South Pole were polar opposites. Even their coloring was different. She had blue eyes and his were dark. She couldn't help staring at her trying to see something that could show her that Blake was really a part of this lovely woman.

"So Chenai, did I say it right?" Marylyn asked and Chenai nodded. "Well, I'm so glad to finally meet you. You seem to be getting through to Blake. He's reading the Bible!"

Chenai stared at Marylyn totally shocked. Blake was reading the Bible?

CHAPTER 26

Sunshine

"Don't despair; you have given birth to a son."

—1 Samuel 4:20

"I like your house," Chenai commented as she stepped into the cool foyer of the white wooden colonial house set on sloping land. The garden was already in full bloom just to be expected at the beginning of summer. Petunias and gardenias swayed in the wind and Chenai noticed flowers that looked like lilies and orchids in shades of white and orange. It was lovely, similar to the other houses in the quiet well-manicured lane. Very different from Blake's modern architecture of a house.

"Thank you, come on in. I'll show you to your rooms. Come on Tyler." Marylyn said.

Chenai and Jodi had to share the room that was right next to Marylyn's and Tyler was sleeping in another smaller room dominated by a double bed in what looked like a flower garden. Marylyn loved her flowers and they were everywhere in the house an explosion of pink roses, gardenias and lilies.

"You two get situated then join us on the porch for some tea. Supper will be ready shortly," Marylyn said, and then left the room.

"Did Andy call you? Are you still going with him up north?" Jodi spoke only after her grandmother had left and she and Chenai were alone.

"Yes." Chenai smiled at Jodi. Jodi's next question surprised her.

"Is he your boyfriend?" Her questions reminded her of Blake's interrogations.

Chenai looked at the bed covered with a quilt in different shades of green. She shook her head.

"I don't have a boyfriend. We are not dating."

"Have you kissed him?"

Chenai laughed, but Jodi was not kidding. Chenai shook her head. At the same time she remembered what had happened with Blake at the camp, not that she ever forgot. "We should go to your grandma."

They left the room quietly. In the hallway, Chenai looked at the photographs and tried to find one of Blake as a young boy, but the photographs on the walls were of scenery. Maybe there was a room where she kept such photos.

"There you are. George should be here soon. That's my husband." Marylyn spoke the last to Chenai. Chenai nodded glancing at the view from the porch. The land behind the house barely had any flowers. Not as much design as the front. Beyond the porch was a stretch of grass that ended by an arch with vines growing around it.

Chenai felt quite at ease in this home, Marylyn was sweet, welcoming. Sunshine came from her eyes, warming all it touched.

How could this lovely serene woman have had a child as mean as Blake?

Later in the evening Marylyn's husband walked in. George Thornton was as big as Marylyn was small, with silver hair and a body that reminded Chenai of an ox. His voice was just as booming, like rumbling thunder. Chenai had been sitting out on the porch that wrapped around the house and over looked the trees.

"Chenai. It's nice to meet you. I've heard so much about you," George said taking her hand. He seemed warm enough until his next words.

"You must be glad to be away from that senseless Blake. He grieves his mother and worries her all the time. He won't even come to his own brother's wedding."

The words hit Chenai so hard she could've gasped. She turned to look at Marylyn and saw the pain.

"He just sends his kids with this stranger from Africa, no offense to you Chenai, but ..." George shook his head.

Chenai could not think of a single word to say when George continued.

"I actually have friends who are blacks. So don't think we are not used to black people."

Chenai smiled and could only manage, "That's nice."

"Anyway I have some work to do after dinner. Feel at home young lady. We are not racist here."

Chenai wondered why he felt the need to say that. *Were many people in the South racist?* She had feared going there. From studying American history, the land she walked on was filled with spilled blood and disturbing events that rattled her. *Was she safe?*

After George walked away, Marylyn stepped closer to Chenai.

"Walk?" she held out her hand towards the path that led to the pond. The sun was shimmering on the silver water and a soft breeze fought a losing battle with the heat. Chenai nodded. Marylyn was dressed in a sharp pencil skirt and red silk top. She looked like she was about to head to the office herself and not someone who was in the kitchen cooking.

"Well, you met my George," Marylyn's tone was filled with apology.

Chenai nodded. She really couldn't think of anything positive to say, so she listened as Marylyn continued.

"That's what Blake ran away from. Yes, I am disappointed in my son for not coming to his brother's wedding or just plain having time for me, but I understand. You'll see when you have children. You try your best and yet sometimes you just get what they offer after the pain of life."

Chenai listened as their feet made a padding sound on the dry path filled with stones and grass. They reached the edge of the grass and stood staring out in the distance, the trees, and the clear blue sky. The gentle breeze seemed to blow some of George's words away and leave Chenai a little breathless.

"Chenai, I know you've been having some tough times with my son. He's difficult. I know he's not that great a father, or even just a person," Marylyn laughed, "But he's never really known what it's like to be a son. Or even seen how fathers are supposed to act. He's been driven. Trying to prove to George that he can make it without going to college or getting a law degree. But most importantly Chenai, he's been trying to prove to his real father, who left him when he was so little, that he could make it on his own without him."

Chenai stared at Marilyn as her voice seemed to catch, shocked at what she had revealed and just as heartbroken at George's words.

Oh God. She wondered why Marylyn was telling her all this. She realized Marylyn's words were breaking her heart. The words seemed to enter the places where she hid her most private emotions, emotions that she kept even from herself, filling up the drum with echoes of injustice, abandoned little boys and tears. The protectiveness over Blake seemed to wash over her, like water from a waterfall. When she thought of Blake as a little boy, lost and confused she could have more sympathy for the big man, insensitive, impatient. When she realized that the little boy was still alive and well in his heart, then she understood him. Just like the vision.

Chenai was beginning to understand something else too. In America, most people blamed their problems on how they were raised, how their mother never listened to them, or how their father never watched them play baseball. In Zimbabwe it was more of a belief in curses. That your whole family was cursed. That's why none of you get married. She wondered if any of them were right. Didn't people still have the ability to make choices? Could Blake have made different choices?

"It's difficult for anyone to feel abandoned," she whispered.

"I'm not making excuses because too many people like to blame their parents for all the wrong in their lives. Which is unfair, right. Either way, I am so glad you are there, at that house with him. God has a plan, Chenai. Blake's changing, softening up. Just like how I knew he could be. Some of the ice around his heart is melting and it's all because of you. He's just had so many years of anger and bitterness."

Chenai remained silent even though she didn't think she was responsible for any changes in Blake. They didn't agree on anything and she was terrified to talk to him about God. Really talk to him. Tell him about God's unfailing love and her own testimony. Her right to bitterness after she lost her mother in a senseless episode.

Chenai didn't know if she was ready to hear anything else about Blake. What she had learned now was hard enough to grasp. A father who just walked away from his son and never ever returned. A man who just disappeared. But just like the lake behind their house in spring, a part of his heart had thawed out. Just around the edges there was still some ice. God in his time and wisdom would thaw the ice in Blake's heart that had hurt too much.

"I feel I need to tell you more so you don't give up and run away from this family because of my son," Marylyn said.

Chenai was stunned. Did she read minds? Did Marylyn know about the Staffords? About the offer to leave Blake and his children?

Marylyn took her face in her hands and forced her to look in her blue eyes. The feeling was unsettling. It was as if she could see in her soul and there was nowhere to hide. That's when she saw the resemblance. There was steely determination beneath her gaze. The look that she would never give up on her son. The look Blake had when he thought about his business. Chenai knew she couldn't hide from that gaze.

"When I talk to you and even now I can sense the stress in you. The tension you try and hide. I know I just met you and I hardly know you, but I prayed about it and you came. You are young, but I sense this wisdom in you. Most probably because of all you've been through. In this country, we think that maturity is to be independent, but the wisest is the one who knows he can't do much without God. Quite contrary to popular belief."

Chenai nodded looking down, wondering if Marylyn was finished. She wasn't.

"You see when Blake got married he was young. I never even came to the wedding or for the birth of my Jodi. I do know though that theirs was not a happy marriage. Were your parents happy together?"

Chenai turned to look at her hands remembering, "Almost every day. They ..." she was trying to think of the best way to describe it. Her parents didn't talk of love. They didn't kiss and hold hands or embrace. She had never seen them kiss, if indeed they did such things. "They were considerate of each other."

Mai would do anything for her father. Sometimes she did too much. At times relatives complained that Frank was passive, was not doing enough to provide for his family. At times she believed it, though her mother never did.

"Marriage is not about doing things exactly the same. It's about two very different people coming together and becoming one complete unit. Your father is my calm and I am his fire. He keeps me from doing crazy things. I know I work too hard. I know, I sometimes take risks, going to South Africa, but I do it because I can. I have it in me. Your father is the anchor of this family. It's very important to remember that," her mother would say.

"That's good," Marylyn said turning back to walk towards the house. "You have to think of the other. Blake and Samantha were not like that. They fought, even in front of me. Initially they fought about money. Then they had a lot of money and they still continued to fight. I'm not saying my son was perfect, but Samantha didn't help."

"I'm sorry," Chenai mumbled.

"It's not your fault. When she died. Well, she was with another man. They both died in the car crash."

Chenai's mouth opened with more shock and disbelief as Marylyn continued to speak. Chenai continued to listen even though Blake had warned her not to listen to his mother.

The next day Chenai met the rest of the family. Blake's younger brother who also looked nothing like him came over for some last minute discussions about the wedding that would take place in just four days. Glen Thornton was blonde and blue eyed, slim and tall. Chenai found his greeting of her friendly, but he seemed to dismiss everyone and focus all his energy on his future bride. His fiancé, Tilly, actually called Nancy Redgrave but preferred the poetic name, was also blonde with blue eyes and as sunny and friendly as her smile. Chenai felt comfortable with her. Tilly had no family and had left her life in New York to settle in Charlotte after meeting and falling in love with Glen at the end of law school.

They held hands as they walked in the dining room and stole kiss-es. Chenai had never seen such affection between two people in love. It made her uncomfortable because even though she knew that her parents were in love they were not like these two.

When Chenai lay down to sleep way before Jodi came to bed, she thought back to Marylyn's full confession about Blake and Samantha. Marylyn's voice came to her, light and lilting, filling in the secrets, and the tales about Blake that seemed to explain everything and nothing too.

"Samantha trapped Blake when he was just nineteen and she was twenty four. She confessed this to me when their marriage was falling apart, a year after Jodi was born. She got pregnant soon after they met and marriage seemed like the natural step."

Chenai had nodded as if she understood, glancing at Marylyn who now seemed to be gazing into the past, and watching a film that was painful.

"The oldest trick in the book. I should know. I did it to Blake's father."

Chenai's head was spinning. She felt like she had been holding out her hand for sand and it kept overflowing and she couldn't hold anymore.

She took her Bible and started reading, turning to her favorite place, The Psalms. She started praying for Blake. She prayed that there would be healing in his heart and that Tyler would not grow up to be like him. Angry, ambitious to the point of obsession. As she prayed for Blake, Marylyn's words kept coming back to her.

"The oldest trick in the book. I should know. I did it to Blake's father."

"And Father in heaven I pray that Tyler and Jodi would know you. Know that even if his earthly father is not there, that you are there. That you are holy and You love him," Chenai said in prayer.

Why had God brought her into this family, only to watch them fall apart? She didn't feel equipped to deal with such brokenness when she was so confused about Blake herself?

CHAPTER 27

Mist

And two shall become one flesh.

—Mark 10:8

Chenai woke up early the next morning. She wasn't sure what time everybody else would get up, or if she was on duty. She planned to take a walk down the street to stretch her legs. Perhaps she would walk to the pond, or sit on the porch and watch the day come alive. When she opened the kitchen door and stepped on the porch she was surprised to see Tilly leaning against the rail, a cup in her hand. She wiped her tears when she spotted Chenai.

"What's wrong?" Chenai asked. Tilly held her phone below her chin standing on the porch staring at the pond. It was beautiful view and the site of her upcoming wedding. The fog that had covered the area had lifted, blown away and melted by the ever present sun. The huge white marquee was being set up. She turned to Chenai and smiled as she wiped more tears that flowed on her cheeks.

"I'm okay," she began, "Well, not quite." She looked down then back at Chenai. Chenai liked Tilly. She was very honest, direct and friendly. They had talked much about the wedding since she arrived. Tilly was also fascinated with Africa.

"My friend, Debbie, just called. She can't be my bridesmaid anymore. She has an opportunity to travel to Paris. She works in fashion and it is the chance of a lifetime for her."

"Oh."

"I just feel horrible that I won't have a bridesmaid while Glen has three of his friends from high school as groomsmen."

"It's okay," Chenai said. She was trying to think of the best thing to say. She had not been to many weddings, or even thought of her own wedding. How would she know what things devastated a bride?

"I'm sure you will still have a beautiful wedding with the man you love," Chenai said.

"You're right. I just wished I had more people to choose from. When I worked in New York it wasn't easy to make friends. It was all work, work and work. Life here is different. The pace is slower but it's not boring. It's all about family here and I like that."

"It is." Chenai looked around and watched the five strong men hoist the tent up. It flapped a little in the wind. Chenai felt a change in mood as Tilly asked the next question.

"So, you stay with Glen's brother? Blake?"

"I help with the kids and go to school."

"What are you studying?"

"Thinking of nursing, though sometimes I hold dreams of becoming a doctor," Chenai laughed. "It's silly."

"You should go for it. I think you'd make a great doctor. From the little I've seen of you, you listen well and you care for others. You are so patient with Jodi. She's not that friendly."

Chenai nodded and Tilly continued.

"Tyler's so sweet, but Jodi. She seems troubled."

"She's going through a tough time, missing her mother and all the teenage problems."

"Yeah I know how that can be. I went through a rebellious stage with my parents too. Did you?"

"A little. Sometimes I hated doing stuff for my brothers. I was the oldest so my- mother would ask me to help her. Sometimes I didn't want to."

"That's rebellious to you?" Tillie teased. "Well, that's good then. So is Blake still going through his rebellious stage?"

Chenai thought about Blake, as she often did. True, he was going through something for sure.

"He's just a busy man," she said, hating the words that she had said to herself over and over again to excuse his behavior.

"He feels a lot of pressure to achieve success like most men do. I think it must be hard to know how to balance it all. Back home, when my – mum passed there were a lot of people who just chipped in and helped. Her sisters…… It kind of cushioned my Dad."

"I'm sorry about your mom. I know how that can be," Tilly said sympathetically. They had talked about their losses the day before.

"God says put Him first and then your family right?" Tilly asked.

"Right." Chenai agreed surprised Tilly had mentioned God. She hadn't given any hints that she wasn't a Christian, so Chenai was very happy to hear her talk about Him.

"Marylyn has been talking to me about her God, about Jesus. I kind of like it."

Wow. For some it was easy to be drawn into to God and for others it took miracles, it took the breaking of chains and forces. Her own mother, Lois, had not really been taught about God. She grew up in a family that believed in the traditional beliefs, the spirits of the dead and ancestors looking after you.

Lois didn't embrace what she referred to as the "white" people's religion. She didn't buy it. It took the war to change her. That moment brought back memories. She remembered her mother telling her the story of how she came to Christ.

"When I was pregnant with you, the war was burning in earnest. It was a difficult time. I had just met your father, we had married, and then he was off to training camps for the war. It was a time when you didn't know who the enemy was. It wasn't whites only fighting for the country, to keep it Rhodesia. To keep it a British state. They had black soldiers too, who were known as *vatengesi*, sell outs. And then it was the people who were left behind like me.

"We also fought the war in our own ways. With your father gone, I had to live with nuns at the Batanai Mission, a compound with a clinic and a school. My parents, though well off, didn't look after me because once you are married; it's the responsibility of the man who married you to take care of you or his family, but his family didn't like me then. I was a city tramp.

"One terrible night when the rivers were dry and the night air crackled with heat, almost the last day of the war, the soldiers came. They usually came and demanded whatever they wanted, food, clothing, money, respect, but that night they were looking for terrorists or wives of terrorists. That would be me. At the mission school, one of the nuns, taught me about God, telling me about how she gave up her life in Europe to come to Africa to spread the word. I was still skeptical, never believing anything at face value until that night. She hid me and lied to the soldiers that I was not there. They hit her, but she never gave me away as I lay under the bed holding you in my arms, praying to God that you would remain at my breast and not cry. After that day, we were able to run away to the city where the fighting was less intense to non-existent, but Sister Catherine wanted to remain.

"Sister Catherine continued to do God's work and completely trusted God to protect her. I remember truly accepting God then and knew that I would serve him the rest of my life and teach my children about Him. Then I knew He wasn't a God of color, but a God for everyone. It took me a while to convince your father. Eventually, after many years, he too accepted Christ. Still, I had one regret, Chenai. I regretted that I needed him to show me some miracle to accept him. That He had to work so hard to convince me. When he knocked in my heart, why didn't I open the door?"

Chenai smiled as she remembered. She also knew that for some they truly needed this, needed big signs from God to show them that He was indeed who He said He was. For others like Tilly, they saw the light in Marylyn's life and they just wanted to be part of that.

"Hey, I have an idea. Oh you're going to love this," Tilly suddenly said.

Tilly's great idea was for Chenai to be a bridesmaid and that meant rushing around finding a dress for her and finding a hair dresser who could work with Chenai's type of hair. So that morning they left Marylyn's neighborhood and drove to another part of town where black people lived. It amazed Chenai how divided America was. There were so many different cultures and yet, right in Detroit part of the church outreach was to Mexicans, who lived in their own area, the Muslims, who had their own city and schools. It's as if touching would contaminate the other. As if each group of people had a secret disease the other was afraid of.

As they got their nails done as part of their full spa day, Marylyn told Chenai about Blake's father.

"I knew he was trouble from the start, or a song just like that. But, the heart wants what it wants right?"

Chenai nodded and Tilly giggled beside her. Chenai had never been to a spa, or painted her nails and put masks on her face. Everything was new and exciting and different. If not scary.

"Ernest was different from any one I had ever seen. His coloring, difficult to pin point however back then we all knew that people from the North could be all mixed races, Greek, Italian, I just wasn't sure what he was. All I knew was he was easy on the eyes. I worked at a diner then. He came in to eat and as you can imagine from that first moment, we were inseparable.

"He came to Raleigh as a traveling salesman for an insurance company. Sure enough, he had not intended to stay. I begged him to stay and as this was the 60s, where women felt liberated. I was pregnant rather quickly. He stayed as long as he could, but from what he told me of his life, father killed in the war, raised by his grandmother there was a restlessness about him. He always talked of seeing the world, maybe taking up jobs in the oil fields or going to find his fortune in California. So, after four years together, he did just leave one day. Just waited for him to come back from work and he never did, leaving me stranded with a young son."

"Marylyn. That is hard," Tilly said. Chenai nodded.

"Did you ever hear from him?"

"Never. Just disappeared into thin air. I didn't even bother searching. My heart had always known that I had just borrowed him from whatever beckoned him. A woman knows. Maybe he had another family."

Marylyn looked into space and the young women knew she was seeing her time with Ernest and wondered if it still hurt.

"I don't know if he is alive or dead, but for a while Blake asked about him each day, until the days buried the memory of his father. Still as he grew some kids made sure he knew his father just ran away. And then I met George, who loved me from the get go."

"Wow."

"Before that I had found God, or God had found me with tears on my cheek and a really broken heart. He put me back together so I could be there for my son. To find God in the 60s is a miracle of its own."

Chenai nodded again, realizing that everybody's love story was complicated. It was never simply that a girl meets boy and they fall in love and live happily ever after. It was just not that easy and happy endings were few. As her eyes met Marylyn's briefly, Chenai wondered if her ending, a life with George was a good substitute for happily ever after.

Chenai was beginning to get excited about the part she had in the wedding until she overheard George's comment that evening before dinner.

"Chenai will be in the wedding? But... how will it look to our friends, clients?"

"It will look beautiful," Marylyn said simply.

He didn't comment again as Marylyn changed the subject, but anxiety grew in Chenai's heart from that moment on.

CHAPTER 28

Scorching

Dark am I, yet lovely.

—Songs of songs 1:5

Blake hadn't planned on going to the wedding. Before he could question his motives he was on the flight to Charlotte. Yes, Glen was his brother, though when Glen was born Blake was already so full of hatred for his mother's new husband that there was no way the birth of their child would make him happy. It hadn't been easy to stay away from his brother, but he had succeeded. The little boy used to follow him everywhere, wanting to be with his big brother even though George discouraged it, calling Blake a bad influence on his son. By the time Glen was ten years old, Blake had left home after angry words with George. Still, Glen was his little brother and his mother expected him there.

Blake arrived at the church several minutes before the wedding was to begin. He walked in and sat right at the back of the church glancing around at the small chapel taking in flowers and candles. To him the church was over decorated and too hot. His chest tightened. He wanted to leave that claustrophobic place, but he forced himself to remain.

The piano music played accompanied by the violin and it failed to calm his senses. Up ahead he saw Tyler and Jodi. Tyler wore a suit and Jodi seemed to be dressed in a dark dress or jacket. He wasn't sure what it was. He thought Chenai would be next to them though he couldn't see her.

Blake tried to ignore the tension in his chest at the anticipation of seeing George and his mother after such a long time. He tried to remember the last time he had seen George and all that came to mind was the last time he left home, words spoken, and walls built thick and hostile.

Glen walked in with a line of his groomsmen and then George followed. George looked the same, big and foreboding and Blake's anger came though he squashed it down with monumental will power, moving his focus to the program in his hand. None of them seemed to notice him. George was staring straight ahead, focused on his goal of getting to the front. His mother walked in to the music and to him she seemed smaller, more fragile. He felt his chest constrict. Before he could figure out why he felt the sadness the back door opened and Chenai stepped in. At least he thought it was her. Blake stared, seeing her as if for the first time. It wasn't just that her hair looked different, but the dress she wore was different too. The gown fell down her body and as she came down the aisle the bottom part twirled with each step she took. The silver dress against her brown skin made a stunning contrast.

She seemed nervous and didn't seem to notice him as she walked past him. He couldn't take his eyes off her. When she stood facing the back door, he stared at her again, not sure why his heart was thudding so hard or why he couldn't seem to see anybody else but her. Even when his future sister-in-law came in to the gentle sound of the piano, Blake's eyes remained focused on Chenai, willing her to find his face, though glad that she didn't. She seemed to be staring somewhere in space, not at anyone directly. Her smile when Tilly walked in seemed to undo him, unfamiliar emotions welling up inside him.

The whole wedding was just a blur and he stepped out soon after the vows had been exchanged. He stood outside for some fresh air before going to check into his hotel. Being back in Charlotte and seeing his step father reminded him of what had happened in the past, the same angry feelings he had as a teenager came bubbling back, like thick lava that threatened to erupt.

The old emotions that churned inside him fit uncomfortably with his new wonderment at Chenai's transformation. He couldn't reconcile the sophisticated woman who stood in the church, to the girl he had picked up at the airport. She seemed like a total stranger. Her confusing image faded to be replaced by George of the past.

"You're just going to be like you father Blake. Do you even know where he is? He doesn't care about anybody, just like you!"

George had spoken the words years before when Blake stole the car and crashed it, and when Blake was caught drinking at school. George always liked to remind him his father, a man named Ernest Pieri had walked out on his wife and son and never looked back.

Blake wanted to hate Ernest Pieri, while on the other hand, always had a desire to meet his father. He really didn't need all those ghosts from the past in his life now. He was now a self-made man who didn't anybody's approval or love.

Even though he was invited to the wedding, Blake still felt like an intruder when he walked towards the marquee that shone with light against the pond. He could hear the music and laughter coming from inside and he hated the feelings that filled his chest. He hated the feeling of always being on the outside looking in. When he was young and he would see his mother, Glen and George sitting together, or going to Glen's plays he'd always felt excluded.

George has no right to keep me away from my family, Blake thought as he neared the tent. Yes, George had married her, but she was his mother.

Blake stepped in the marque at what appeared to be the mother son dance. The tent was dimly lit by the candles at each table, a spot light on the dance floor. He guessed that most of the people were his mother's friends and George's clients and business associates because he didn't recognize anyone at first glance. No one recognized him.

The song ended and then other people moved to the dance floor. Glen and his bride, Tilly danced together, holding each other close. George danced with his mother. She looked older, smaller than he remembered, but looking glamorous as she always did since George married her.

He turned towards the back and saw Chenai. She sat alone watching the people on the dance floor moving to 'Love Changes

Everything.' She looked calm, beautiful, and exotic all at the same time. The glow from her was soft, pure and fresh. She just seemed so clean and untouched. Before he reached her Tyler came running and ran into his arms. When he held him close he looked at Chenai over Tyler's head because she had seen him and the way she looked at him, part joy, part questioning surprise, set his heart racing.

Jodi saw him and just gave a quick unfriendly wave then turned away to nobody in particular. Before he could reach Chenai his mother had come unable to hide her excitement of seeing him. She held out her arms.

"Oh Blake. I knew you would come. My son. Oh my two boys are here." Marylyn held out her hand to Glen who had moved towards the exciting reunion on the edge of the dance floor. He walked towards his mother's embrace and Marylyn looked at them both, one on either side. Both were tall. Blake dark haired and brooding and Glen, blond haired and smiling. It was the first time they had been together in almost twenty years. She glanced at one then the other, the occasion adding more emotion and drama to her actions. Glen spoke first.

"I'm glad you made it Blake. It's good to see you."

"Yeah. Congratulations," Blake said wanting to extricate himself from his mother's embrace, but not sure how to do so. She held on tightly.

"You should meet my wife. Well, it's hard to believe that she's my wife."

"Can you please come for the cutting of the cake," the wedding planner, who had been standing by patiently, said. "We would like to move the program along."

Glen nodded still looking at his brother then moved towards his bride as the music that had been selected for the cutting of the cake came on. Somehow George had managed to miss the reunion and Tilly was having her face redone. After that she made her way towards the cake in her billowing white gown. As they cut the cake Blake turned around again to Chenai who had been watching the whole thing with tears swimming in her eyes.

"Will you sit with us?" Marylyn asked.

"Later, I'll come by. You go ahead and take your place with your family," Blake said trying not to make it sound too harsh.

"Then we can talk?" she asked.

He nodded and Marylyn walked over to sit next to George right near the front. For some annoying reason, he still felt sixteen again. Unwanted. All his accomplishments seemed to fade to dust. No , he felt like a loser.

He watched the cake cutting, something he considered dumb, then Glen and Tilly were back on the dance floor again, swaying to the music, the lights even dimmer now, almost turning the tent into darkness, the only light the flickering candles. Other couples joined them and that's when Blake turned toward Chenai. As he walked towards her she sat up straighter, her eyes on him, questioningly. He reached her then held out his hand. Chenai took a moment, but when he kept his hand there, steadily outstretched she must have felt as if it didn't ask, but command her to take it. And she did.

CHAPTER 29

Rain

Do not rouse or awaken love until it so desires.

—Songs of songs 2:7

"Tyler did you write your grandma the thank you letter?" Chenai asked leaving the office and walking into the family room. She stopped short, surprised to see Andy. He never usually just arrived. He always called first.

"Hello," she said. Tyler didn't look up from the game that his grandmother had bought him. It was hand held and it seemed to preoccupy him too much. She turned her questioning eyes to Andy.

"Hi Andy," Jodi said. Chenai noticed the extra sweet voice from Jodi. She had seen it countless times with the girls at church. She wondered if they were not shy to show their interest in a man so blatantly. The way her mother had done. Dancing to the sound of the drum was even worse!

"It's a beautiful day, thought we could take a walk and grab ice-cream." Andy said. Chenai was supervising the new cleaning lady who was almost done and was ready to leave, standing by the door. She had dinner to throw in the oven. Frozen lasagna. Jodi removed her earphones when she saw Andy.

"Hey Jodi," Andy said smiling. He was always polite and kind to all those who seemed to adore him and his good looks and to those who admired his gifts as a musician. "How's summer camp?"

"Fine. Can you help me with my Chemistry project?" Jodi asked.

"Okay."

"Go ahead Andy. I have to cut some veggies for a salad any-way," Chenai said.

"I was about to go for a walk with Chenai. I can help you a little now and then when we come back?"

Jodi nodded, but she looked at Chenai with what seemed like a challenge. Chenai had noticed Jodi's crush on Andy. Was it just an innocent crush? She had to talk to her about it. Andy was way too old for her. She watched them settle on the kitchen tables as Andy read the direction for the project, Jodi's eyes intently on him. He gave her some instructions when he noticed Chenai was ready.

"You want to go now?"

"Let's go." Andy said taking her hand. She wore a simple sun dress that flowed around her body in a sunny yellow color and pale wavy lines. Chenai patted her new hair style, still not used to the way it hung past her chin, thin and straight.

They walked side by side in silence for a while and when they were halfway to the lake Andy broke the silence.

"I like your devotion to this family, but you should also have a life outside them. You are really like their mother and I'm not sure it's healthy."

"I do have a life. I have church," Chenai reassured him. Andy didn't seem convinced. They stopped briefly and examined the logs for the tree house that was never built. Andy shook his head and didn't say anything. He knew that Blake had promised his children to build the tree house, but hadn't even begun it. The tree house was a symbol of Blake's broken promises.

Andy changed the subject abruptly before they reached the lane that circled the lake.

"So you never really wanted to talk about the wedding. How was it? I know you said you were a bridesmaid."

"A last minute one." She took a step next to Andy as they began to walk towards the water. They planned on taking a trail that would go part way past the lake and then out to the paved roads.

"So Blake came too?"

Chenai nodded. She didn't want to talk about it. Andy would wonder why. She could tell him part of it and leave out the rest. Thinking about what happened warmed her face. If she had lighter skin he would see her blush. This was getting too complicated.

"Well, Blake kind of ruined the wedding. It wasn't his fault," Chenai said.

"What did he do?"

"He punched his stepfather. Well, Marylyn's husband."

"You didn't get caught up in it did you?" Andy asked stopping to turn to her. Chenai wouldn't look at him for a long time. "I worry about you. I still think you should leave this house. The Staffords still want you."

"I can't Andy. What will Tyler do? And Jodi is getting much better. I just can't up and leave them."

"I know. I worry."

Chenai realized Andy didn't know how right he was to be concerned about her. After what happened at the wedding, she knew that she couldn't stay at the house much longer, though at the same time she couldn't leave the kids alone just yet. She would never be able to live with herself if she walked away from Tyler and Jodi. She loved them both. She had to admit that it was much easier to love Tyler. Marylyn had said to her that the people who were hardest to love needed it most. Jodi and Blake.

The more she spent time with Tyler though, sacrificed her own free time for him when he needed her at baseball or going to see his teachers and counselors, the more she loved him. Real love only came with sacrifice. You had to give up something, and when you did the reward was a heart filled with love. She was bursting with it. When you sacrificed for someone, you truly loved them more.

"Remember who is in control," Chenai said looking up at the sky.

Andy smiled then leaned against a tree.

"So what about you? Are you still refusing to sign with the record company?"

"Yep. I made up my mind a long time ago. I just don't feel right, selling God's music," Andy said.

Chenai nodded. Then something struck her.

"But you listen to recorded music by Christian artists. You listen to Casting Crowns, Israel Houghton, Hillsongs…."

"I enjoy it. Most of it is great and honest and true….. It's just not right for me I guess. I'm not speaking for everyone. I just want to sing for God, alone or in church. Worship Him alone and not get confused with any commercial stuff."

"I admire that. You don't need the fame…"

"Definitely not."

"I hope your friends understand now."

Andy shook his head then flicked her new hair.

"You changed your hair?"

Chenai shook her head, feeling the hair move freely. She didn't think he had noticed. She was often surprised that Andy seemed to notice things about her.

"It was for the wedding. What do you think?"

"It's fine. I liked your other hair. Now you just look like every-body else."

Chenai didn't know what to say. She was still thinking of a smart response when the first drops of rain hit her square on the nose.

"What was that?"

"It looks like a freak summer storm." Even as Andy said the words the rain started coming down fast like a bucket had been poured down from heaven, warm and persistent.

"Oh my goodness!" Chenai cried and started running ahead of Andy laughing. Andy soon followed and caught up with her. He took her hand as he led her up towards the house.

"My hair will be ruined!"

"What do you mean? It looks great."

"Andy wait and see. Wait until we get back home. It'll be a mess!"

He reached and ran his hands over it and she squealed as she increased her pace up the path. They were now in view of the house, breathless from the run and their laughter.

Blake arrived home, driving through the long winding driveway just as the sun settled comfortably on the water. Chenai's car was there, though after checking the office where she liked to study, he realized she wasn't there. Jodi typed on her cell phone and had her head phones plugged into her ears. He didn't want to talk to Jodi. He was still angry that she had lost her first summer job at camp because she was caught smoking. He saw Tyler busy on his video game.

"I'm about to go to the next level, Dad," Tyler called out. He was totally focused on his game. Blake decided to find Chenai.

Daily now, when he arrived home he longed to see her face, his thirst for her sight, deeper than a man stuck in the dessert longing for water. He was also trying to spend more time with Tyler and Jodi, but his daughter seemed totally lost, a stranger. He hated to admit it, but he didn't like her very much. Now it bothered him that he had let her become a stranger. He had missed the signals. He didn't know why he now feared that he may never have a relationship with her. She hated him, hated life and would never look at him with adoration as she did as a little girl.

With Chenai, he knew that things were shifting between them. In fact they had made a leap. He was surprised at how much pleasure her greeting gave him when he was home. Even the wariness and the shy light in her eyes when she looked at him gave him satisfied something in him that he couldn't name. They couldn't deny that something had happened at the wedding. He knew it and he knew she knew it, though she pretended otherwise.

His cell phone rang and he sighed. It was Penny.

"Penny. I thought you said I could meet your contact from the bank later this week. That it was all finalized."

He refrained from asking her why she was calling.

"Yeah I did. I wanted to talk to you in person. Can I come to your house this evening?"

Blake was quiet for a moment. Penny had been on to him about coming to his house, to meet his kids. He always had a reason why they should meet anywhere, but at his home. He had to find time to end this thing. Maybe after he met her contact. He knew that his response to her question could make her cancel her contact. She was that brutal.

"I'll let you know, alright."

After he hung up, Blake walked into his office and powered up his laptop. He gazed outside as the machine came on. He felt as if he had knots in his stomach when he thought about his construction company. He was going to lose it all if Penny didn't come through. His client wasn't happy with the report from an independent inspector. The new medical center wasn't up to code. His lenders were not happy either and still the building wasn't done. To him, the sight of that building actually made him feel physically ill. It looked like a grave where he was going to bury is future and self-respect.

He made a couple more calls just as he saw the rain begin to pound outside. He wanted to see Chenai. She alone could calm the storms and make him forget the mess of his life. How she did it he didn't know, but he couldn't stop thinking about his brother's wedding, because of Chenai.

The wedding was two weeks ago for goodness sakes, he admonished himself, *get over it!*

Blake got up and walked back to the family room.

"Where is Chenai anyway?"

"She went walking with Andy."

In the rain?

Blake opened the sliding doors that led outside and stepped out. It seemed like just as quickly as the rain had come down it had suddenly stopped. Chenai and Andy walked towards him holding hands.

Chenai stopped abruptly when she saw him standing on the porch watching them. Blake knew he couldn't look happy, even if he tried. Why did he feel like punching that young boy in the face and watching him roll right into the lake, never to be seen again? Blake looked at Chenai. His eyes roamed over her, from her plastered hair down to her wet clinging dress. Chenai looked down and her eyes widened as she took deep breaths and covered her chest with her hands.

"I better go change," Chenai said. She attempted to wring the water out of her dress and quickly strode past Blake. Blake didn't turn around to follow as she walked in. He just stared at Andy who also seemed captivated by Chenai's clinging dress as she disappeared into the house. Andy stood with his wet hair hanging across his face looking youthful and lustful in Blake's eyes.

What Blake said made Andy narrow his eyes with shock. It seemed disrespectful to Chenai and at that moment he wanted to whisk her away from this dangerous and miserable man.

"No. I don't want to *sleep* with her," Andy said instead of repeating the foul word Blake had used. "I care about her and I respect her." Andy replied trying to keep his anger under control.

The sun still shone, though the darkness that had appeared over the two men could start another storm.

"That's not what I saw in your eyes."

"I don't need to hear this. I'm outa here."

"Don't come back here Andy. You should stay away from Chenai."

"No. I think Chenai needs to leave this house."

"And stay with you?" Blake laughed. "You wouldn't even know what to do with her. She's not some toy, Andy she's a real woman."

Andy followed Blake's gesture towards the house.

"She's not that kind of girl," Andy argued, his left temple throbbing with anger. Andy had never felt like punching anyone as he felt his anger accelerate. What good would that do?

"Any girl is that kind of girl with me," Blake said..

"You need prayer," Andy turned away from Blake walking away instead even as he spied Chenai in the window, staring at them.

"No. You need to stop being so holy and admit you are a man," Blake shouted after him. Andy didn't turn around or respond as he got in his car and drove away.

"What's going on?" Chenai asked sliding the door open. Her hair still looked damp, but she had removed her revealing dress and wore another cotton dress that billowed around her body. She could tell that Blake and Andy were arguing, but had not heard and was grateful that Jodi was wearing her head phones upstairs and Tyler was in the living room with his video game.

"He said some inappropriate things about you."

"Andy?" she queried watching his blue truck disappear from the drive.

"Have you slept with him?" he asked when the car disappeared. Chenai spun round, knowing exactly what he meant.

"What?"

They stared each other. Chenai could feel a deep tremble from down in her belly. Stronger than the way she had felt at the wedding. More unsettling.

Before she could answer a red Lexus drove up the drive way, its soft purring barely audible over Chenai's drumming heart. Chenai and Blake both turned to see Penny's blonde head through the windshield.

"Surprise! I just had to come and tell you in person. I made manager," Penny said.

CHAPTER 30

Sweltering

Whoever loves money never has money enough; whoever loves wealth is never satisfied with his income. This too is meaningless.

—Ecclesiastes 5:10

Blake would later tell himself that the accident could have been avoided if it wasn't for the chaos happening with his new project and the problems in his company. But he had to give it one more push. He had to stop his life from being swept into the ocean of failure and mediocrity.

"How did she get in an accident?" Marylyn asked.

All he wanted to say was, "It was my fault. My entire fault."

"Blake. What is going on with you? Is there something you are not telling me? Is Chenai alright? What happened?"

How could he explain? He wished he could turn back the time and not call her, but he had called her and that call had resulted in the worst decision of his life.

The day begun like most of his days, dealing with one stressful situation after another. First, his other business partner came to see him from Windsor. Jason Pittsman had worked with Blake on several housing projects in the past and they had maintained a good relationship, until now. Their families had even been on vacation together. All that was over now. Jason had trusted Blake by investing hundreds of thousands and then allowed Blake to run everything.

"Blake, this was supposed to be easy money. I am supposed to have my payoff by now. What's going on?"

"Just as I explained on the phone, Jason. We have just been unlucky."

"No Blake. I don't believe in being unlucky."

"I know that. It's not just being unlucky, the builder messed up, before that, the architect.."

Jason shook his head, his dark eyes glistening with anger. Only Blake knew the extent of his anger. He had seen it directed at someone else, not him.

"Don't give me excuses. Save that for the tooth fairy. I don't want to hear it."

"Jason. You know I gave everything to this project," Blake stood up and walked to his office window loosening his tie. "I have no life. I live to get this project done, and done well."

"I don't care how hard you are working. It's all about the results. You promised.."

"I know what I promised," Blake growled back.

"I went to the site today, Blake. Nobody is working. It's a ruin."

Blake stared at Jason. Jason took a deep breath then spoke in a menacing tone.

"I don't care that we have been friends for ten years Blake. Don't mess with my money. I expect good news soon. Or the threatening notes you were receiving, will punch you in the face."

"So you've been making threats like a coward. You've been in this business for years. You know how unpredictable it can be," Blake shouted.

"Do you know what your problem is Blake? You have no business acumen. You just thought you could move from being a bricklayer to a business savvy tycoon in a matter of seconds. Show some humility."

"You. Get out of my office. At least I had the guts to try it out, while you will be a brick layer for the rest of your life!"

After Jason left, Blake stared out the window for a few minutes. It was a relief to know where the notes had been coming from, but that didn't make him feel any safer. How well did he really know Jason? Was he capable of hurting his children because of a bad investment?

What could he do about it? Right now every avenue seemed closed.

His phone rang immediately. Blake fished it from under a pile of papers. His assistant spoke quickly.

"You have a Mr. Martin from AGP Barnex waiting for you and also Rick Scottstrye is on line 1."

"I'll talk to Rick."

"Mr. Pieri. It's been a long time," Rick said.

"Listen. What's going on? Why are the guys at your office taking so long to finalize my permits? This is the last stage of this project."

"Blake. I think you made some people angry. In this business it's not just about what's right. It's about keeping people happy who have the power to give you the go ahead. You made someone angry."

"That may be, but I need to get this moving, Rick. Today."

"Well. If you can get some payment to Jackson before the holiday maybe you can go ahead on Monday. But he leaves for Florida tomorrow and may leave the office in an hour or so. You need to get payment there as soon as possible. They can move it along faster for you. It's like paying for expedited work."

"Fine Rick. I get the picture. I'm about two hours away right now. I can send someone over."

"Just make it quick."

"Fine." His office line beeped again, but he ignored it. Instead he dialed Chenai's cell phone.

Chenai picked up her phone on the fifth ring. "Hello."

"Where are you?" Blake asked. He would have liked to be polite, but he didn't have the luxury of time. This had to be done an hour ago!

"I'm on my way home."

"I need you to do something. Do you have the debit card I gave you?"

A while back he had given her an ATM card for emergencies. He knew she had never used it. It accessed his account.

"I do," Chenai responded. "I need to park and talk to you. I'm driving."

"No, keep driving. I need you to withdraw some money from my account. My limit is $1,000. I need you to go to the bank down town. I'm calling my banker right now and he'll give you the rest. Get $10, 000 from him and I need you to take it to an address. Can you do that for me?"

"What bank? I'm on the highway going North."

"Turn back around. Where are you?"

"On the highway."

Blake had to bite his tongue to keep from cursing. "I mean close to what. I know the road pretty well."

"I've just passed the Candlewood Tech…,"

"Oh good you can exit. I'll tell you where to go."

"Blake. It's really hard for me to talk on the phone and drive. I'm not very good….."

"Anybody can do it. Even Tyler could talk to on the phone and drive. Just pay attention okay."

"Okay," Chenai agreed reluctantly. He heard the fear and trembling in her voice. He planned to make it up to her later. Right now she had to help him and do it fast.

"Which highway is coming up? Anything?"

"696 I think,"

"You need to take it," Blake ordered.

"I think I'm too late."

"Just go, Chenai. Show your signal."

"Oh oh."

"What?"

"East, West,"

"East of course!"

"I can't. Oh ahhhh…."

Blake heard the scream and the horrific sound that sounded

like a blast going off, then silence. He stood there, still as death holding the phone in silence for a second. "Chenai. Chenai!" but there was no response. No other ideas could form in his mind but the words, "Oh God, Oh God."

Then the most terrifying thought of all. He had killed her. "Oh God. Oh God!" She had to be alright.

"Hang on," he started towards the door. Stopped. Realized he didn't have his car keys. He picked them up and left his office. Martin Barnex and his business partner stood up when they saw him. He had forgotten that they were in the waiting area, until he saw their frustrated faces.

"About time," they said in unison, but Blake waved them out of the way and walked past his secretary towards the exit. Cathy remained calm. She had throughout this storm.

"What the …," Martin yelled. "Where do you think you're going?"

"I have to go," Blake mumbled almost incoherently.

"If you leave this room Blake you are asking for trouble. You'll lose everything …,"

"Fine," Blake's voice was harsh and he walked away not even registering much around him.

"You'll never work in this town again!" Martin's voice followed him outside, angry and dangerous, with a few expletives thrown in. The words barely reached his ears.

Blake doesn't remember how he drove or what he saw along the way. He started praying. He hadn't prayed since he was a little boy when he asked God to bring his Dad back. But God hadn't answered and since then he didn't see the use for it. Now he started to pray again, knowing that he would do anything to make sure that Chenai didn't die.

"Oh God if you are there, please let Chenai be okay. I'm sorry. It's my fault. I'll do anything. Take my company, but please let her be okay. Please God."

He heard her scream again and he imagined her car tumbling and her body being mashed by oncoming traffic or hitting against the walls of the highway. He shut his eyes for a second trying to stop the terrifying images.

Instead, his mind filled with her in his arms in North Carolina. He remembered how it felt to hold her at the reception. How at some point during the song they danced to at the wedding she had melted into him, relaxing her tense body in a form of surrender. At that time he had felt a powerful emotion unlike any he had ever felt. Protective, love, comfort, passion all in those few seconds. He had fought it and denied it. Still the love seeped into him, over-flowing, threatening to drown him and at that time he had been relieved when his dreadful step father stepped in and caused the fight, the moment his mother had looked on him with the kind of disappointment he hadn't seen in years.

After what seemed like an eternity he reached the 696 exit his brain burning with worry. He parked his truck on the side lane where he wasn't supposed to and just as the traffic cleared he saw Chenai's car being pulled away from the wreckage area. It barely looked recognizable all bent out shape and flattened.

He finally managed to get his brain to work, to think of the nearest hospital. Once at Beaumont, he'd been told to wait. Wait. Wait for news. Wait to see Chenai and tell her the truth. He focused on that thought not on possible serious injuries. Or death.

Sitting on the uncomfortable chairs in the hospital waiting room, Blake shifted, thinking back to the wedding, the moment he knew how he felt, though he refused to admit it. He wanted to distract himself from the fear and yet what he had to face was just as terrifying.

When he held out his hand and she took it he had been relieved. She'd been stiff at first, but after the chorus to a bluesy, jazzy version of the Billie Holiday's "Original Romance in the Dark" she began to melt. It was a fast song, but they moved slowly. He could feel her let go of something that had her in knots and they had moved, his heart beating, his hands wanting to press her close, but still continue to hold her gently like she was fragile and could break like glass.

He felt the tap on his shoulder and when he turned around he came face to face with his stepfather. He hadn't seen his step father in over ten years and seeing him took away the peace he had felt in Chenai's arms to replace it with his ever growing anger.

"What are you doing here Blake?" George's voice was hoarse with anger.

"My brother's wedding."

"It's my son's wedding and you want to ruin it don't you?"

"That's bull!" Blake yelled back. He knew he sounded sixteen again. He felt like a kid. He still had his hand of the small of Chenai's back. She tensed and he could tell she wanted to be anywhere, but in that tent.

"And what are you doing with this child. Leave Chenai alone. She's not some floozy you can just play around with…"

"Chenai's not your concern," Blake said.

"She is if she's going to get caught up with a skunk like you."

The words were barely out of his mouth when Blake punched him hard. George turned his head and was about to lurch forward when his brother held his hand and Marylyn came close, too.

"Stop it both of you," Marylyn cried, looking from Blake to George. Her expression when she looked at Blake was accusing.

How could you? How could you ruin this day?

"I'm leaving," Blake said and walked towards the exit. He disappeared behind the tent and started making his way up from the pond. He could hear someone following him, but he didn't turn around.

"Blake."

He carried on walking. Chenai persisted. No one said Blake like *Belake* but her. "Blake."

When he reached his car, in a line of many other cars, he stopped and she caught up with him, out of breath.

"Didn't you hear me" she asked.

"I did. I must go."

She looked down. He waited for her to say something. She didn't. She just stood there, looking at the ground and then somewhere near his shirt. Never his face. He could hear the music from the wedding. It seemed the dancing was going on without him. Like he didn't matter. Somehow he didn't care. Chenai was here with him. She wasn't with them. The people who wanted to leave him out.

"Sorry you had to see that," Blake finally spoke, his breathing slowing. He still wore the rage like a comfortable coat, snug and perfect.

"Oh. The fight?"

"Well, he didn't really hit me back."

"Because he was being held back," Chenai reminded him. He smiled.

"I shouldn't have done that. Though I think he had it coming for many years."

"Did it make you feel better?"

"No."

He regarded her. She had her hands behind her back, one leg slightly forward coming through the split in the front of her gown. She looked amazing to him under the lights in the long circular drive way and his anger disappeared. Her straightened hair danced in the breeze. He liked it straight. He had to admit that he also liked it puffy on her head like black clouds.

"You look beautiful," he said. She laughed shyly and brought her hand up to her collar bone.

"Thanks."

They stood there again for another minute until she spoke first this time.

"Blake."

He loved the way she said his name.

"What."

"Why are you so angry? So-so mad."

Blake loosened his tie then put his hands in his pockets.

"I seem angry?"

"No. You are. You scare me sometimes."

Blake let out a breath in whoosh that sounded like a whistle.

"I do?"

She nodded. "I'm sorry, Chenai. I don't want to be. I'm driven. I want to be successful, to reach my goals."

"And if you don't?"

"I won't stop."

"And then what? What after you have all the money you ever needed?"

Blake stared at her, wondering what to say. And then what? Then he would be happy? Then he could focus on his kids?

"I worry that you will have all the money, but no one to even care besides you. And your kids will be the casualties."

They were silent for a while. Blake wanted to say what he would normally say. Tell her she didn't know what she was talking about. That she was just this girl from Africa who didn't understand life. Didn't understand the world, but tonight he felt the words die before they reached his mouth. She was right. He had refused to see how Jodi was suffering from his neglect.

Chenai didn't know it but Sam, his dead wife Samantha had been the first casualty. She had tried to do so much just to get his attention, to get him to notice her. She had surgeries to improve her looks, bleached her hair and then started having affairs that only made her more miserable and eventually killed her. But he had been immune to her efforts. He'd been so focused on his ambitions. To what end?

"I don't know, Chenai. I have to try."

The music floated to them again.

"We never finished our dance," he said. "I like dancing with you."

Her smile was wide, like a grin. He had to ask.

"Do you?"

"What?" she asked.

"Do you like dancing with me?"

She nodded looking down at their feet and he reached for her again.

"Excuse me sir. Are you here for the girl who was in the car accident?" Blake was brought back to the present by the doctor standing in front him.

Blake nodded standing on unsteady feet.

God of Chenai. Please don't take her, I beg you please, please. Not like this.

CHAPTER 31

Fiery

He stood beside me and said, "Brother Paul, receive your sight!" And
at that very moment I was able to see him.

—*Acts 22:13*

Andy kept trying Chenai's cell phone, but it went straight to
voice mail. He was getting worried. They were supposed to
meet at the coffee shop that evening with friends, but she hadn't
showed up and Amanda had informed him that she had missed
Pregnancy center committee meeting. This was so unlike her.
Chenai always called if she was running late or couldn't come.

He took his role of protecting her seriously. She was living in a
lion's den. If anything happened to her, he would feel responsible.
She was so naïve, trusting and unbelievably vulnerable. She just
didn't get men like Blake.

"Where are you?" he spoke to the wind then put his cell phone
back in his pocket. Frustrated, he picked up his computer back
pack and stuffed the present he had bought for her inside. It was
silly anyway. It was a CD of a women's conference that focused on
faith. She needed to build her faith living in a house with Blake.

I should go and check at her place, Andy thought. It was almost

8pm. He knew he wouldn't be able to go back to campus without talking to her. This was not like Chenai to just stay quiet like this. He got into his truck and started driving. He decided to try the house. It was only a few minutes away, but he wanted to call first even though he was worried that maybe Blake would pick up the phone. Andy decided to take the chance.

"Hello."

"It's Andy is Chenai there?"

"Hi Andy!" Jodi cried. Andy could hear the excitement in her voice. Andy ignored it.

"Is Chenai there, Jodi?"

"Yes."

"Can she come to the phone?"

"She's not well. I'll tell her you wanted to see her."

"I'll be right there," Andy said. Chenai was sick. All he could think was that that monster Blake had done something to make her sick. He didn't care that Blake had banned him from going to his house. He had to see if Chenai was okay.

"Chenai," Blake called softly, holding her hand. She lay on the bed, her skin a stark contrast to the white pillow. He looked at her face and her arm. He touched her skin with his finger. She opened her eyes slowly and he looked at her expectantly.

"Hi," his voice broke when he spoke.

"I'm so sorry. The car…," Chenai whispered.

"No no. Don't worry about it. Are you okay?"

She nodded imperceptibly. It was such a slight movement. "Head hurts."

Blake leaned over and touched her forehead gently. She closed her eyes again. The doctor had explained her injuries. She was fine now, but would probably feel more pain the next day. They were keeping her over night for observations. She had bruised her ribs and sprained her leg when she tried to break. Her arm was fractured; thankfully a closed fracture so there was little fear of infection. She still would need a cast or something to keep her immobile. So far they didn't think the head injury was serious, though she might have a mild concussion. Still his heart had not stopped racing because he had seen the car. Only a miracle saved her.

"It's my fault. I'm so sorry. I should never have asked you to do that for me."

He reached for her hand and she gripped his fingers. He liked the pressure. She was strong though she seemed groggy.

"It's okay. Is it bad?" she asked after a while.

"What?"

"The company. Will you be in trouble?"

"No. It's fine. Not bad at all."

"Good," she whispered with her eyes closed.

"It's not important any more, Chenai. I think I've given my life to God. At least I started praying to him and it was incredible," Blake began then stopped and squeezed her hand. She didn't squeeze back. "Chenai. I can see clearly the path I was taking was leading me nowhere. I just didn't know how to stop."

Blake paused, filled with gratitude that Chenai would be okay. He felt incredible relief though he still felt lightheaded whenever he thought that he could have lost her.

"I didn't see it before. I think I really felt God's presence today. I was terrified that something had happened to you. That you had been killed. I begged God to save you and I felt his peace, like a hand on my shoulder."

Blake shook his head smiling. When he looked he could see Chenai had not heard a word he had said. She was sleeping. He was reassured by the rise and fall of her chest.

He held her hand and leaned closer, resting his forehead on her palm. He stayed like that for nearly an hour and the nurses encouraged him to go home and come back in the morning as she was likely to sleep all night. It was hard to leave her When he stood up he kissed her hand.

"I love you," he whispered close to her forehead as he leaned in and kissed it. He straightened up but she never opened her eye.

"Where's Chenai?" Andy asked once Jodi opened the door. Something wasn't right. Jodi wore a strange expression, like a dress that didn't fit, a knowing light in her eyes that raised alarm bells in Andy. Andy was too worried to try and figure it out.

"Come upstairs and I'll tell you," Jodi said closing the front door. Andy looked at the stairs. The house was quiet and the only sound he could hear was his heart beating as he worried that maybe Blake had done something to Chenai. Often he prayed that she would leave the house even though he understood her desire to remain loyal. Though at times he wondered. Was she making sure the kids were okay or their father?

"Just tell me Jodi. Is Chenai up there? Is she okay?"

"She was in a car accident, but she's fine. Come on up."

"What? When?" Andy demanded shocked.

"She's fine. Come, I'll show you." Jodi said and started climbing the stairs.

"Fine," Andy agreed and followed Jodi up his heart still racing. Chenai was in a car accident, but she was upstairs. So she was fine.

Jodi led him towards Chenai's room and opened the door. He walked in ahead of her, struck by the perfection of the room. The bed was made and everything looked in place, perfectly organized. He hardly came up to Chenai's room and when he did her Bible would be on her bed or her college books. Not this perfect space. There was no sign of Chenai in the room.

"Chenai," he called then walked to the adjoining bathroom and opened the door.

Nothing.

"Where is she?" Andy asked then turned back in the room. He nearly fell down with shock when he saw Jodi standing before him with her T-shirt off and her jeans unzipped.

"What are you doing?" he asked, shock and dismay making his voice tremble. "Jodi?"

"I- I just wanted you to come here so we could be together," she said. "I love you Andy. I want you to hold me."

"No." Andy recoiled as if from a snake and ran his hands through his hair. Yes, he had been in situations like this before, but not with a child! She was what? Fourteen? And she had told the story about Chenai just to get him alone? How stupid he had been. He should've just waited.

"Please Andy. I love you! Why do you bother with Chenai. Chenai loves my Dad!"

"Get dressed," Andy ordered walking towards her. "Cover yourself, little girl."

"No!" she screamed and pulled at his shirt, ripping all the buttons off. Andy pulled back so roughly, Jodi stumbled forward.

"Jodi!" It was Blake's voice.

Before Andy could react Jodi let out another scream and ran out of the room yelling, "Daddy!"

Blake caught her as she left Chenai's room and then he noticed her state of undress. He lifted his head towards Andy who had just walked out of the room. Blake's eyes turned dark with rage. Andy immediately realized what Blake perceived and he felt sick with worry.

"You!" Blake cursed and lunged towards him. All Andy remembered was that he now really knew what it felt like to be attacked by a bear.

CHAPTER 32

Torrid

*But no human being can tame the tongue. It is a restless evil, full of
deadly poison.*

—James 3:8,

Chenai woke up with a fright when the nurse opened the door.
It took her a while to understand where she was and why she
was lying in this narrow hospital bed. Her head felt like it was being squeezed between two very strong unyielding walls. The nurse
moved closer to her and touched her arm.

"Are you alright?" she asked, and then checked the IV next to
her bed.

Chenai tried to nod. Instead she managed a small smile as her
eyes darted around the room, taking in the big TV set, and the big
windows. The hospital room was clean and almost luxurious. It
could have been a hotel room.

"How's your head? That was our biggest concern."

"Sore." She croaked then cleared her throat.

The nurse gave her a glass of water and helped her drink it. Her
manner was gentle, almost motherly and Chenai felt comforted.
Still, she longed for her mother more than ever before. She tried to
stifle the overwhelming emotions. God was with her. He promised

never to leave her.

"I'll tell the doctor to increase your pain medication. You had some visitors earlier. You were fast asleep, so I told them not to stay in here. They are outside. Can I send them in?"

Visitors. Andy? Blake? Oh Blake. Blake had said something to her. He had told her that he … he loved her. Chenai felt her head hurt more. She couldn't believe it. Blake had said that he had prayed to God and now he knew that he loved her. Was that true? No, he didn't love her and she certainly didn't love him. Did she? No! She feared him and cared at the same time but love? No.

"They can come. Thank you."

"You're welcome. Now would you like to try something more solid to eat? Maybe some breakfast?"

Chenai nodded slightly and caught the clock next to the TV. It was already 9 am. Had she slept that long?

It was Blake. Her heart jumped like frogs after a storm at the sight of him. He stood by the door, hesitant. His eyes were shadowed as if he hadn't slept and he hadn't shaved either. Even his jeans and shirt just seemed carelessly thrown on. Still, she wondered why her heart was racing and she knew that if she had had a heart monitor the nurses would all be running in and calling the doctors to tend to her.

"Hi." His greeting was hesitant. Chenai was amazed at how a simple 'hi' could be felt deep in her belly and leave her weak.

She was also confused by this suddenly unsure man who was as awkward as a teenager, a stranger to her. The old, mean Blake she could deal with, not this, this unsettled, insecure one.

"Hello," she responded and swallowed. Her throat was dry again. Blake moved in and slowly closed the door.

"How are you today? You feel okay?"

"Okay," Chenai responded still afraid to look at him. His rumpled look that somehow looked more appealing than his usual put together one.

Why was he coming to see her? He wasn't making her feel any better. In fact he was increasing her stress.

"The doctor thinks you can come home today or tomorrow."

"How are the kids?" she ventured to ask and stole a glance at him. He was looking at his feet, hands in his jean pockets. His hesitation had her worried.

"Is everything okay?"

"Fine. Fine. Don't worry. They are fine."

"Something's wrong?" she tried to sit up, but winced in pain. Blake rushed to her, and then he sat on the bed. He adjusted her pillows. Being that close, his warm breath touching her cheek added to her anxiety. Something had flickered in Blake's eyes. Was he in trouble because she couldn't deliver the money? Had he lost everything and now blamed her?

"Nothing's wrong. I'm glad you can come home. We have things to talk about."

She tried to nod, but moving her head felt like knives were jousting in her brain. She looked at the water and Blake reached for it and held the cup while she drank. After he put the cup back beside her bed, she settled back on the pillows.

"Do you have a phone?" she asked.

"Yes. You need to call someone?"

"Andy."

When she said those words, his expression changed. She could see that he wasn't amused.

"I think you should rest, okay. You can call him later." His eyes searched hers for any resistance. None was coming. "Tyler wanted to come and see you. I told him you would be home soon."

"Where are they?"

"With their grandparents," Blake said then looked at her fractured arm. Chenai followed his eyes to her still arm then flinched when she felt his touch on her fingers.

"Sorry. Did I hurt you?"

"No."

His hand reached for her face and she turned away overwhelmed.

"I'm sorry about the accident. It was my fault."

"No it wasn't."

"I was a greedy fool. Trying to fix my messes by adding more shit to it.. sorry for that, too. I need to watch my language."

Chenai felt laughter bubbling inside her, but she held it in. Was he going to spend all day apologizing because Blake's mouth did need to be cleaned with soap? How long would it take to clean layers of his filthy, angry language? With God it could happen in a day, she knew that.

"I'm going to look after you." Blake's words filled her with strange sensations as she swallowed nervously.

After being discharged and ordered to rest her arm until she got her cast, Blake took Chenai home. He settled her in the car and she leaned back, eyes closed as he drove from the hospital, just as it started to rain. When they got home, she was struck by how quiet it was as they drove in and then she remembered that Tyler and Jodi had gone to their grandmother.

Blake walked to her side to help her out of the car. Chenai wanted to tell him she could manage, but realized it wasn't easy to move with only one hand. He helped her out and she held her breath until she realized she would die unless she allowed herself to breathe which she did, however her loud exhales caused Blake to look at her with even more concern in his dark eyes.

"I can walk," she said and he let her good arm go and opened the door that led her to the laundry area and then to the kitchen.

When she reached the stairs, she stumbled a little and Blake dropped the keys while he reached for her hand. She gasped when he held her hand and she turned to his face beside her then quickly looked down at his shirt.

"Let me help you," he said and before she could protest she found herself scooped up in his arms, one arm under her knees and the other supporting her upper back. Her arm was in a sling on her chest.

Before she could say anything he was half way up the stairs and she was looking at the ceiling, heart racing. The last time she had been carried like this was when she had been at school and stepped on a shard of glass during cross country running. The blood had poured like a waterfall and the sports teacher who had been monitoring them while they ran through the forest had picked her up and ran with her to the school clinic, her blood making a trail of red dots all over the sand. By the time they arrived at the clinic she had almost passed out and barely heard the nurse scolding the man after she was laid on the cot and something pressed on her foot.

"You halfwit. You should have covered the wound first instead of carrying her bleeding and messing up my floor and almost emptying her small body of all her blood. Go away. Let me take care of her."

With that memory Blake opened her bedroom door with his hand. She barely registered her leg hitting against the frame.

"Sorry," he muttered and then he placed her on the bed gently, she felt like she was some fragile being. He rubbed the side of her head. She removed his hand.

She still felt tense as she watched him move around her room and opened her cabinet. She stared at his back, T-shirt and jeans and running shoes. He touched his dark head then reached for something. She saw him bring out the blanket that she liked to wrap herself in. A gift form Amanda. He unfolded it and placed over her. Watching him do such domestic stuff had a dream like quality.

Chenai tried to relax though she wondered if he could hear her heart beating. The sound was so loud in her ears that she felt light headed. His patience reminded him of the way her mother would make peanut butter to sell. The long arduous grinding between two stones.

"Are you okay?" he asked.

Chenai tried to smile and nodded. He spoke again.

"Want some food? I'll get you something. Soup okay?"

Before she could respond again he pulled out his phone and called the same Italian restaurant from which he liked to order his food.

"Can I have an order of two chicken soups, a salad—Is that okay?"

Chenai nodded. She wanted her phone. She wanted to see Tyler and Andy and Jodi too. She didn't think it was a good idea to be alone with Blake.

"Where, where are the kids?"

"Gross Pointe. With their grandma."

She nodded. He had told her that at the hospital. Shouldn't they be back by now? It was too quiet. She didn't know how to ask for the phone. Hers was probably in pieces out on the highway.

"You need anything else? I'm going to pick up the food."

"Thanks. Can you please- I need the phone."

She noticed that Blake looked uncomfortable when she asked. It was a quick flash across his face.

"Relax for now Chenai, alright. I'll bring you dinner; we'll eat and then get you the phone."

"Ah."

"It's alright. You need to stay relaxed. Feel better."

He saw her questioning look.

"Okay?" His command reminded her of the old Blake. The real Blake.

She nodded and watched him walk out. She heard his footsteps and when the garage door closed and she heard his car leave she relaxed. She didn't realize how tightly she had been holding herself until he left. She felt light hearted- a leaf floating gently from the tallest tree in the forest and she knew why. She turned and saw her Bible and reached for it like a life line. She hugged it and felt tears roll down her cheeks. It was a warm sweetness that washed over her as she tasted the salty flavor of her tears. She felt like she had come out of the wringer and something became clear to her. When Blake walked out of the door with the promise to return something exploded inside. It was so powerful, it drew her in and she knew her life would never be the same.

CHAPTER 33

Cooling

Is anyone among you in trouble? Let them pray. Is anyone happy?
Let them sing songs of praise.

—James 5:13

Chenai struggled to open her eyes. She remembered falling asleep, the sweet dreams demanding her mind and body to surrender. Something nagged at the fringes of her mind though she couldn't think of what it was. It worried her even more that she couldn't remember what it was that had her stomach in knots. Slowly, more memories of the night before came to her.

Oh God, she thought as she felt her heart do its somersault again. Is this the emotion Mai told me about? *I feel like I'm falling from the highest tree, not sure how I will land and yet I want to …*

She turned her head abruptly.

Blake was in her room. He slept on the chair, legs hanging down, and slippers on his feet. His dark hair was ruffled and she found herself smiling. He looked like a little boy. His features were relaxed, and his whole demeanor was sweeter.

He had run around for her last night, after he went to get the food he dug around the kitchen and found a tray for her. He had brought her food. The rich aroma of the soup filled her room.

That had brought memories of her father, when her mother had been ill, so ill in fact they feared she would not make it. Her father had tried to make her mother her favorite okra and somehow in the process had cut his hand and bled all over the green vegetable. But his effort had made her mother smile though she had not smiled for weeks. In this instance, Blake had not cooked the food, but he had ordered it, and he had fed her though she insisted she could eat on her own. She had not been able to eat much and he helped himself to her leftovers. He gave her medication and while he sat on the chair she had succumbed to it and fell asleep.

Blake stirred and his eyes locked on hers. His sharp gaze penetrated her soul. She couldn't look away at first. Finally, she looked down, her heart pounding.

When she looked at Blake again he stood up and seemed to be stretching out in pain. It couldn't have been comfortable sleeping on the couch. If she had known he would also fall asleep she would have told him to sleep in his bed. Not that he ever listened to her anyway.

"Morning,' he said.

"Morning."

"How you feeling now? How's your headache?"

"Better."

Blake nodded and yawned again and that triggered a yawn from her, too.

"You slept there?"

"I guess I did," Blake replied glancing behind him at the couch. "Wanted to make sure you were okay."

"I'm fine. Really."

"Let me get you some breakfast. We have food in the house right?"

"Don't worry about me. I'll come down and get something," Chenai said quickly. "Please."

"Chenai. Not worry about you?" he chuckled and moved close to her. "You don't get it do you?"

"Get what?"

"I'm not just worrying about you. I- I can't stop thinking about you."

She looked down and Blake walked to her and lifted her chin.

"Look at me," his voice was gentle. When she looked up at him her eyes were wet. He reached for her hand.

"Something changed in me two days ago. I'm still trying to figure it out. I may lose my company, but – I don't care. I may lose this house-it doesn't matter. I could see clearly the man I had become. I just hadn't seen it before or- refused to. I never stopped to reflect—I kept moving, faster and faster each day, after my dreams." Chenai nodded. He squeezed her hands more as if he was willing her to understand.

"When you were in hospital I started reading the Bible, right from the beginning and then I rushed to the New Testament, but nothing is new is it. Men getting lost, moving away from God trying to do everything on their own, but God – He is merciful. It means he loves me as bad as I am?"

Blake paused and Chenai thought her heart would explode. "I don't know why He will forgive me for my deceit, my neglect of my kids, Tyler, Jodi…my wife. I never cared about any of them.

Just my dreams and many people told me, but I never saw. When God opened my eyes everything became clear. Do you understand?"

Chenai nodded again tears falling from her eyes. She knew. God let you see things with spiritual eyes.

"And he let me see it all.. and you.."

Blake's cell phone rang and he picked it up from the table where he had placed it and glanced at the number.

"Yes," he spoke into the phone. Chenai wiped her eyes with her good hand.

"Okay."

Blake pressed the end button then stood up.

"Let me get you breakfast. I'll go to a restaurant and get you something fresh"

"Okay."

After Blake left Chenai slowly rolled out of bed and walked to the bathroom. She dreaded to see herself in the mirror. She hadn't gotten a chance to do so since the accident, but now she wondered. Blake was looking at her as if she was something special.

She stood by the mirror then took a deep breath before opening her eyes. Her eyes still looked too big for her face and her mouth too full for her too high cheekbones. But somehow Blake enjoyed looking at her face. She tried to smile, then she did letting it reach her eyes. Chenai used her one good hand to wash her face and then she tried to smooth her hair that now looked flattened at the back and straight up like Skyscraper in the front. Stubbornly, it just sprung back up. She would need to wash it, but she couldn't do that and would never want Blake to help her with that chore.

She shrugged helplessly and then decided to get a phone before trying to bath or get dressed. Maybe someone from Church could help her with things. God, why did she always need people?

She left the room and walked slowly downstairs then found the phone. Without her cell phone she tried to remember Andy's number. She dialed, but there was no answer. When the voicemail picked up she disconnected the line. She had to speak to him and leaving a message wouldn't work. She had missed appointments with him, Church and today they were supposed to meet again and discuss the Walk for Hunger fundraiser.

She decided to try Amanda's number.

"Chenai! Where have you been?" Amanda spoke as soon as Chenai identified herself.

"I was in an accident."

"That's awful. Are you okay?"

"I'm fine. I'm home now. Is everything alright?"

"Chenai. You don't know?"

"Know what?"

Chenai slid to the ground with shock as Amanda began to explain.

CHAPTER 34

Calm

*If one of you should wander from the truth and someone should
bring him back.*

—James 5:19

Blake picked up his phone and when he heard the voice he
wished he hadn't.

"Kimberly?"

"Blake. What's going on with you? Why have you dumped
the kids at Ma and Pa when clearly you have a nanny? Is that you
again shucking your responsibilities?"

"You don't know what you are talking about."

"I don't? Where are you now? I imagine you are at work."

Blake looked around the parking lot as he left the restaurant
with breakfast for Chenai. He hadn't been at work for three days.

"It's a long story Kimberly, but you are right. I have been a
terrible father and that is going to change."

There was silence on the other side. Kimberly must have been
surprised by his admission, Blake thought.

"How? How will you change?"

"Can I tell you later? I will need help on how to do it. Kim,

I'm so sorry for everything. I was a terrible husband. Bad dad. I probably don't know how to be a good one. Maybe you can help me with Jodi, since she probably talks to you more."

Silence.

"Kimberly."

He realized she was crying when he heard her sniff.

"I'll talk to you later, Blake."

When Blake arrived home he found Chenai sitting by the kitchen table the phone in front of her. She turned to look at him when he walked in. He froze when he saw the look in her eyes.

The moment he saw her eyes he knew that she knew about Andy. They looked wounded. Blake didn't want to assess how he felt, the fear that she would blame him for what happened to Andy. He closed the door and took slow hesitant steps towards her, not sure what to do or say. He stepped closer and closer and saw the disappointment in her eyes closely and it seemed to stab him in its silent accusation.

"Why?" the word came out strained.

"I should have told you."

"I had every right to know." She said then broke off as if the horror was fresh in her mind again and she seemed to get dizzy. Blake rushed to her, but she moved away from him shaking her head.

What was she thinking? Was she blaming him?

"I can't believe it? Andy's in jail?" Her voice sounded shaky and she cleared her throat. "This is a nightmare. Is Jodi okay?"

"That's partly why she is at her grandparents. She wanted to leave."

"You saw?"

"I came in just as it happened."

Chenai shook her head again and she wore the news like a burning heavy cloak. She gnawed at her lip and Blake reached for her trembling hands.

"It's okay."

"No it's not. I'm so sorry. He was, is my friend and I'm just so shocked that he would do something like that. Why?"

"I don't know."

"You should've told me…I need to know these things."

"I know, Chenai but …you were not in the state to hear these things. You don't need the stress right now and whoever told you shouldn't have."

"And I just go on believing that Andy is a good person when he's dangerous?"

"No. You are very fragile right now."

She stepped away from him holding out her good arm.

"I just need to go outside for a while."

"Okay."

"Alone."

Chenai walked towards the door and Blake watched her struggle with the latch, eventually the sliding door moved. He walked to her and closed the door for her watching as she began walking on unsteady feet towards the lake. He saw her glance at the logs for the tree house and Blake winced remembering. How long had those logs been there?

Blake wanted to follow her. He wanted to comfort her, but right now he knew she was confused and wanted to be alone. To pray. He needed to pray.

"Oh God. Umm help Chenai deal with this," Blake said as he walked towards the room. He remembered what Chenai had told him. That she talked to God as if she was talking to her most trusted friend. She didn't try and hide anything because she knew that God already knew anyway. She was as transparent as she could be. Blake wondered if he could be as transparent as Chenai was.

He had asked her about kneeling. If that was also a requirement. Chenai had smiled, her beautiful smile.

"Sometimes. It's not how you look physically, but your heart. Kneeling is good because, somehow, that physical act, your heart just follows. On your knees, you are at the highest point. I feel closer to God."

"Hi there," he said, feeling foolish, but determined as he went and knelt down. That was humbling. Going on his knees like this. His head wanted to resist, to tell him he was foolish. He embraced being foolish, soaking it like a glass of water after a long run. Blake felt his heart lift. He had never done this, not since he was maybe four. All his arrogance, his own strength, meant nothing. Not in light of God Almighty. "You see the mess we are in right now? We need you. Please give my family hope."

As the minutes ticked into an hour, Blake ached with the need to be with Chenai, but she needed to be alone so he tried to keep busy by calling Tyler. Jodi didn't want to talk to him and then he called his mother. All the while he would walk to the window and look at Chenai's tiny figure in the distance, sitting as if frozen in time.

CHAPTER 35

Heat

I am the vine; you are the branches. If you remain in me and I in you, you will bear much fruit; apart from me you can do nothing.

—John 15:5

A Christian. How does a man just change overnight? Penny typed the word 'Christian' on her computer and started to read the second post that talked about people who followed Jesus. She had known many Christians and some of them were weird, like Chenai herself. Some didn't touch alcohol. She didn't know too many of them. She avoided them really. After all Christianity in its purest form was dying anyway. Like the Amish, penny reasoned.

Blake becoming one of those holier than thou who profess to believe in a heaven was a little hard to swallow. And yet, Blake had seemed completely genuine. It annoyed her how "kind" he was being. It made her want to puke. Who was this stranger, she wondered. Was it all an act?

Chenai. That girl had done something to him. She had used her big innocent eyes to seduce her man.

Penny wanted to laugh if she wasn't so annoyed. So Blake now liked unsophisticated, innocent and totally clueless women. What on earth could he talk to her about? She wasn't educated. She didn't know business and Blake was very successful because he lived and breathed his company.

That morning while drinking her coffee Penny had read her magazines and found an article on the types of women men fell for. The writer had hinted that men liked women they could rescue, women that made them feel like warriors. The thought of being that kind of woman totally disgusted her. She didn't need a man to do anything for her that she could do herself. She could kill her spiders and slay her own dragons. No. What Blake needed was an equal to him. A woman who could be his equal in thinking and strengths, not some frail, giggling woman like Chenai. That magazine was wrong and she had thankfully tossed it in the trash. But now she wondered if she needed to change the kind of woman she was. Be the damsel in distress so he could feel more of a man. The thought sickened her and she knew Blake would probably see through it. She had to do something.

So what if he was going to lose millions in a bad deal that was now a horror. Everybody lost money sometimes, but you just had to get up and move on again. Well, Penny could also play nice. She could play the Christian holy person too if that's what Blake now liked. *How hard could it be?*

Two days after Chenai got home Blake finally decided to go to the office. He hadn't abandoned a sinking ship. Cathy greeted him as if it was a normal day. She was still confident, though he was sure she must have been dealing with calls all day long.

"Mr. Pieri. I've put all your messages on your desk," she said after he had greeted her.

"Thank you. Please hold the calls for me," he said, then before he got in his office he turned to her.

"How are you Cathy? I have never asked you, have I?"

Cathy smiled. She was a gift to his company. The only person who seemed to manage the storm without going insane.

"I'm very well. I always enjoy a bit of uncertainty here and there. Keeps life interesting."

Blake nodded and walked in his office. He saw the stack of messages neatly held together by a clip. He pushed them behind his desk and picked up the phone.

He dialed his old friend, Jim Litgee. Jim had already left the business when he started attending some Bible study. Blake remembered the contempt he had felt for the man back then.

"Blake. What a surprise. How are you? How is business?"

"Business is not good man."

"Sorry to hear that."

"That's not why I'm calling."

Jim was quiet. Yes, he would be surprised to hear what Blake had to say.

"What's going on? You are not in trouble are you?"

Blake didn't know how else to tell him, but just to come right out and say it.

"God has found me, Jim."

"What? Do you mean what I think Blake?"

"That's right. Something happened and now I don't know what to do next."

"Blake. That is the best news I've heard in my life. Do you

know how wonderful that is?"

Blake laughed when he heard his old friend's laughter. Blake remembered how Jim had changed right in front of him. Now he understood how.

"It's as if I've had a heart transplant, yet it's also complicated."

"You must come to church, Blake. Today. Don't waste time. We have a men's Bible study. What God is doing, that's great man."

"Well, and something else too."

"What?"

"I think I've fallen in love with someone."

"That's great. Who?"

"Chenai."

"Isn't that the kids' nanny from Africa."

"That's her."

"Phew. That's a lot going on. Does she know?"

"I've told her. I think she heard me."

"Well, man now that you are born again you know relationships need be different. Everything you knew about relationships. Toss out. You can't do your old things…"

"I know. I know. I'm not stupid. Chenai is like no one I've ever known. I can't wait to be with her, be married to her, once I have my life sorted. Just to talk to her now is incredible, even though I do desire her all the time. . Man it's like I want to protect her, I want to be better, but I also want to know her God more. It's as if.."

"You fell in love twice at the same time. First with God and then with her."

"That's it man. I knew you would understand."

"Well, this is the best news I've heard all year. How is the company?"

"Now, that's what's falling apart."

"And yet you are so happy."

"And yet I am."

"I would like to pray for you, if you will let me. Have you heard of the sinner's prayer?"

"No. What's that?"

"It's just something you say to acknowledge out loud what you have already done in your heart. If you want we can say it together."

"Over the phone?"

"That's right. We can. Or I can come over there?"

"Why wait. I would like to try it."

"Alright. So most of us do this the first time we accept Jesus into our hearts. It makes it official."

"Alright."

"So are you ready?"

"Of course man. I want to do everything I can to make sure."

"Okay. Repeat after me. Jesus."

"Jesus," Blake said and in that instant something seemed to shift inside him.

"I repent of my sins." Jim spoke.

"I repent of my sins."

"I ask you to come into my life."

"I ask you to come into my life"

"I make you Lord and Savior of my life."

"I make you Lord and Savior of my Life."

"Amen."

"Amen."

There was silence then Blake asked. "That's it?"

"That's it man. You have made God the Lord of your life. That's only the first step. You have planted a good seed in your life. Now you will need to stay watered, in good soil."

"Alright. What do I do?"

"You need to find other like-minded people, come to our Bible study or find another one that suits you, maybe at Chenai's church."

"That's good. I'll see what I can do."

"And with all the new 'loves' in your life, I am guessing you do know the dating protocols right?"

"I won't touch her. I have an idea."

Jim laughed. "All the best man. I'm here if you need to talk. Remember I've been exactly where you are and I am still learning. Each day God reveals himself in new and wonderful ways."

"I know. I'm seeing my kids like it's the first time. I have some messes to clean up. Can God save me from my own foolishness? Do I even deserve a second chance? I've messed up man."

"God will give you a million chances. He is now a part of you. It's hard to understand, but He is. And remember you are not on your own. Jesus says in John 15, "Remain in me, as I also remain in you. No branch can bear fruit but itself; it must remain in the vine" and He is our true vine, Blake. You now have the whole of God's army and whatever happens, it will all be for your own good."

"Keep telling me that. Bye Jim."

The stacks of messages still stared at him. The phone blinked with the usual messages. He owed money. His company was most likely bankrupt. All this was true last week, and last month. Yet everything was different.

CHAPTER 36

Cozy

They followed worthless idols and became worthless themselves.

—Jeremiah 2:5

The days that followed were tense, sometimes he imagined what it felt like to look at your home after it had been destroyed by a storm, a house built on sand. With Chenai next to him, he felt like they were a team, facing the distraction together. The medical center was now truly going to be taken from Blake. He would lose everything he put into it, time, money energy, friends but worse, he could be sued.

Blake accepted all this, somehow the stressed man she had met at the airport had mellowed out. Chenai tried to find him, searched in his eyes, but he was gone. God is that good, Chenai thought with wonder.

When she found out about Andy, Chenai knew that the ground shook, and Blake seemed to hold her steady. The betrayal was so deep. Andy might as well have tried to harm her. It was hard to reconcile the monster and Andy. How could he have hidden his true colors from her so well, Chenai wondered. Many people at church looked up to him, maybe too much. When she confronted

Blake about it, how he had kept the truth from her, she had gone outside to cry and pray alone. After nearly two hours Blake had followed her outside, worried that she was losing her mind or the injuries from the accident were making her too stressed out. She had startled when he sat down next to her. She breathed in the damp air and the man next to her. For a while they both just sat down, silently. The water danced from the breeze that occasionally blew from the sky otherwise all was quiet. After a while Chenai had leaned on his shoulder and that seemed to be a peace offering to them. Maybe all would be well.

Besides the Andy problems, they also had to deal with Jodi. Chenai could only imagine how terrible the whole ordeal had been. Each day Blake went to spend some time with his children in Grosse Point. Each day when he came back he was disturbed by Jodi's lack of warmth towards him.

"It's okay, Blake. These things take time," Chenai told him when he told her about Jodi's lack of respect while he cleaned up after the dinner he had bought on his way home.

Now that Blake was more attentive to his daughter and wanted to spend more time with her, Jodi seemed even more withdrawn, her hostility strong enough to destroy any bridge Blake tried to build. Chenai sat on the couch with her legs resting on the otto-man, watching Blake. At her last doctor visit her doctor told her to take it easy, but with all that was happening in their lives it was hard to just relax.

"Jodi told me she knew I would lose everything. That I was a loser," Blake said, shaking his head. He walked and stood behind her couch and rested his hands on her shoulders.

"She's hurting. Look how long it took you to turn to God, when he had been chasing you since you were a baby. And he's your heavenly father."

"That wasn't easy for me. I'm surprised he didn't give up on me."

Chenai smiled, "He won't give up on you."

She gazed at him, tilting her head up, "You have much work to do with Jodi. You will have to woo her. I tried to woo her too, and slowly she was warming up to me and then I lost her again. We are fighting against all the other influences she has, that we all have."

"Woo her. I like that. Keep trying even if she slaps me in the face."

Chenai nodded. "We can both keep trying."

Chenai remembered something else that she had to ask him.

"So when will the kids come back? Are you still worried about the threats?"

"Maybe next week. I've had to disclose my bad business dealings to my partners, especially Jason. They are not happy, but I've come out honestly and told them I'll find a way to pay them back. I'm hoping that they won't make any more threats against my kids or insist on suing my company."

"I see. But if they really wanted to do something to hurt you or them won't they find out where they are?"

"I don't think they will do anything, but I will take precautions."

She could tell he had something more to tell her. She sensed it, see it like a floating bubble, waiting to burst.

"I knew,"

"Knew what?" she asked. Blake walked around and sat on a separate couch. She turned to him, confused.

"My wife. Samantha. I knew she was having an affair and the weekend she went away with her boyfriend, I knew. I could have stopped her, but I pretended not to know."

Chenai stared at him.

"You see how bad I am…"

"Was," she said. "Why are you telling me this?"

"I just remembered. I caused her accident. I caused yours."

"Blake,"

"It's fine. I just need more forgiveness than regular people."

Chenai had never been to his offices. He took her first to the medical center that lay in ruins under the clouds. Chenai had been trying to understand everything he had been involved with in his company. It was a long list of unscrupulousness that she didn't even understand. He didn't leave any of the ugliness out when he confessed to her, the cutting corners, bribing, cheating, all to have more and more money in the bank and keep his magnificent life and build security. She discovered he had a home in Florida too and another one up north that he had not visited in years.

"I wanted it all; Chenai but it never satisfied me. I had the latest cars. I was trying to fill the hole left by my father I think, why else. I was trying, always trying but …"

"I know," she had said, overwhelmed by his openness.

"I hurt a lot of people with my ambition. My wife, my mother, my brothers, mostly Tyler and Jodi."

She nodded again. Her heart raced whenever she thought of him, how close they were becoming. It terrified her because he was opening up to her and she felt the weight of it on her shoulders, though she wouldn't have it any other way.

As she walked through the different rooms of Blake's medical center, she marveled at how she had once looked at him as the enemy, how there was so much against them to be together. His age, his kids, his lifestyle, his skin color. She loved her family, he was estranged from his whole family. Would he understand her need to be there for her father, her brothers? How would her father react?

In Zimbabwe there were very few mixed relationships because often black and white people lived in two parallel worlds. They rarely mixed. She remembered the Millards. Her only picture of a white family. The Millards didn't see blacks as people and her father had always told her that it was reflection on them, not her. And strangely enough, America it wasn't as bad. People could be racist, but they didn't show it as much, until they did, of course. She had not come across it though she heard about it. Her friends were all races. Maybe she was naïve.

And yet, here they were. So close. Pulled together by a force that destroyed all the barriers. She turned to Blake as he talked and her heart filled, overflowed and she thought she couldn't catch her breath. They now stood outside the building the potential of the medical center before them.

"I didn't know how to deal with Jodi's grief and her growing pains. I still don't."

"You will figure it out. It might not be a perfect relationship, but you will try your best."

"Hell, yeah." He caught her eye. "I mean yes."

Chenai laughed, "You won't suddenly stop cursing like you do. I'm sure you will try your best."

"Especially in front of you I will give it my da.. I mean best."

Now she wondered if the people he owed money would forgive him. Figuring what to do next, Blake wasn't letting the details consume him, because he knew it could swallow him up again and he could find himself back to it, chasing something that just didn't satisfy.

Her heart breaking, Chenai realized something else. Even though God forgave him and gave peace, there were still the consequences of his decisions. He still had to face those.

Now, the castle he had built on the sand was tumbling down and yet Blake seemed more at peace. She marveled at God's power. She marveled at his peace. That's all she ever prayed about, peace in the midst of the storm and to her utter surprise, Blake had it. He was now fighting for what was important, his children. True freedom and joy came from self-denial. Focusing on others, would bring joy to him. That's not what the world usually taught, Chenai realized. God had changed one man's priorities before it was too late. How many never sought those answers?

Chenai was also getting used to another idea. It seemed she was also included in the list of the important people to Blake, though she was tempted to tell him to focus on his kids and not so much on her. She also knew he needed her or felt guilty about the accident. She had no idea what the future held, but Blake seemed to want her in it. And as much as his past behavior had scared and upset her, she had also forgiven him. Only God could do that.

Chenai was unable to believe how relaxed she had become with Blake. They talked for hours when he was home and she tried to give him ideas about Jodi though she herself had not really been able to reach his daughter. Tyler was enjoying time with his Dad, with no questions about the previous neglect.

The next day, their fourth day since he brought her from the hospital, Blake came in after his run and shower. "Can I sit by you?"

Chenai froze at his words, still holding her assignment. He had kept his physical distance the past few days, but now his question filled her stomach with a thousand butterflies.

She watched him walk towards her. He wasn't waiting for an answer. She sat up when he sat next to her and the movement dipped her towards him. When she tried to move away he stopped her. He took her hand then slowly traced along the scar on her left hand.

"What happened here?" he asked. His voice seemed to send a trickle of shockwaves through her body. Seeing his hand, not white, but tan, on hers, his finger tracing her scar, her heart seemed to stop. They were so different and yet his hands on hers were firm, comforting and terrifying. Feeling lightheaded she had to blink a few times and force her brain to work. The scar. Where was it?

"I was cut on a wire when taking a short cut from school."

"You were trespassing? Breaking the law?"

"Yes."

"Is that the worst you've done in life? I can't even tell you my worst."

"I have committed many sins daily. We can't compare them. They are the same in God's eyes."

"Really. That's good. It must be unfair that I get forgiven of so much and you did so little." Blake grinned.

"Most of what God does doesn't make sense."

Blake nodded. Chenai knew that falling for Blake didn't make sense. The fact that he seemed to be falling for her certainly baffled her. It seemed what he had enjoyed before no longer enticed him. The places he went to drown his sorrows. The company he liked to keep..

"Lean on me Chenai. It's okay."

She remained tense. It was not a bad kind of tense, she noted as his scent wafted towards her, his soap or shampoo that reminded her of grass after the rain. Her injured arm was away from him, her good arm under his back. She moved it around him and he brought her closer into his arms.

"There you go," he said and she noted the sensation of his voice so close, traveling inside her. She wanted to pray, but her brain wasn't forming any words because it seemed that Blake being that close took over her whole world. She realized with trepidation that in his arms she seemed to lose track of her thoughts or remember how to breathe.

"Relax Cheny," he teased and she giggled. "You remember."

"That you couldn't say my name?"

"Yep. I was an idiot. I'm surprised you stayed as long as you did."

"I stayed for the kids."

"I'm glad you did. Now can you stay here for me and forever?"

She was silent then he looked at her. She was looking down. She rarely looked at him. She tilted her head up to him when his fingers lifted her chin. This close, she realized Blake could see the other scar on her chin, where an angry hen had scratched her protecting its young. He traced it, but then something seemed to happen to him. She noticed the flicker in his eyes when their eyes met. Now it seemed as if he was frightened.

He stood up so abruptly she toppled over where he had had been sitting.

"Sorry Chenai. I shouldn't do that. We'll need to make other arrangements so we – we date properly. This is insane."

Chenai was astonished when he walked out and left her there alone. She was further confused when she heard the door close.

He had actually left the house. What had scared him? Did he now fear her? Did she have a profound effect on him?

Chenai shook her head. Impossible.

She watched him gather tools and take them to the tree house by the lake. Unbelievably he began to work on the tree house, chain saw buzzing, hammers hitting, and drills buzzing. She could hear the sound from the kitchen as she moved about, even upstairs she could hear him work. Somehow she knew that he didn't need interruptions, and that he would not stop until that house was built. Chenai's love for Blake grew and exploded like a wave that threw her on sand, sparkling gold dust and tantalizing. The fact that he loved her too, made her gasp.

CHAPTER 37

Fall

For there is nothing hidden that will not be disclosed, and nothing concealed that will not be known or brought out into the open.

—Luke 8:17

"Chenai!" Tyler stood up shyly. Chenai waved at him and after a few seconds of hesitation he ran into her arms for a hug. She closed her eyes as she held him then looked up. She had never entered the home of Louis and Debbie Shelby before. When she and Blake picked up the kids she noticed that they didn't seem too happy to see Blake and remembered why. The Shelbys probably blamed him for their daughter's death. They blamed him for Jodi's behavior and now probably were angry at him for the mess he had made of his life. How much of that could Blake take? All the blame. All the disappointment that people seemed to throw at him like grenades. She glanced at him noticing how he kept his face impassive, and thought a quick prayer for him. She didn't want this visit to end up exploding in her face.

Their two dogs and cats remained close to the father, thankfully. One of the dogs was as big as a horse.

"Hello again," Chenai said.

"How are you? I heard you were in an accident," Debbie spoke first. She walked and reached out her hand to shake Chenai's. She smiled warmly at her. When Debbie looked up at Blake she just said, "Blake."

"Debbie," Blake muttered back.

"Are you okay?" Tyler asked. "Can we come back home now. You promised that I could teach you to play baseball."

"Soon. I promise," Chenai said quietly. Tyler touched her cast that now reached her fingertips.

"Can I write on it?" Tyler asked.

"Sure." Chenai looked around hoping to see Jodi. Where was she? She was nervous to see her. Chenai knew she had to apologize for what happened.

"Are you looking for Jodi?" Louis asked. "I'll go and get her. Where are you going to eat?" Debbie asked.

"Little Italy," Blake responded. He still stood close to the door as if he wanted to run out.

"Hey Ty want to take a walk with me?" Blake asked. Tyler nodded and walked up to him. He put his arm around his father awkwardly and the gesture almost brought tears to Chenai's eyes.

"We'll be back," Blake said and walked out.

"She'll be up," Debbie said coming from the basement.

"So how long have you been in American for?"

"Just a few months," Chenai replied.

"You are from Zimbabwe right," Louis said. "Please have a seat."

Chenai perched on the edge of the sofa glancing around the comfortable living room where the TV was flanked by a fine cabinet filled with ornaments. Their home was also very big, though not as big as Blake's stone house.

"Yes," she said.

"I've been reading about it, when Tyler told me. Bad things are happening there."

"Yes."

"You have family still living there?"

"I do. My father and brothers," Chenai replied. She was getting used to this curiosity about her in a way. Those who were curious asked many questions. Those who were uncomfortable ignored her.

Jodi emerged before Louis could ask his next question. The moment their eyes met, Chenai noticed something flash across her face. Why did she look guilty? Jodi usually wore a look of defiance. Guilt hardly ever crossed her face even if she had done something wrong at school or home. That was shocking to her. Jodi's hesitant smile also put Chenai on edge. What was going on?

"Hi Jodi," Chenai spoke first.

"Hi. Oh you got a cast," Jodi said. "Does it hurt?"

"No. Just itches."

"So we are going for dinner? Where?"

"Little Italy," Debbie replied.

"That's lame," Jodi said.

"Where do you want to go?" Debbie asked.

"Gram you know I hate pasta. Little Italy is boring."

Chenai realized she couldn't talk to Jodi right there. But could she talk to her at the restaurant? She had to know the details. Andy wouldn't take her calls, and it seemed like everyone at church no longer wanted to talk to her. She wondered if they blamed her or if they had only been interested in her at all because of how much they all loved Andy.

"Gramps are you coming to dinner with us?" Jodi asked.

"No sweetie. We have dinner with our friends, remember," Debbie responded. "You all have a good dinner. Your father's already outside."

"Fine."

Chenai and Jodi stepped outside. It was a cool evening and the sun was on its way down. Chenai glanced at the trees that were starting to turn orange and brown and shivered dreading the winter.

They reached the car in silence and Jodi stood by the car. Chenai noted her black tights hidden in biker boots and short jacket. Her hair was tied in a ponytail and she also noted the new earring piercing by the top of her ear.

Chenai wondered what Andy had been thinking. How could he do that to a mere child? She felt betrayed. How could she have misjudged him so?

Chenai glanced down the road and she could see Blake and Tyler walking back. They had gone far.

The neighborhood was quiet, only one car passed by them. Nobody walked around and there were no signs of children playing though almost each house had a basketball hoop. Jodi seemed reluctant to look at Chenai.

"Jodi," Chenai began. "I need to talk to you."

"What?" Jodi turned her face wearing it's defiance like a well-worn coat. Chenai looked down ready to give up. She to face the girl. This was too important.

"It's about what happened with Andy."

"What?" Jodi spoke a bit too loudly. "What?" Chenai felt her heart begin to race. Something was not right. Jodi recognized something in her face then began to yell.

"He just came into the house looking for you. What on earth does he see in you? He deserves it. I didn't mean to lie, but then he just refused to even touch me like I was scum or something. I hate him!"

Chenai listened to her tirade, her heart sinking with horror. Oh God. Oh my God. What had happened? Still she had never felt like slapping anyone in her life as she did that moment. She held her good hand in a tight fist, listening to the crying, the deep wounding words Jodi had spoken. Her anger grew with each second.

"I wanted him to hurt just like I did and Dad he just called the police. I didn't think he would call the police. And he hit him. He wouldn't even look at me. He kept looking for you."

Chenai was so horrified she didn't even notice Blake standing watching them. When she turned to him his face mirrored hers. She could feel it in his stillness, the way a man with a mask might look, alien to all those around him.

CHAPTER 38

Gale

Return, faithless people;

— Jeremiah 3:22

Every time Chenai thought of what happened, which was all the time, she felt sick. The whole situation was a nightmare. Andy had been out on bond and she couldn't imagine his anger, the terror and anguish he felt. The wheels of justice were slow and Jodi's admittance of lying was surely going to get her into serious legal trouble.

Chenai was astounded at how much bad publicity the story had garnered for the church, for Andy. She had been so busy healing after her accident and dealing with Blake and his family she had not realized the magnitude of what could happen. Andy could have spent years in jail for something he didn't do and be labeled a registered sex offender. What if Blake had not over heard the whole confession? Would Jodi have told him the truth?

She talked it out with Blake. He recalled the day it happened. How he had just been so angry. What else could he think? She tried to soothe him even though she was going through her own guilt of ever thinking Andy would commit such a crime.

Jodi had no choice. She had to confess to the cops. Tell the truth and deal with the consequence. Blake had to drop the charges. Still the damage was done. Ruva talked about it, as everyone at the hospital did. They had watched the news and of course it was all they talked about it.

"Andy is a broken man, Chenai. He's not the same. We should pray for him." Blake was talking of prayer. That comforted her. Still she was eaten up inside with guilt and anger at Blake and Jodi.

Chenai tossed and turned night after night her heart hurting from every move. She prayed each night that she would forgive Jodi and try and be there for her, but when she imagined Andy is some prison cell for something he didn't do, her anger returned. "Do not judge." She would tell herself.

Blake and Chenai seemed to have naturally decided to keep their distance. He was finalizing things with the building and it was also a slow process. He had told her the day before that Penny had offered to come and see her and help her with things.

Penny.

Penny arrived at Blake's house, singing her motto in her head. Keep your friends close, but your enemies even closer.

She rang the doorbell.

"Hi Chenai," she greeted. "I've brought you some food."

"Hello," Chenai said still standing by the door. Was this girl blocking her entry? Did she really think that she had driven all the way to Bloomfield Hills from Royal Oak just to drop off the food and run with her tail between her legs?

"I'll bring it in," Penny said and Chenai stepped aside. Penny couldn't believe what Blake saw in that drab African girl. She had no style. She wore some long shapeless skirt and sweater. Oh my goodness. Men could be so blind. It took all her effort not to scream at the foolish girl.

Penny caught a reflection of herself in the hall mirror. She had dressed in her best and tightest jeans and a black blouse with ruffles. She knew that everywhere she walked, heads turned. Her blonde hair was flying in the wind, recently styled and wavy. She was not wearing her work chignon. If Blake walked in and saw both of them, surely he would realize that she was something special. She was the one he should spend the rest of his life with, not this unsophisticated alien. She really wished that America would close its borders and not just allow ignorant people like Chenai in to steal her man.

"I'm so sorry I didn't come and see you sooner," Penny began putting the tubs of Chinese food on the table. "But you look so much better now."

"I do. Just have to wait for the proper cast."

"How long will that take?"

"Six weeks or so. It was not as good a break as they initially thought," Chenai said sitting by the kitchen tables. Penny glanced around and looked at Chenai as she straightened the boxes. She looked really young right then. What was Blake thinking?

"I'm so sorry about that."

"It's okay."

"So you are here alone, all day?" Penny glanced around as Chenai began to speak. Those cabinets will have to go, she thought.

Dark wood was in.

"Well, Blake is here sometimes."

Penny cringed at the way she said his name. She couldn't even say it properly. So they were now playing house. Just the two of them. No kids. What was Blake playing at taking this innocent girl? Men were such imbeciles. What could they talk about? They could only talk about God for so long then what?

"Eat up. Do you know how to use chopsticks?"

"No I don't."

"Here. They have forks, too," Penny said, and then dug in the plastic bag and produced a fork. It was chicken and rice and Penny took her box and took a bite.

"I can stay as long you want. I really don't want you to be taken advantage of."

Chenai stopped eating then looked at Penny.

"What do you mean?"

"I mean that I know you have been working here and sometimes, some men take advantage of women, you know."

Chenai seemed embarrassed, but didn't say anything.

"Chenai can I ask you something?" When Chenai nodded then Penny continued. "Have you ever been intimate with a man?"

She shook her head and coughed. Was she blushing? It was impossible to tell of course. Chenai was perfectly embarrassed.

"I figured as much. When you have, it ties you together. It's in the Bible. It makes you one."

"I know."

"That's how Blake and I are. We've been intimate for over a year now. Our bodies joined and so did our spirits. We just didn't get married yet, but to me, in my heart, we already are."

Penny watched the effect of her words on Chenai. Her face fell and she could see that her words had a huge impact. She smiled.

"Relationships are complicated, aren't they? I know you must have the same complications right now with your boyfriend. Is it Andy?"

Chenai tried to smile. Penny could tell by the way she put her fork down that Chenai had lost her appetite.

Was it that easy?

"He's my friend," Chenai began.

"It's okay. You don't have to share yet, but he is perfect for you." Penny took a bite of meat then chewed slowly, trying to re-member what she had tried to memorize in the Bible just for this moment. Oh yes. It was coming back to her. She had done her research well. "You know your Bible talks about not being yoked to unbelievers. That's why you and Andy are good for each oth-er. Cut from the same cloth. Blake and I. Well, we are definitely yoked nicely together."

Chenai stared outside at the Lake, her fork now abandoned. Penny followed her gaze, imagining her life in the house as Blake's wife. She could already see the two of them taking a boat out while the kids slept and making love under the moonlight. She would give Blake a good, well balanced life. She turned to Chenai. The purpose for her visit was not over.

"So what are your plans for the future? I don't think it's a good idea to stay here forever. I know when Blake and I get married we won't need help. I can take care of the kids and they are pretty big. There are many after school programs when I have to work late."

"I got a scholarship to start school next fall for premed."

"Wow. You are going to be a doctor. That's fantastic."

"I don't know yet. It takes a long time."

"What eight years. That's a really long time. But it goes by fast."

Chenai nodded.

"Well, you are young. Which school?"

"It's in Kalamazoo. A private college."

"That's great! So what are you going to do until then?"

"I was thinking of going home. Spend a year at home but.."

"You should!"

"I have my return ticket."

"That's nice. I can help you when you need to come back."

"Thank you. You are kind."

Penny reached for her hand, "I've been there. Struggling to go to school. I lived in a small town in Ohio with very few prospects, maybe like your country, but now I am in a position to help. I make good money, I work hard."

Penny paused and saw that Chenai was drowning in some kind of misery. Serves her right to think she could just waltz in here and steal Blake from her. Over my dead body.

Chenai didn't say anything. Penny imagined the food turning sour in her stomach while hers tasted sweeter and sweeter. Life was funny like that.

"When did you want to leave?" Penny asked.

"I guess soon. I miss my family. I want to go and help them. I sent them all my money, but they need me there."

"Good. Tyler and Jodi will be just fine. I'll make sure of it."

Penny looked into the young woman's eyes and felt a little tinge of guilt when she saw the sadness there, but she shrugged it off.

When she drove away she had all but helped Chenai pack her bags.

CHAPTER 39

Nippy

He heals the brokenhearted and binds up their wounds.

—Psalm 147:3

"What does my son mean that you are leaving? What's happened?" Marylyn sounded confused.

"Nothing at all. I had already planned to go home before starting classes next year."

"I thought, you and Blake?"

"I know. But it's not right for us. I have school, he has things to deal with…"

"He just accepted God into his life and you just leave him? He needs you."

"I – I understand, but he's going to Bible study. I don't want to be a distraction."

"That's hogwash. Do you love him Chenai?"

Did she love him? She loved him too much. He was her waking thought now, overpowering everything else, but she had to accept that her place wasn't with him. It hurt. It continued to hurt to face facts that were as clear as the sky.

She could see all the moments they had spent together, lately. She could see him sitting in a chair far away from her, his eyes burning hers, making her smile and tremble at the same time. How was it that when he just brushed by her, her heart raced, her neck muscles tightened, pleasurable and unbearable. Even the first time she met him now made her smile or laugh. He had been so impatient, so wrapped up in his own world. And the way he called her "Cheny" was now so sweet to her.

She wiped the tears from her eyes. She had told him she was leaving and he had concluded that it was because she loved Andy. She had not corrected him.

Chenai had prayed. Still no answers had come or had she refused to see them. She just knew that Blake had to find his way with God without her. He had to rebuild his family alone. Or with Penny.

She also wondered if she was taking the easy path, just giving up.

"Chenai. I know you do. I knew it at the wedding. I understand there are many obstacles, that love doesn't always come in convenient packages. Packages where you are the same color, you love the same things and you knew God at the same time. But it's still love."

Chenai didn't respond, fearing if she did, Marylyn would hear her sobs. Now that she'd said goodbye to Marylyn, her next task would be unpleasant. She had to go and see Andy.

⁂

Amanda came to pick her up in her Ford Focus. Chenai probably could drive and Blake had purchased a new car. She just didn't want to, yet. As Amanda drove, she was chatty, telling her about her life.

"We are planning to go to Florida for Thanksgiving to visit my grandmother," she said. "What are your plans?"

"I don't know yet." There was no thanksgiving in Zimbabwe. She would be long gone by Thanksgiving. Her flight was already booked.

Andy opened the door to his apartment and Chenai was shocked by the change in him. He looked like a stranger, the former smiling eyes dull and broken.

"Hi Andy," Amanda said cheerfully. Chenai tried to smile though all she wanted to do was cry.

"Chenai." He glanced at her hand. "Come in."

Andy sat on the couch and pushed his hair back. His hair had grown long and unruly. Chenai sat down opposite him and Amanda sat on one of the bar stools. She didn't know how to begin. She was fighting tears.

Andy looked broken. No matter how much she searched his face, he wasn't there, a frame without a painting. Chenai had prayed for wisdom for the right things to say, but now her tongue wouldn't move and no words came.

"I'll be back," Amanda said suddenly and left the apartment. Chenai barely noticed that she had left. The silence was thick. Was it with accusation? Did he hate her?

"I'm sorry about everything, Andy."

"It's not your fault."

After those words Chenai fell silent. In her heart she asked God for wisdom. She just couldn't come and sit and look at him and not offer him any comfort. He needed her, just as she needed him all those months before.

"Andy. Can we…..um do you want to go for a walk?"

He seemed ready to shake his head, but got up and pulled a wind breaker from the closet. Chenai had not removed her jacket.

They made their way out the door into the windy day. The sun fought a losing battle against the clouds that rolled in with the wind. Andy turned to the right where a path led them to a park not far from his place. They walked in silence watching the leaves fly ahead of them from the strong wind. Chenai braced herself against it, but Andy just seemed to let it push him forward his lanky frame taking the blast. Why did he feel like a stranger to her? Could it be that easy to destroy the love he had for Jesus. That passion that inspired so many?

At the park they stopped by the swings that moved in the wind, facing one another.

"Talk to me," she implored. "I want to help."

"No one can help," he said. "I mean, Yeah I was angry that you believed I would do such a thing."

"I'm sorry."

He finally looked at her. His eyes were no longer clear and sure, but were clouded as if his vision for his life had been distorted. He looked really dejected and Chenai had to fight not to weep. She had to be strong, because for once, Andy looked like he needed her strength.

How can such a short time change a man, that words between them seemed frozen when just weeks before she could talk to him about anything, laugh and work together with those in need? Ruva's words came to her.

"I would never date a white man," she said, "At least not the ones from here. They are not that strong. They grow up spoilt. They buckle under pressure. Life has been too easy for them."

Chenai shook those words off like leaves on her head. She didn't want to think those words. Blake was white. He wasn't buckling. Andy didn't need to be judged and in that moment she resented Ruva for saying that. Blanket statements like that never ever considered the person. The individual.

"I felt my world tumbling down. I thought God had abandoned me." The words poured out, angry and strange. He must have seen the unspoken questions in her eyes. He had often told her that she wore all her emotions on her face like a magazine cover.

"No. He never does that."

"Chenai, when you are getting your finger prints, your mug shot and everyone thinks you molested a child. You feel dirty, guilty, the world is over." Chenai nodded as he opened up finally, not sure she could even say anything to make him feel better, not sure she could hold his words. They burned and she could only try and imagine how they must have burned him.

"And I was mad at God. Maybe still am, because there will always be some people who doubt."

"They don't matter."

"They do. At church, there are whispers. I want to go back, but I know that sometimes being accused of something and having your face on television is enough for many to think you are guilty."

With those terrible words, Andy sat on the swing his legs in front of him. She sat down facing away from him, her good hand holding the chain on the swing.

Chenai wiped the tears from her cheeks. She had done a lot of crying since the truth came out, since she had decided she would leave.

"But it's all over now right? You are not convicted of anything or even charged."

"I know," he said still looking down. So far away.

"Andy. I want us to pray that God restores your love for Him. That you don't let this hardship take you away from Him."

"My heart is hard Chenai. I'm not doing anything stupid. My life is a mess and I am at the bottom of the pit."

Chenai spoke quickly, afraid she was losing him. "Think of Joseph. He was thrown in the pit by the brothers who loved him, falsely accused by Potiphar's wife, but he lived to reign as ruler and delivered God's people from poverty and death. I believe you can do that too."

Andy gave a harsh laugh and shook his head, still far from her. How could this be happening? How could Blake be coming to God in his darkest hour and Andy who had so loved Him so was now pushing Him away is his storm. She thought she could feel God's tears fill the park, raining on them, but she also felt hope. She had noticed the alcohol on his counter from the corner of her eye when she arrived in his sparsely furnished one bedroom. Andy had never drunk.

She tried to say one more thing to him, the way he would have done had she been in his shoes, desolate, lost, and angry. "We are made for God. No matter what. Nothing. Nothing else will ever satisfy you."

Andy turned his cloudy eyes on her, "I know it all, Chenai. But right now it's just in my head. It's not in my heart."

The helplessness filled Chenai as they walked back to Andy's apartment. Seeing him so lost and angry terrified Chenai. That a man can just toss his identity just like that? That life can change just like that? But messing with his eternity was not something she would take lightly. She would be on her knees every night praying for Andy, praying for Blake, and others who lost their way due to the injustices of life.

"I have a question for you," Andy said when the silence seemed to grow into a being. They stopped just before the path leading to his apartment building. It was colder. Darker now. The wind picked up the fallen leaves swirling them around their feet.

"Yes. Anything," Chenai said.

"What's going on with you and Mr. Pieri?"

Chenai's mouth opened slightly, but no words came.

"This is so twisted. Are you involved with him?"

The disbelief in Andy's voice alarmed Chenai and she knew that she couldn't hide the stress, the shadow of loss that passed her face.

"That's why I didn't want to see you Chenai. Seems to me you are siding with the enemy. The people who want to ruin my life. You think we can still be friends."

"Andy. Jodi's a lost soul."

"She almost ruined my life. Probably did. Now it's her turn."

"What will you do? You know what The Bible says about vengeance."

"It's God's. Don't forget I teach the Bible. It's Mine, sayeth the Lord. I'm not thinking of revenge right now. So if you came to plead for your boyfriend."

"No. I came for you. You have always been there for me."

Andy's laugh was harsh.

"Blake should have known I didn't do anything. When my lawyer started investigating the whole sordid mess Jodi's skeletons came out. Her sleeping around. Nude pictures on the internet. Expelled from school. Smoking… and Blake still thought I did something to her."

"Imagine a father walking in on that. He made a mistake. I did too. I am so sorry Andy."

"Blake never liked me. He has said some terrible things about you and I. He's a sick man, probably pretending to be born again so he can get what he wants. You probably think you can change him. He will change you. Men like that don't change."

Chenai bit back the sob. They both stood the wind howling between them.

"You must be careful. Falling for Blake. Chenai, you must be crazy"

"Nothing like that, Andy. Nothing at all." *Everything.*

Andy didn't say anything and his silence was full of anger and accusations that Chenai couldn't even face. His words had done the damage intended.

Chenai you must be crazy.

When they reached his warm apartment, Chenai remembered something else.

"Andy. I know you didn't want me to know," Chenai began,

not sure she should say it.

"What?" he stood by his kitchen counter. She detected concern in his face, but she wasn't sure. Could his face be the reflection of someone who had been to war, and lost.

"I know you paid my fees for the semester," she finally got it out. "I want to say thank you."

"What are you talking about? Who said that?"

"Oh," Chenai was flustered now as she played with her scarf. "My mistake. I thought it was you."

Amanda came back with cups of coffee from a local coffee shop. There were no more questions about Blake or his daughter. Certainly no discussion about her fees. When she left, Andy had become a stranger to Chenai, and she feared that if he wasn't careful, he would still be in prison even if all the charges were dropped.

When Amanda and Chenai drove off, Chenai gazed into the deepening darkness. She was confused, but the butterflies danced in her stomach at the realization that Blake had paid for her semester even back when he treated her like garbage, he had cared. It could only have been him.

Drizzle

My people will live in peaceful dwelling places, in secure homes, in undisturbed places of rest.

—Isaiah 32:18

Bindura, Zimbabwe.

This was the first dry day in weeks. Incessantly, the rains had fallen while they were forced to stay indoors. Chenai woke up one morning and the sun was out at last. Desperately needed sun.

Chenai sat with her father outside on the verandah, the sounds of tractors, farm workers dying down. In the distance she could see the smoke go up as the fires for cooking sailed to the sky. Yes, her home was small, humble, and yet her heart was at ease. This was the only place where she could be truly herself. Her year in America had opened her eyes to her need for a place that's hers. Home.

Her perspective had changed too. Her home, compared to the Pieri home was a shack. The farm house was tiny. Her father seemed smaller too, her room plain and simple. The only thing bigger was the hole left by the loss of her mother.

Still it felt so good to be back home, sitting on the verandah with her father just as butterflies began their journey, escaping form the maize fields with a few landing right on her hand.

"Baba look," Chenai said giving her father a picture of him and her mother, a faded black and white taken in a make shift studio, right after they married. "Mai told me about how you two met. That was so strange."

Frank smiled, "She told you didn't she? My dancing Queen."

Chenai sighed and looked at another photo, "This one is one of my favorites."

Frank nodded at the photo of Lois and himself, holding baby Chenai, after he returned from the war. He drank his water. The boys were in the kitchen washing the dishes. Evans had actually come to visit when he heard Chenai was coming. He had changed too. Seemed older, but beaten by life in those mines where they found gold, but didn't really make enough money to improve their lives. Now he was planning to go to South Africa, or Zambia, or Namibia. Evans was done with Zimbabwe.

Chenai had cooked the food and she insisted that they do the cleaning. They grumbled, though she knew that they respected her, Evans, fighting tears had told her that seeing her was a little like having his mother back.

"It's good to have you back home, my child. But you've been home for what…a month and you don't really tell us what happened."

"Nothing much. I had a good year in America."

"And Aunty Rutendo?"

"She's fine. Staying with her just didn't work out."

Chenai glanced at the only photograph she had of the Pieris.

It was a photo Marylyn had taken of Blake with Tyler and Jodi. Blake had his jacket on, his superman jacket and he also wore his serious face, the way some wore make up. Tyler was smiling, the happy boy who never let life's storms take away his joy. Oh, she missed him. Jodi was sulking. Her time with them seemed like something she had dreamt, all those days living with Blake's children, and then the final days when they had been just the two of them, like little kids, talking, whispering, and trying not to touch.

Her heart ached at the memory. Then came the day she had left, her arm still in a cast. Tyler cried uncontrollably, not being consoled by the fact that she would visit them, that she would be back. A year did seem like a life time away she knew. So much can happen in a year. Penny and Blake could get married. Tyler could have a new nanny and Jodi could be born again.

"And that family was good?" Her father's voice cut into the thoughts.

"They were."

She couldn't tell her father all the details. He wouldn't understand would he? She could have told her mother. She missed her mother more deeply then and each corner of the house was filled with memories of her. Her geraniums were not doing as well. She broke off the dead leaves and now they would thrive again. Memories.

What did she have with Blake? It had been so brief, so fragile, a flickering candle that Penny had blown out with one blow and it had died.

She had done nothing, but think about Blake on her flight back, wondering how she had believed Penny. She knew she was fragile then. So soon after the accident. So soon after Andy's ordeal. The Devil knew the Bible and could quote it and she should have been more alert where Penny was concerned.

Had she given up on Blake too easily? Had he given up on her?

He had his children to save, his relationship with God to nurture, problems to solve in his company. Where did she fit? She refused to believe that he needed her, too. And now it seemed they were really through. A candle blown out in the wind of adversity.

Well, her love for Blake still fought to survive, just as her mother's plants had done. Her feelings remained even though she brutally squashed that hope, that longing that made her gasp. Sometimes, she wished she was like her mother, a woman who could dance her way into a man's heart. Have the courage to fight for what she wanted, gather the drums, sing songs and dance her heart out until the man noticed and fell in love with her.

Chenai shook herself out of her painful memories and got up suddenly, dropping the photos on the table.

"Baba I'm going to see if we have letters. I'll check at the store."

Chenai walked out the gate, once again wondering what Blake would think of her humble home. Would he be disgusted?

It was a sunny evening, a few days before Christmas. She remembered what Christmas would have been like in Michigan. Snow. Cold, but maybe a fake fire in the fireplace.

She had received a letter from Amanda. There was no email or phone at home. Chenai had opened with trembling fingers. In the letter Amanda informed her that Andy was doing better, had actually come to church and shared his testimony about his months of being lost and coming back to God again. Chenai had danced with joy, realizing that God had never left Andy and glad that Andy had accepted his unconditional love. Amanda didn't know anything about Blake and the kids, except she had seen Blake at church. Chenai's heart lurched at the mention of Blake's name and she traced his name on the letter, as if that could bring him back to her.

She started walking on the path that used to take her to and from school. The Millards were gone and the house seemed abandoned. Things had changed. The landscape of the farm was still the same, corn beginning to flower, cows grazing and smoke from the cooking at the farm areas. She was glad they had electricity at their school house even though often the power got turned off. At least they could sometimes watch TV and cook on her mother's stove instead of on the fire outside.

Her feet crunched on the sand as she walked, her mind filling with similar walks, breathing in the familiar air, her mother's footsteps echoing from years past. She had been looking down for a while then she glanced up. She was surprised to see the front of a taxi come from around the bend. It stopped by the side of the road.

Who would hire a taxi all the way here? A man stepped out, a figure in the distance that began to walk in her direction. The man wore khaki trousers and a white shirt and cap.

A white man. He seemed familiar and she felt her knees weaken as the figure became clear. She stood still, staring wondering if her eyes were playing tricks on her. Her step seemed to falter, as if she had stepped in a gaping hole in the road. Why was her heart racing? What did it know? When he got closer he stood still. Everything had supported their apartness. Age difference, race, cultural, education, children, Penny, but all that melted when she saw him, on her road, carrying a backpack, coming to her. She felt the bursting of stars deep in her belly, a profound joy that set her in motion.

With exhilaration Chenai felt something strong in her stomach. She didn't have to dance for the man. He would dance for her.

"Blake!" As if she couldn't move fast enough she took off running towards him. With laughter and tears he was running toward her.

Acknowledgements

When I wrote this book my hope was that I would study more of God's word, understand his promises and get my life closer to his will. That, to me was more important than completing this book. Am I there yet? No. I still need to immerse myself in The Word and continue to grow day by day. God is good and faithful because once again, when I needed help, guidance, inspiration and confidence, He provided the people.

God gave me a husband who is patient, who wants what's best for me in every way. With him by side, I know I can accomplish anything.

My son saw me putting together a media kit of all my books and he said to me, "Mummy lets pray for your books." He's four and he prayed for them and I knew then that God had blessed them and they would go where he opens doors and He will give them wings. I am grateful for this little guy's wisdom and all the beautiful prayers he says for me every day.

My wonderful mother, Agnes Denenga is always the first to read my books. She continued to encourage me and share stories with me that added richness to my story. I am also grateful to Maria McKenzie who also read early drafts and with her words, I had renewed energy. She is a great, because she truly believes in me.

I am also super thankful for my sisters who contributed in amazing ways.

I am truly grateful to all the readers around the world who kept asking for my next book. Those words gave me the strength to work harder and finish this book for them. It's amazing how encouraging it is to hear questions about future books, because they are a much needed boost of determination to keep on working at what I love.

About the Author

Miriam Shumba fell in love with writing as a young girl, beginning with comics and then full, hand written novels in school exercise books. These she shared with very few friends in school. As a college student her first short stories appeared in Drum magazine South Africa and then while teaching she regularly wrote short stories for Parade Magazine in Zimbabwe and Jive in the United States. Her stories have also been published in literary magazines online. Her top selling novels, *That Which Has Horns* and *Show Me The Sun* are celebrated by audiences in several countries. She is currently working on two other novels and developing screenplays.

You can learn more about her on www.miriamshumba.com

Other novels by award winning author, **Miriam Shumba.**

That Which Has Horns

I devoured the book in two evenings. It was interesting, gripping and entertaining.

—*Diasporan Darlings*

Show Me The Sun

SHOW ME THE SUN is a heartwarming novel about how one woman's low self-esteem almost got in the way of obtaining her goals.

—Rawsistaz reviewers